THE
FOREVERS

Books by Chris Whitaker for Adults

Tall Oaks
All the Wicked Girls
We Begin at the End

THE
FOREVERS

CHRIS WHITAKER

HOT
KEY
BOOKS

First published in Great Britain in 2021 by
HOT KEY BOOKS
80–81 Wimpole St, London W1G 9RE
Owned by Bonnier Books
Sveavägen 56, Stockholm, Sweden
www.hotkeybooks.com

A CIP catalogue record for this book is available from the British Library.

HARDBACK ISBN: 978-1-4714-1095-6
EXPORT PAPERBACK ISBN: 978-1-4714-1099-4
Also available as an ebook and in audio

1

This book is typeset using Atomik ePublisher
Printed and bound in Great Britain by Clays Ltd, Elcograf S.p.A.

Hot Key Books is an imprint of Bonnier Books UK
www.bonnierbooks.co.uk

For Isabella, who never lets me sleep

'The chances that an asteroid or comet of potentially catastrophic size will come hurtling towards Earth are exactly 1-in-1. It's 100 percent, a sure thing, a lead-pipe cinch. The only variable is when.'

Gordon L. Dillow

1

Mae expected to feel more the first time she saw a dead body. Blind panic, breathlessness, dark clouds and thunder.

Instead gentle waves rolled in beneath a sky so bright she raised a hand to dull it. The world turned like it didn't know, like it didn't care.

She'd skipped English and crossed the hockey pitch to the woodland beyond, found the cliff edge and followed the track down to the beach.

It used to be her place, where she went to forget.

She glanced back and saw him following.

Hugo Prince was everything she hated. 'We need to talk about last night.' He flashed a practised smile, but when he saw the body he staggered back, the golden tan drained from his face.

'What is it? Is that –' He tried to grab her arm but she shook him off.

'Go and get someone,' she said.

Too calm, that's what Hugo would later tell the policeman. Mae was too calm, like nothing about her was human.

He went to speak but she cut him off. 'You really want people to know why you followed me down here?' She watched the shame fill his eyes. 'You heard me screaming. You came to help.'

'Listen, Mae . . .'

She hated that he knew her name, that he looked at her at all. He existed in an alternate dimension where being good at sport meant you were good. Where girls laughed at your crappy jokes, twirled their hair and played at being dumb so you could feel superior.

'Go.' She screamed it, so loud he broke into a sprint, climbing higher, sending birds from the treetops as he burned through the woodland.

The dead girl lay face down, ashen hair fanned out like she'd been posed. Some kind of terrible masterpiece Mae knew she'd never forget.

She found a school bag on the rocks, inside was a purse. Mae pulled out the notes and stuffed them into her pocket.

Waves crossed and broke, a thousand blues pared back to white as she reached down and turned her.

Abi Manton's eyes were as empty as her soul.

Mae saw the tattoo creeping from behind Abi's gold wristwatch.

Dark scrawl over blue veins.

On Mae's wrist was that same word, like they were two parts of one whole.

The third body in a month.

James Wilson and Melissa Rowen, they'd been found together, hanging from the oak tree by the school gates.

Mr Silver talked about suicide like it was contagious, some kind of pollutant that smoked through impressionable minds, replacing hope with despair. He told them inner strength was a choice, during the kinds of assemblies where teachers dabbed at their eyes and shook their heads in disbelief.

All the while Mae saw the others exchanging wary glances.

They all knew it would come.

They all knew it was just the beginning.

2

They said when the news broke Mae walked out into the garden and looked to the sky like it was on fire.

Seven years old, first day of summer, her worries limited to mastering cursive, number bonds and what to wear to Abi Manton's party.

It seemed like a hundred years back, not ten.

Sometimes she would close her eyes and try to remember before, when minutes and hours dripped into an endless pool of future and history. But then she thought maybe life began and ended the night her parents stood side by side in front of the television as BREAKING NEWS edged out the movie they'd been watching.

She felt her father turn and stare at her.

He held her mother's hand tightly, their fingers interlinked. They didn't tell her, not till later, but hearing talk of space, she dropped her book to the floor and walked outside.

She stood barefoot on the grass and faced the moon as fireflies sparked from the heathland behind.

Either side the neighbours did the same.

Stan and Mary. Luke and Lydia.

And Abi.

They stood in a line separated by low picket fences and watched the dusk air like Selena wasn't a billion miles from them. It didn't feel like the end then, more like a phenomenon, a miracle born from impossible fate, odds so spectacularly long they could only have been preordained.

'Are we going to die?' Abi said.

'No,' Mae said.

Abi reached through the fence.

Mae took her hand.

Over the coming days the newspapers bulged with expert opinions, doomsday preachers and armchair scientists. The man who first saw it, he worked for NASA and his name was Juan Martin Morales. He was the person who stood in front of the microphones, dabbed sweat from his forehead and rubbed at three-day stubble while a selection of carefully vetted journalists lobbed questions at him.

Morales named it Selena.

Its real name was Asteroid 8050XF11.

They would later learn Selena was the name of his daughter, and that she'd died at the age of three, from a disease so secular Morales ignored all reference to Last Judgement and laid out simple fact.

If this was ever going to happen, we'd always hoped to spot it early enough to do something about it.

We have a decade to save our planet.

That last sentence would echo through Mae's childhood and beyond. She would see it graffitied on the bus stop each morning as she walked to school. They would play it on the radio, on the television, and print it on the cover of a thousand magazines.

Though they looked at time differently, it went on, unknowing, uncaring. Seasons changed, sun to snow, trees shed leaves as school years ended and began.

Mae watched the trouble from her coastal town, so far from the cities it was like the rioting faces belonged to another species. Each night the news was painted with rage, fear and faith.

On the morning of Mae's tenth birthday she huddled on the sofa, her hand on her mother's growing stomach. The dawn chorus sang as they switched on the television and watched a rocket break the sky but nothing more.

Morales became the face of the world, the combined hope of every nation. After each attempt at salvation he would take to the podium and field questions like an ailing politician, while most would read the failure in his tired eyes. He'd scratch his beard, long and peppered with grey now, and he'd say Selena would be easier to tackle the nearer she came.

And come she did.

She blazed a relentless trail, shrugging off solar storms and recoil. Millions of miles away but her impact was felt each day in countless ways. In science Mae would learn about gravity tractors and impactor probes, in maths it was relative velocity and the necessary angle of deflection. She learned they would need to slow Selena by a centimetre per second to send her off course. Each night Mae would hold her thumb and forefinger a little apart.

A centimetre is almost nothing, she would say, as her father stood by the window and watched the stars like they were blinking out before his eyes.

As the world reeled from a new kind of terror, Morales and his team sent up the Saviour 3 spacecraft in another attempt to change its fate.

Mae went into London to watch the launch on the large screen by Tower Bridge. In a crowd of a million her grandmother gripped her arm tightly as fireworks lit the Thames and weary men peddled glowsticks and commemorative T-shirts. Her sister slept through it all, at peace in her pram, too young to breathe the panic in their fleeting air.

The carnival lasted two weeks.

And then Morales took to the world stage and once more shook his head.

Before then Mae had never seen her grandmother cry.

Most nights Mae would lie on the beach with Abi and Felix and watch the night sky in all its perfect, endless glory. She wondered about faith and its limitations, its blindness to everything she knew and everything she hoped for.

Lauda finem, the Sacred Heart school motto.

Praise to the end.

In philosophy Mae stared at the whiteboard and the bold lettering:

If you take away consequence, if you can do anything, right any wrong, however slight, how would you spend your final days?

The topic was ethics. The debate turned so fierce Mr Norton had to hold Liam Carter and Sullivan Reed apart.

It was a question that Mae dwelled on. It was the answer that kept her awake at night. Though it would take until the failure of Saviour 9 before she allowed herself to face up to the overriding, overwhelming facts.

She was seventeen years old.

She would die in one month.

3

WELCOME TO WONDERFUL WEST-ON-SEA.

The sign swung gently in the breeze as Mae smoked the last of a cigarette and watched a storm cloud edge in.

Rusting fishing boats bobbed in a marina that opened on to a vista of girls turning cartwheels on the beach, the falling sun blinding through the Vs of their legs.

When the heavens opened they screamed and lay back on the sand, arced like angels as rain pinned them down.

They hadn't yet heard.

Another dead girl.

Another reminder of paradise lost.

In the small police station she took a seat opposite Beau Walters, whose uniform swamped him so totally he looked like a child dressing up in his father's clothes.

He placed an old tape recorder on the desk and hit record with a trembling hand.

'Was Abi Manton depressed?'

Mae picked dark varnish from her nails. 'Depression is the inability to construct a future. Seeing as we have no future, we're an army of depressives, Beau.'

He cleared his throat. 'It's Sergeant Walters now . . . till my dad comes back from the city.'

She glanced up at the photograph on the wall, Beau's father, the chief constable, glared back. The kind of man who looked cold to the touch, who bled judgement from his unforgiving eyes.

'We'll stop Selena,' Beau said. His hair was the colour of sand, his cheeks reddened by acne.

She wondered where that hope came from, that belief. She guessed it was what Morales told people to keep from total social breakdown.

This was a close call.

Life had stalled, but this was not the end.

This was a time for self-reflection.

'What were you doing in the woods with Hugo Prince?'

'You want me to draw you a picture?'

He slid a pencil and paper across the desk, calling her bluff.

She got to work, then slid it back.

He glanced down once, then again. 'That's disgusting.'

She stared at him through damp hair, unflinching till he looked away.

'I need you to tell me what you saw.'

Rain drummed on the roof. Her arms were scratched, she licked at a small cut on the inside of her lip. Sometimes she drank so much she lost a whole night.

'There was blood by her head. Her foot was twisted.' She spoke without emotion, like she was reading from a schoolbook.

'When was the last time you talked to her?'

Mae turned from him, though remembered Abi's sweet

10

sixteen. Abi's father hired a yacht, seventy feet of gleaming white. The invitation had been placed in her locker, a long time after Abi left her behind. Mae put on the only decent dress she owned and headed down to the marina, only to see the boat leaving without her. Abi stood on the deck, raised a hand and mouthed, Sorry, like it was an accident Mae's invite showed the wrong time.

'Hugo said he heard you scream and came to help. I'm not sure I believe him.'

'Why not?'

'I can't imagine you screaming.'

An old fan turned the close summer air.

'You and Hugo, it doesn't make sense to me. I see him with Hunter Silver, the headmaster's daughter. And she's . . . I don't want to say the opposite of you, but . . . she's the opposite of you.'

Mae swallowed. 'Maybe I'll do things Hunter won't.'

Dusk fell.

Bruised sky over purple water.

She caught her reflection, dark hair and light eyes and too much attitude for a body that clung hard to a childhood she'd never known.

'Tell me about Abi.'

Mae took a cigarette from her bag and gripped it between her teeth. 'She was a bitch.'

He snatched it from her. 'I know you don't get on with my father, and you think he looks at you every time something bad happens in this town, but the Mantons . . . they're broken.'

She felt her jaw tighten as she stared at the desk and finally talked. Abi used to live in the house next door. Her father built shelters, panic rooms, bunkers. Saviour 8 made him rich overnight as people scrambled for the illusion of safety. The Mantons moved to an Ocean Drive beach house and Abi jumped several rungs up the social ladder. Her hair, her clothes, the parties she held.

'You're saying she was popular.'

'She was bland and beautiful and hateful. So, yeah, Abi was popular.'

Mae watched a fishing boat carve waves. On her arm were other tattoos, a moon and star, some dates that meant something to no one but her.

'Abi's boyfriend is . . .' he checked his notes, 'Theodore Sandford. The boy from the choir. I saw him sing last autumn at St Cecelia. That voice . . .' He tapped his pen on the desk like he was lost in the memory. 'I forget where the song is from –'

'*The Marriage of Figaro.*'

She wore a short skirt and beneath that an old hunting knife strapped high on her thigh. People talked about her like they didn't know, like she ever stood a chance.

'Abi would have left before the dance. The Final – morbid name. Are you going?'

She ignored that.

'She was wearing a purity ring. Theodore wears a matching one.'

'Everyone's looking for their angle.'

'You know you can talk to the school counsellor,' he said.

Mae thought of Counsellor Jane and her taut church smile, imploring eyes and beige trouser suits. 'She's not a real counsellor. She records the conversations. If she's worried, if she thinks we might blow our brains out, then she sends them to someone qualified.'

'Resources are stretched.'

She glanced at his badge. 'No shit.'

'Hugo . . . he said the popular kids have targets on their backs now. What does that mean?'

She spoke more to herself than him. 'Maybe they're trophies. Maybe the kid that gets bullied finally brings his father's shotgun to school. Maybe the hot girl that treated the boy like dirt is finally forced to see him. What's the worst that can happen? Maybe it'll all be over long before punishment is served.'

'It's not the end, Mae.'

'The way things are going, maybe we should all pray that it is.'

'One last question. It's just a formality. Where were you last night, Mae?'

She felt sweat roll down her spine.

And then the windows began to rattle as the ground shook beneath her feet.

4

She followed him out into the street.

The first rumble was slight.

The second stopped the town dead.

Mae crouched low and pressed a hand to the road, the trees across barely swayed, the air too calm.

She imagined the clouds parting right then, catching them all unawares.

A streak of red and yellow, a white flash bright enough to blind.

And then the roar.

Thermonuclear.

The Earth so broken not a thing would survive.

Mrs Abbott came out of the hairdressers', the foils still in her hair as she looked at the sky, then the ground. 'Just a tremor.'

Dog walkers moved on, beach girls lit a fire as a plane crossed their sky, the air thick despite the shine of rainwater on the road.

Mae stood in the haloed shadow of the church clock tower and watched the creeping minute hand cut swathes from her life.

A board sat outside the newsagent's, a bold red 31 splashed across it.

Beside was West Video, where Mae worked shifts alternating between flipping through magazines and pointing prescient summer people towards the ARMAGEDDON display, where they could get their fix of last-gasp salvation against a banging score.

An old Vauxhall pulled onto the driveway of the rectory.

'Did you feel it?' Mrs Baxter said, climbing out. 'Global warming, Mae. It's like we've broken our world.'

Mae opened the boot and grabbed a shopping bag.

'Pineapple this week, gone like it never was.'

'I don't remember the taste,' Mae said.

'I saw you in the police station. Are you in trouble again?'

Mae lived with the judgement, no longer feeling it.

'Is it true what they're saying?'

'Abi Manton.'

'Lord.' Mrs Baxter wore emotion like a badge. 'Three children.'

Mae opened the garage. The boxes were stacked. Crates of food rose floor to ceiling, packets of rice, cereal, tins of soup and vegetables. Freezer chests lined the far wall.

'He takes it to the shelter in Newport,' Mrs Baxter said.

They turned as an ambulance crawled up the hill, no lights flashing. Mrs Baxter dipped her head.

Mae walked out onto the street as it passed, her face mirrored in the smoked glass. She thought of Abi in there, zipped into a bag. She wondered where they'd take her; if they'd lay her on a cold metal table, slice her open and see there was nothing inside.

'Jesus,' Mrs Baxter whispered. 'She was seventeen. There'll be nothing left to save. Nothing at all.'

Inside Mae climbed the creaking staircase and found Felix by the window, his forehead pressed to the glass. He stood six five, wore glasses too large for his face and was the kind of skinny that had old ladies trying to feed him after Sunday service.

'It's not true, is it?' he said. 'Tell me it isn't true.'

She nodded.

'Jesus, Mae. What the hell is going on in this town? She jumped? That's what I heard. But then Sullivan said she was pushed. And Jeet said . . .' He looked down at her, eyes as dark as his skin. 'Jeet said you found her.'

A group gathered by the church. Abi's friends huddled as their mothers stared off towards the cliffs.

'He also said you were with Hugo Prince. Don't tell me you were –'

'Maybe I was.' She said it coldly, her eyes on the hurt and the pain across the street.

'Sleeping with the enemy. You know he hangs around with Liam Carter. And you know Liam goes out with –'

'Candice Harper.'

'And she should be going out with –'

'Felix Baxter. But he's too much of a pussy to talk to her.'

'I'm biding my time.'

'Because we have so much of it.'

Felix ran a hand through hair slicked back at the top and falling to tight curls over his neck. A poster of Barry White filled the far wall.

Sergeant Walters arrived at the church. Mae guessed he confirmed it because a Lycra-clad blonde crumpled as her husband rushed to prop her up.

16

'People are falling apart,' Felix said.

'They weren't whole to begin with.'

'What happened to our Forever?' He looked down at the solitary *F* tattooed on his wrist.

'You cried before I could finish.'

'You said stick and poke, nothing about actual needles. And they weren't tears, I told you. The ink won't take. My skin is too pure for it. My father's the goddam Reverend. That practically makes me an angel.'

Mae grabbed a copy of *Playboy* from beneath the bed and held it up. 'Angelic.'

'I just read the articles. Not much else I can do. I can't . . . any more.'

She followed his eye to the small, wooden crucifix above his bed. The Reverend's latest attempt to capture his son's lost soul.

'He's fixed it with glue. My father is a sadist.' He reached for a small bottle, shook out a pill and swallowed it dry.

Mae didn't know exactly what was in them, just that Felix took one every night, and that one pill was powerful enough to keep him from sleeping.

The theory was as simple as it was stupid. Time was running out, Felix didn't want to waste a single moment of it.

He snatched the magazine from her and looked longingly at Vanna White. ''87 was a fine vintage.'

'Bathroom?'

'Mother Teresa watches down from above the toilet.'

Mae shrugged. 'She's bound to have seen worse on her travels. Lepers and shit –'

17

'What if there's a murderer in town? What if he comes for me next? I can't die a virgin, Mae. That'd be the real tragedy.'

Felix checked his watch then switched on the television. Morales stood before a dozen microphones as cameras flashed in his eyes. He raised a quietening hand.

We don't stand by and wait. We have the most capable minds studying every part of her. The probe we landed, it sends back data every second, and from that data we have formulated Saviour 10.

It will be different. There will be casualties but the devastation won't be total.

'I'd rather he just said we're all doomed, go have some fun,' Felix said, frowning at the television.

'Panic sex, it's your only hope now.'

'I've got Candice right where I want her.'

'Unaware of your existence?'

'I just need to summon my inner Barry White and then she'll –'

Mae silenced him by reaching into her bag and taking out a piece of paper.

His mouth fell open. 'You got it?'

'Printed it during my last shift. A list of every single movie Candice Harper has ever rented.'

He went to take it but she snatched it back. Felix took a bottle of communion wine from his wardrobe and the exchange was made.

Mae went back to the window and watched Abi's parents arrive. Her father, hands shoved deep in his pockets as he looked around like he was in some kind of daze. Abi's mother was swallowed by the group, all keen to hug the shock out of her.

And then Mae saw Theodore. Instead of joining them, he crossed the road, dropped his head low and walked away.

'No way she jumped,' said Felix. 'Abi was a Forever. Sometimes I miss –'

'What?'

'You. There was the Mae before, and she was messed up, but at least she smiled sometimes. She was living.'

She looked to the sky, mouth tight. 'So I'm not?'

'You're existing, Mae. We've got, like, no time left, and you just waste each day. Alone. You know he's out there.'

'Who?'

'Everyone gets one, and one only. I'm talking gut-wrenching, all-consuming, never never gonna give you up, true love.' With that Felix turned, blew the dust from a record and closed his eyes to the deep baritone voice.

Mae turned back to the TV, to a still of Saviour 9, the trail of fire and light like a nebula hanging in the predawn sky.

'I remember the Forevers,' he said, lying back on the bed and pushing his glasses up his nose. 'We did it for the creeps and the weirdos.'

She reached a hand out and felt rain on the rooftop.

'You and Abi, you said we didn't belong here. So we do belong some place. But I'm scared we don't have the time to find it.'

'We were that place.'

'Some days I feel invisible. Candice doesn't see me. My father doesn't see me. I bet Barry never had that problem.' He took off his glasses and yawned.

'Get some sleep,' she said, as she headed for the door.

'I'll sleep when I'm dead.'

'And that will be . . .'

'Thirty days.'

'And sixteen hours.'

5

The house was old and maybe once was grander but Mae did not allow herself to remember before.

Inside, her grandmother followed her through to the tired kitchen. She wore a dressing gown pinched at her skeletal waist, close to gaunt, skin painted her bones like any flesh between would be wasteful. A sky watcher, all day, every day. Mae remembered a time when she was soft, red-cheeked from working her allotment, her kitchen filled with the homely smell of minted lamb and apple pie.

'Mrs Abbott called to say she saw you come out of the police station. What did you do now? Were you on the beach with a boy?'

Mae said nothing.

'You know there's a name for girls that do things like that.' Every cabinet door was opened and slammed. She carried a note pad and pen and kept track of each can and packet, her hand shaking, the writing illegible. 'Think of your sister.'

'I do.'

'This town. You get a name and it sticks, Margaret.'

Mae hadn't always hated her given name, but right then it reminded her of her mother, the memory so sharp it hurt.

'My granddaughter, the slut.'

'I didn't do –'

Mae wasn't ready for the slap. It caught her so hard she dropped to her knees, her hair falling over her face.

She closed her eyes, counted, that's what she did when she couldn't take it any more. She counted, and each number brought her nearer to the end.

'Who used a plaster? We had thirteen mediums.'

'Stella grazed her knee,' Mae said, the sting in her cheek brought tears to her eyes.

'She fell?'

Mae nodded.

'You have to take her arm.'

'She hates that.'

'Why are you on the floor?'

Mae took a deep breath. 'I slipped.'

'A girl died. Is that right? Mrs Abbott said it was Abi Manton. It couldn't be, she came by here just last night.'

Mae felt her pulse quicken as she followed her grandmother towards the stairs. A dozen leaflets sat piled by the front door. A hundred more were plastered across the doctor's surgery. Some nights Mae scanned TV channels, the high numbers rolled live every hour of the day with meditation techniques, deep-breathing exercises and mindfulness.

'She said sorry.'

Mae looked into her eyes, trying to read her. 'Abi said sorry?'

'Yes. I asked her to come in. I wanted to make her a hot milk. That always worked when you had a nightmare.'

'A nightmare?'

'Poor girl looked scared to death.'

Mae stood there beside the peeling paint, her feet on the bare floorboards.

She cracked the door to her sister's bedroom, took in the dark walls, the starred ceiling, the papier-mâché planets that hung from wire that criss-crossed the room.

'Did you feel it, Mae? The earth shook again.'

'Yeah, I felt it.'

They climbed from Stella's window and lay on the flat roof of the kitchen.

'You know there's bunkers,' Stella said.

'I know.'

'If you've got enough money, they'll let you in. Or if you're clever enough, or beautiful enough.'

'That's bullshit.'

'Teddy Lawson said I'm not pretty enough. And his mum laughed at my clothes. They think I don't know, because I can't see. And he said Daisy wouldn't get in because her daddy has a boyfriend. And he said –'

'One, Teddy Lawson's mother is a toxic dirtbag. And two, the way you look . . . your sexuality, your gender, they're the least interesting things about you.'

'The Prince family are building one,' Stella said, excitement reaching her words. 'Missy Wright lives next door and she says they dig all night long. You know his mother has gone.'

The leavers. Those who said their goodbyes or those that simply tired of the wait and disappeared in search of more. Sometimes Mae wondered what more looked like. Maybe it was a sailing boat in the South Pacific, maybe it was drinking yourself to death in a Vegas hotel room. Whatever it was, it had to be more than sitting in a classroom listening to a weary teacher preach ethics when they'd never mattered less.

'Is it true there's a dead girl?' She was eight, too small to speak those words.

'Yes.'

Mae glanced over at the flat roof next to theirs. She used to lie there across from Abi. They'd try and touch hands but the gap was too vast.

Do you think we'll ever stop watching the sky?

Even if they stop her, we'll still wish on stars.

'Was it Abi Manton?'

'Yes.'

Mae placed an arm around her sister. Small for her age. Stella wore dark glasses to hide eyes that had never seen, hair cut by Mae, a smile too big for their world. She chose her own clothes, the brightest she could find, a technicolour dream to Mae's eternal dark.

'Paint the sky for me.'

'The sky is white tonight. The brightest white I've ever seen. And the stars are black, like pepper on mashed potato. And the moon . . . the moon is green like it's grown grass.'

'Green.' Stella smiled.

The silhouette of her, too small, too breakable.

'Sometimes people in class talk about the future,' Stella said. 'It's like they don't know. Does anyone not know?'

'Some kids have parents that lie to them. Would you rather I lied to you?'

'I think maybe Miss Hart has parents like that. She's getting married in autumn and she tells us about her wedding plans.'

Mae thought of Stella's teacher, her smile so fragile, like the coming days would shatter it. 'It's a directive. We choose to live. To go on like it isn't happening, like Morales will save us. That works to a point, and then it stops.'

'And then what happens?'

'I think we're starting to find out.'

'Those men in the butcher's. They fought over that piece of steak. Sometimes words are so hard I can feel their edges, their points and their sharpness.'

Punches had been thrown. *It might be the last fillet I ever eat.*

'Will you go to the Final?' Stella said.

'No.'

'Felix can teach you to dance.'

'Felix is an idiot.'

'He's teaching me, for the play. I have to waltz with Prince Charming but Felix keeps making us listen to Barry White.'

'You don't need a boy to dance with.'

'But it's in the –'

'Boys make everything worse, Stella. Never forget that.'

Stella nodded.

'Cinderella, huh? They must think you're pretty special if you got the lead.'

'A blind Cinderella – they'll sell more tickets.' Stella reached out and touched Mae's face. 'Your cheek is hot. Did Grandma hit you again?'

'No.'

She traced her small thumb across the tattoo on Mae's wrist. 'Can I be a Forever?'

'It doesn't mean anything, Stell.'

They climbed back through and lay on Stella's bed.

'Did you find Abi?'

'Yes.'

'Paint her for me.'

'She was wearing white. Her brown hair fanned out. And she had this look on her face . . . like she was sleeping. But more than that, like she'd found peace. Her lips were curved into the slightest smile. She was the Abi you remember.'

'Did her eyes look empty like mine?'

'Your eyes are full of life.'

'Was there a time . . . before?'

'Yeah.'

'Was it everything?'

Mae felt her sister's small hand find her own. She wanted to tell her yes, it was everything.

Mae slipped into black jeans and a dark zip-top. She hid her necklace under a scarf, tied up her hair and buried it beneath a baseball cap.

Streetlights glowed as West slept. The zigzag of bats skimming trees, the distant wave of beach fire.

Mae walked down the middle of the road like the town belonged only to her.

Ocean Drive, the road winding above the town, each house punctuated by the water behind, so black it might as well be the edge of her universe.

The white house was the grandest on a street where grandiose was an art form. Each night she'd stop outside, lose her nerve and choose less intimidating prey.

The house had long been the subject of rumours. Three summers to build it, kids rode their bikes to the fence and looked on as fully grown trees were craned in. Stella said it belonged to a family of vampires, immortalists who thought nothing of burning millions of pounds before the place was decimated.

She found footholds in the stone wall, her arms strong, the muscles lean and tight.

Mae dropped down into another world.

Lanterns hung from trees that snaked up a twisting driveway.

She stayed in shadowed borders, rare flowers sweetened the air.

She passed marble statues of winged children.

A large fountain erupted in the centre of a sweeping carriage driveway.

The house could be glimpsed from the water, if you swam out to the second buoy, but here, up close, it felt as if the owners had dared to build something so beautiful it couldn't possibly be destroyed, like the crime was too great.

A downstairs window was open to balmy night air.

She didn't like to go in when people were there, but time weighed her down now, the press of each minute so acute sometimes she could not breathe.

Mae crossed fast and kept low, each step carefully measured. She pulled her scarf up over her nose, only her eyes on show as she climbed through the window and found herself in a home office.

Everything was so crisp and so startlingly white, from the walls to the carpets, for a moment she just stared.

Mae opened each drawer in a large white desk, found stacks of papers so moved on to the bookshelves. She carried a small bag and shoved in a laptop, stalled by a drinks cabinet, and then she saw it. On the bookshelf, the copy pristine, the half-naked lady on the cover, 'D.H. Lawrence' scrawled on the spine.

She lay unconscious of the wild little cries . . .

Mae remembered sitting at the back of the library, reading those scenes with Abi, both of them laughing so hard the old librarian shot them the death stare.

The memory was so vivid she didn't hear the door open.

And then she turned.

And paused.

Frozen.

The boy stood there, tall and slim, full lips, eyes so dark she almost looked away.

She felt her heartbeat in the tips of her fingers.

I don't want to be here.

I don't want to be anywhere.

He wore a dark suit, white shirt and black tie, like he'd come straight from saying a final goodbye.

She heard noise outside and her breath caught.

He looked at her bag and saw the laptop poking from the top. There was a moment when he seemed to weigh things. He looked at her with such sadness she almost broke in two, then he'd see it, that she had nothing inside, no good or bad, just nothing at all.

She willed herself to disappear.

And then he opened his mouth to call out.

Mae moved fast and slammed into him, her scarf falling to the floor.

They fell back against the wall, her lips on his. She pushed her tongue into his mouth and grabbed a fistful of his shirt collar.

Hard and frantic.

As they broke she stood breathless.

A voice right outside. 'Jack, are you in there?'

She tasted vodka on her lips.

Flecks of orange lit his eyes, like fire on the darkest night.

He reached up and gently took off her baseball cap.

Her hair tumbled down.

'Jack?'

She heard the tick of the white clock on the wall beside them as she pressed a hand to his chest and felt the beat of his heart.

'Are you in there, Jack? I heard a noise.'

He moved the hair from her eyes. 'Yeah. Just looking for something.'

She breathed again, her lips inches from him, her breath warm on his.

Footsteps faded.

Mae backed away, towards the window.

'You can't take that,' he said.

'Watch me.'

She picked up the bag, climbed out and met with the shadows.

6

The news of Abi Manton ravaged the town, smoking through the morning air, racing down streets and slapping the complacency from parents who thought the only threat came from the sky.

Mae hadn't slept, just twisted and sweated in the sheets, Abi's broken body there whenever she closed her eyes. At dawn she climbed onto the roof and watched sunlight christen the dark as she sliced Abi neatly in two. Her friend with the lopsided smile, mousy brown hair, eternal optimism. And the dead girl, with the golden tan, platinum locks, cool-as-hell demeanour.

She dropped Stella at West Primary, waited for Felix for five minutes, guessed he'd finally passed out cold so headed to school without him.

Sacred Heart sprawled along the top of a white cliff. Victorian buildings, bleached stone and steepled rooftops that rose high above the cliff edge.

Mae passed the remains of the felled oak Hugo Prince had christened the Death Tree. Kids took to staring at it, like they could still see James and Melissa swinging from its limbs.

Inside she cut her own path, head down, content to disappear. People said she was trouble, she did nothing to prove them wrong.

The speaker above crackled with Mr Silver's voice as he told them to head to the chapel for assembly.

Abi's locker had been turned into a shrine of paper hearts, flowers and perfumed notes. A lone candle lit and extinguished, smoke ghosting towards a poster for the Final school dance.

As Mae passed she saw a poem scrawled and taped in place. She knew grief wasn't measured in tears or sleepless nights. It was colder, the knot in your stomach, the taste in your mouth, so bitter it ruined the sweetest moment. Mae knew grief. Better than most, she knew grief.

Each pew was filled, heads low beneath painted saints. Hunter Silver and her friends flooded the front benches with the sharpness of their sorrow.

We knew the dead girl.

She was ours.

If West was their galaxy, Hunter Silver was a supernova. The kind of nuclear fusion that sucked in wide-eyed boys like startled deer in the bright lights of Wonderbra cleavage and silken legs. That she was the headmaster's haloed daughter only added to the appeal.

She was flanked by a posse that bowed to her almost as low as the boys did. Distinct by their dead-straight hair and severe eye-skimming fringes. The colour was a uniform ashen steel that gave them a robotic edge. Girls from each year, some as young as eleven, raided the chemist's for peroxide and hair dye, keen to follow, keen for Hunter to baptise them with a lingering glance, or if they pulled it off right, a smile.

Hastily arranged slides of Abi were scored to *'Ave verum corpus'*.

The orchestra led out, a chair was left empty where Abi had once sat and played her violin, in a tribute that had a dozen teachers reaching for tissues and dabbing the regret from their eyes.

Maybe I missed something.

Maybe I could've done more.

Abi had helped elevate the kids on stage from tragic to tolerated, rebranding them the Sacreds, and without her they all looked lost, till Sally Sweeny sat down at the piano and took them on a journey out of the chapel and into the crashing sky. Had Sally's future not been written, it would've dazzled with the kind of greatness that came from practising ten hours each day, till her fingers bruised and she dreamed in arpeggios.

She played with a grace that belied her size. Her weight gain had been legendary. Petite until a year prior, rumour circulated, and then died, that she might be pregnant. Her pale stomach squeezed between the buttons of her shirt. She'd been unceremoniously dumped from Hunter's circle, her hair returning to a fiery red.

Theodore Sandford kept his blue eyes down as he missed his cue and stood there in pained silence till Jeet Patel, his all-smiling understudy, filled the gaps.

When they were done Mr Silver took to the front, blandly handsome, he said everything and nothing, his voice rising above the anguished cries of a dozen girls that didn't really know Abi, just the idea of her.

Sergeant Walters stood, clutched his hat and told them to wait behind if they knew anything.

Mae could see the begging in his eyes.

Tell me it was suicide.

Tell me she was depressed.

As he talked Mae glanced back, and that's when she saw him.

He sat alone in the far corner, wearing that same black suit and tie. There, beneath the light from the stained glass.

'Who is *that*?' a girl behind her said, close to combustion.

'New kid,' came another voice.

'He lives in the white house.'

'Hot *and* rich.'

At that moment he looked over.

Mae stared back, unashamed, unafraid.

'So what's his story?'

'Duh. His family want to die somewhere beautiful.'

Sergeant Walters was cut short as the large speakers beside him burst into life.

Five hundred heads turned towards them as the screech of feedback turned to the steady crackle of a tape being played.

Sergeant Walters looked to Mr Silver, who looked to Miss Holmes, the music teacher. All three shrugged in confusion.

And then the voice echoed around the chapel, high and haunting.

We built the swing on the edge of the cut-out. Thirty feet above waves so gentle and blue we stood there mesmerised.

Everyone stared at the speakers.

'It's Abi,' someone said. 'It's Abi's voice.'

I asked them if they'd seen it. Felix nodded. Mae nodded.

Then the saccharine voice of Jane, the school counsellor.

And you remember this clearly?

Like it was yesterday. Those moments in life, you don't realise they're important till after, when you look back. When you're in them, when you're living, it's like the sweetest nothing.

Miss Holmes looked around desperately, then rattled the locked door at the back.

The night before, we'd watched Saviour 5. Mum cried. Dad squeezed my hand and told me everything would be all right. That's what parents do though. They dress up their lies as promises.

You think your parents lie to you?

Not as much as they lie to each other.

Mr Silver tried to dismiss them. They stayed rooted to their seats.

I asked Felix and Mae if they thought we'd die.

And what did they say?

Felix said no. He knows about science, he puts all his faith in it. Which is ironic, because faith and science are kind of at odds. Like, it's totally messed up. His father –

The Reverend Baxter?

He doesn't . . . He can't take it. That his only son doesn't believe. I told Felix to just lie or something, isn't that what we all do? We go to church and bow our heads and think about how screwed we'd be if there really was someone in control of this shitshow. Begging his forgiveness, that ought to be the real sin.

And what did Mae say?

Mae felt the eyes on her, the hot stares as kids turned in their seats, as teachers strained to see the girl they'd long ago written off.

Mae never begs for anything. The idea of original sin – we can never make amends so why even bother. Mae thinks we'll die. She's casual about it. Like it's a certainty. I love her. She's strong, she's like, so small but so goddam strong. Considering what she's been through. Most people would've broken. But . . . she always knew we were going to die. And she made peace while others went to war.

You said before she was like a sister.

Closer than that. You don't get to choose your sister. But Mae, I mean, we chose each other.

You were eleven years old at this time?

Six weeks of pure and perfect summer. Marshmallows on the beach and barbecue evenings. Swimming out to the furthest line and seeing who could tread water the longest. Sometimes I think we're too goddam golden to even exist.

Mr Silver tried again, desperate. No one moved.

Felix threw himself, and he swung far out over the water, screaming as he dropped into the sea.

Then it was me and Mae.

We stood close, our bare arms touching.

Sun cream and bubble gum.

I asked Mae if she thought it could take both of us.

She said no.

I asked if she wanted to try. She said yes.

We held hands and launched ourselves.

Mae glanced back, this time the boy saw her.

I can see by your smile it's a good memory.

It's funny that they hurt the most.

Are you afraid of dying, Abi?

That question they'd asked themselves a thousand times.

I was fearless in that way only kids can be. Because they don't know, the world and the kinds of people in it. Selena, she seemed so far away, not just in miles or time. She just seemed like this thing, this cautionary tale about making each day count, about living some kind of idealised best life. And each Saviour, each failure, brought us closer to the edge of decency, closer to basal, wants and needs – that line has never been thinner. So, to answer your question, Counsellor Jane, no, I wasn't. Back then I wasn't afraid of dying.

And now?

Now I'm terrified. Because I know for sure where I'm heading. And who isn't afraid of burning.

7

They were hauled out of class and into interviews with frantic faculty members.

Mae drew the shortest of straws.

Edward Silver, head teacher, gestured to the leather armchairs in his office. Mae took a seat as he walked over to the window and cracked the blind.

'When something bad happens, people look at you, Mae. You think that's unfair?'

There was a time when she might've said yes.

He wore a fitted suit, expensive watch. His hair was neatly parted, his skin too smooth, like he'd never needed to shave.

'We live in an age of miracles, Mae. Every day is more wondrous than the last. Copernicus was on his deathbed when he published his theory that planets revolved around the sun. Before that we thought we were the centre of the universe.'

'Some of us still do.'

He tapped the window and shook his head at someone outside. 'People wonder what we're still doing here. I don't mean now, us as a school. I mean, people wonder how humanity has survived this long. We're so intent on self-destruction.' He took a moment, then finally turned.

He had the kind of blue eyes that held no secrets. He appraised her tattoos, the faded denim skirt, the grazes on her legs. Like she was an entirely different species to his daughter.

'Counsellor Jane is . . . Someone broke into her office and stole that tape. A cruel prank. Was it you?'

She shook her head.

On his desk was a photo of Hunter beside her mother. There was something inhuman about their smiles, their white teeth, their glow. Like they'd come with the frame to project an ideal. *Look at the life you could have lost.*

'Did Abi talk to you, maybe tell you why?'

'I don't know anything about Abi Manton or her life.'

He looked sad. 'You were friends once?'

'I was a lot of things once.'

'James and Melissa. And now Abi. I thought they were stronger than –'

'I can't think of anything braver than taking your own life.'

'When we wake up on the twenty-first of July, we'll have to live with the things we've done.'

'And if we don't wake up?'

He looked towards the sky. 'Then we'll have to answer for the things we've done.'

On the wall was a painting in a heavy frame. A woman laid out in white, some kind of demon on her chest.

'*The Nightmare,*' he said. 'Abi used to stare at it too. You know she was a talented artist?'

When they were fourteen they'd taken the train to London,

38

wandered the Tate and stopped before Warhol and Picasso and Rothko. Abi had stood facing Dali's mountain lake and cried.

Sometimes it was too much.

As she reached for the door he spoke.

'These next weeks, they're a test of resolve. Make sure you don't fail.'

She ate lunch alone, in the shade of a willow that faced the water. She flipped the pages of her book, her eyes skimming Atticus Finch's words, Scout's unblemished soul.

Mae wondered if people really did only see what they looked for, and hear what they listened for.

Hugo Prince made his way towards her, glanced back over his shoulder then took a seat on the grass.

He wore shorts in all weather, ran daily, swam, kicked a football. A few days ago that's all she would've seen, how perfectly he fit together. But then she broke into his home, hid in his wardrobe when she heard noise, and watched him, Hugo all-star Prince, take a razor blade and cut neat lines into his thighs. He did it without emotion, no tears or pain or acknowledgement that what he was doing pushed him from being nothing to something more than the sum of his pristine parts. And then he'd reached for a box from beneath his bed, taken out a brush, a selection of small containers, and expertly made up his face. He'd been carefully applying lipstick when he heard her.

'You get Mr Silver?' he said, like it was normal they were talking.

She said nothing.

'He thinks it's me or Liam. Like it's a prank. Like I'd do

that, after what we saw.' He fussed with his trainers. 'You'd think he'd go easy on me.'

'Because you're nailing his daughter?'

Blond hair cropped short, cupid's bow lips; now and then girls stole looks at the boy Hunter Silver deemed worthy enough.

He ran a thumb and forefinger over the square of his jaw. 'I didn't sleep. I wanted to talk to someone, but . . . So that's what you do now? You take stuff that isn't yours. You're a thief.'

'Yes.'

He nodded, like it made sense. 'I keep thinking they'll announce it. Morales . . . those guys. They must be working on something we don't know about. Like, we'll just hear on the radio that she'll miss us. Skew off or something.' He pulled at the grass. 'Maybe we'll lie on the beach and she'll pass so close, right over us, like a plane or something. For a moment we'll be shadowed. All of us. And then –'

'We'll die, Hugo. We'll all die.'

He stood. 'I just wanted to . . . make sure our story is straight.' As he reached down to pick up his bag, his vest rode up. The bruises were angry, blue-black.

She swallowed. 'Your father. Is that why you –'

'We've all got our shit to deal with, Mae. A giant space rock doesn't change that.'

She watched him walk away. He shoved Jeet Patel because the kid was walking too slow in front of him.

Move, bitch.

Normal order resumed.

As she walked back into the building a long line of kids stood outside the old careers office. Like they hadn't received the memo. Mae could only imagine the kind of pseudo psychobabble being spewed by Counsellor Jane.

And how does that make you feel?

Felix grabbed her shoulders, shoved her into a doorway and pointed.

She followed his eyes to Candice Harper, who opened her locker to a hundred rose petals landing at her feet.

'*American Beauty*,' Felix said. 'She rented it two years ago.'

'Where did you get the roses?'

'Mrs Preston gave them to me.'

'Didn't she die last week?' Mae said, staring at him. 'You robbed her grave?'

'Hush now, Mavis. Don't sour this moment with your –'

Felix fell silent as Candice ran into the arms of Liam and kissed him.

'He's taking credit. I sat out till midnight to get those flowers. I had to wait for Mr Preston to cry himself out.'

Mae shook her head and began to walk the hallway.

'Creep.'

She stopped, turned and felt the silence fall.

A path cleared for Hunter and Lexi.

'You're a creep,' Hunter said. 'Creeping on my boyfriend at lunch. Like he'd look at you.'

Mae saw kids watching as Hunter played for them.

'Hugo said you didn't scream when you found Abi. You didn't cry. I always said you were a weirdo. A freak.'

A younger girl crossed towards them, a streak of sunburn across her nose, her hair neatly parted down the centre.

'You're the head girl.'

Hunter placed a hand on her hip and fixed a smile in place.

'I was told I could come to you if I needed guidance.'

'Ugh,' Hunter said. 'Fuck off, you little shit. You'll be dead in a month.'

The girl fought back tears and sloped towards the toilets as Felix came to stand beside Mae.

'You think Hugo sees you,' Hunter said, stepping ever closer, 'but there's a name for girls like you.'

'Slut?' Felix offered.

Mae frowned at him.

'Nothing,' Hunter whispered. 'Just like Abi Manton.'

'I thought Abi was part of your cult.'

Hunter raised her voice. 'Abi was troubled. I tried to counsel her.'

Mae got it then. They cried when they needed to, but now Hunter Silver wanted no further part of Abi Manton. Hunter sometimes led assemblies, stood at the front and preached courage and resolve. Abi's death had pissed on her parade. Hunter's group were fallible, just like the mortals.

She whispered again. 'Abi killed herself, maybe you'll be next.'

'I'm thinking an overdose,' Lexi said, running a hand through her hair, so long it stopped just short of her knees. Her mother was the town pharmacist, her boyfriend, Callum, played rugby. She fit neatly beside Hunter.

Hunter smiled. 'Or maybe you'll slit your wrists. Maybe your crazy grandmother will find you in the bathtub, the water all red.'

Mae tensed a little as Felix shook his head.

They turned to see Mr Starling, the science teacher. Hunter and Lexi linked arms and walked out into the sunshine, Mae and Felix slowly followed.

'Are you okay?'

Mae nodded. A lifetime of Hunter, a lifetime of being reminded of her place, like she wasn't acutely aware.

'You know I had your back, right.'

'Yeah, way back.'

'Seriously. And if Hugo or Liam jump in I'll mess them up. You know I've been learning karate online. Every night at eleven I webcam with Tenaka. He's old but deadly. He doesn't stop till I'm proper sweating.'

'One-on-one time with an old man who gets you sweaty in your bedroom? You do know you're being groomed.'

Mr Starling led them to the football pitch. He was old, his skin a shade darker than Felix's. His brown tasselled loafers sank into the leaves. He spoke briefly of Abi, told them he was sorry and said it with tears in his eyes. And then he clapped his hands and handed out helium-filled balloons and marker pens.

'The International Astronomical Union once stated that asteroids' names had to begin with the year they were discovered, and traditionally they were named after Greek gods, but you can call yours pretty much anything you like.'

They formed a large circle and held their asteroids in the air. Mr Starling read out some of the names.

Invincible.

Hercules.

Hugo snatched Jeet Patel's balloon and scrawled *Bitch* on it as Jeet rolled his eyes like he was in on the joke.

Mae glanced at them, kids like Jeet and Sally Sweeny. And Sullivan Reed, who stood apart, always, his cheek so badly scarred he took to standing side on.

'Imagine your asteroids are hurtling through space. Some of them are the size of pebbles. Some are the size of cars. Some collide and pass harmlessly by us.' He popped a couple of asteroids with his pencil. 'Solar storms can make them change direction.' He popped more. 'Some will hit other planets, or add more craters to our moon.'

'What about that massive asteroid?' Hugo said, pointing at Sally Sweeny, who turned away.

'So that's it, we just go on without Abi,' Felix said. 'One assembly, and then back to class.'

'Sergeant Walters will go with suicide. James and Melissa, the Death Tree – they laid the groundwork.'

'That was a pact. This was Abi Manton. Our Abi.'

'Remind me when you last spoke to her?'

Felix looked down. 'It doesn't matter. We're Forevers.'

'We're nothing, Felix. Just ask Hunter. The Forevers was childish crap.'

'I know you don't mean that.'

Mr Starling quieted them. 'Some of these asteroids have burned up. But a few larger ones remain intact. And those are the ones that will hit Earth. But you can see how they've been reduced in size. They may land in the sea or the desert or even a city. But the odds are small, and when it does happen it's rare that human lives are lost.'

He popped all but Mae's asteroid.

'So that leaves one,' he said.

'And how big is that that one?' Jeet Patel asked.

They gathered around and looked at it.

Mr Starling stuttered, 'It's . . . It's the size of . . . It's seventy miles wide.'

Everyone sobered, even Liam and Hugo, Candice and Hunter.

Mae let the balloon go.

They watched it float gently towards the clouds.

Just high enough that they could still read the name scrawled across it.

Selena.

8

Mae wasn't sure how she got to the gates.

One minute she was walking towards home, the next she was on Ocean Drive, staring at the solid wood, the number thirteen, the sprawling glass beach house behind.

Abi's father led her through to a galleried kitchen, the picture windows filled with breaking waves. She looked around for some kind of trace, anything that hinted at the family whose table she used to eat at, whose daughter was closer than a sister. She found nothing.

Luke Manton drank straight from a bottle of vodka, his voice mechanical, the words so leaden they fell from his mouth and shattered on the perfect stone floor.

'It's supposed to lessen it. Less than a month to go. People live through worse. Kids get cancer. You believe in heaven, Mae?'

'No,' she said, cold.

Laid out on the counter were stacks of photographs.

At the window she saw the obligatory telescope.

'Money.' He waved a hand around like he was answering a question. 'Maybe it made Lydia happy.'

Lydia Manton drove Abi the short distance to school the

day she got her new Benz, stood at the gates the day she got her new lips.

The phone rang and he moved into the hallway.

Mae grabbed the vodka bottle and drank, that familiar heat warming her throat and her cheeks. She picked up photos. Some were from holidays over the years. A young Abi smiling in front of a caravan. A more recent shot, Abi standing on a large terrace, an infinity pool disappeared into crystal ocean behind her.

'That was Abi's personal trainer,' Luke Manton said as he came back in.' 'Everyone calls, like there's anything left to say.'

Abi had a trainer. Mae wondered what had happened to the girl that used to eat a whole tub of ice cream when they watched a movie, the girl who dressed in worn jeans and didn't so much as glance in a mirror before she left the house.

Mae picked up a brochure. 'The bunkers, will they work?'

He drank again. 'Nowhere in Europe. Maybe we should've gone before they closed the borders. Maybe none of it matters.' He pressed the bottle to his forehead like he was fighting a fever. 'They wouldn't . . . We didn't see her till they got her to the hospital. But was . . . I know this is difficult, but was she okay? When you found her, was she –'

Mae thought of the blood by Abi's head. Her leg bent, the life gone from her eyes. 'She looked peaceful.'

He nodded like he saw through the lie but was still grateful, then fished out a photo of Mae and Abi, insisted she take it.

'Do you know where Abi was, on the night?' she asked.

'She said she was going to see you. I've been going through her things. She was messy.' He smiled. 'Lydia was always telling her to tidy her bedroom. I found this in there.' He held it up.

47

The memory flooded her mind with such force she felt herself drowning. She and Abi walking along the beach at sunset, arms around each other, each carrying a bucket of shells. Most were broken crowns, shards stripped of colour. Abi would thread them, Mae would make the sign. Each summer they sold them to summer people from a small table by the marina. ASTEROID CHARMS.

'You can take it. Please, Mae. She'd have wanted you to have it.'

Mae took the bracelet and held it tightly. 'Has Theodore stopped by?'

'No. Just the other kid. With the . . . the scars.'

'Sullivan Reed.' She wondered at his connection to Abi.

'Last night. He didn't come in, just stood in the rain and looked at the house.' He drank some more. 'A month. I don't even think I can make it through that.' He cried then, his shoulders shaking as he buried his face in his hands.

Lydia Manton breezed into the room, trailed by a strong smell of bleach. She stripped off rubber gloves, her cheeks slightly red like she'd been scrubbing away the pain. Luke shrugged off his wife's hand. The sound of his cries followed Mae from their home. Whatever was coming could be no worse than what they had already been through.

She headed towards the beach and threw the bracelet into the sea.

And then she lay back on the sand and watched the day bleed out above her.

Mr Starling told them to watch every sunset like it was a gift, to grasp every minute as tightly as they could. At the marina she saw a dozen others doing the same, couples holding hands, a little boy on his father's shoulders.

The last blazes of the last days of June. When it was time, when the water drowned the last rays of sun, she looked across the twilit coast and watched the boy from the white house ghost back into her life.

In his dark suit and tie, he stopped by the water's edge and kicked off his shoes. And then he looked up at the sky, and he walked into the water.

Ankle deep.

Knee deep.

Mae sat up.

He dived into a wave.

She glanced around but saw the beach empty, the marina now quiet. As she got to her feet and crossed the warm sand, starlight met the waves, so dazzling she lost sight of him.

Again she looked around wildly for someone to help.

He emerged by the buoys. And then he sank.

She scanned the water, mentally counting off seconds, each one lingered, each one told her it had been too long.

Mae kicked off her shoes, then stripped off her jeans and T-shirt.

The water was cold. She moved with purpose. A West girl, swimming in the sea was her childhood.

She cut through gentle waves with silent grace, dropped beneath the water and powered her way towards the buoy.

She looked around, treading water, the shore lights blinked. Mae dropped again, the salt burning her eyes as she felt the pressure build in her ears. When her lungs started to hurt she swam up.

Another dive and she pulled herself deeper.

For a moment their eyes met, the water like ink, she reached a hand out but he just watched her.

She grabbed a fistful of his shirt, felt his hand on hers but kicked hard.

He coughed as they met the air, the moonlight finding his flawless face.

She clutched the buoy with her free hand and fought for breath.

He coughed again, then took his own weight, reached around the buoy and breathed.

In the half-light his skin almost glowed.

'Can you swim?' she said.

He nodded.

They swam together, she kept him by her side.

When they made it to shore they collapsed on the sand.

They lay side by side.

The stars opened above them like some kind of show.

'What the hell was that?' she said, still panting.

He turned to look at her.

It was then she realised she wore only her underwear. This time he leaned in, and he kissed her so hard she lost all the air in her lungs.

She pushed him, her hand on his chest, her eyes blazing as water dripped from her hair.

Behind them the town shone.

Above them the sky fell a little lower.

9

'Your hair is wet.'

'I went swimming.'

'At night?' Stella said, pressing the clock beside her. It spoke out the time and she raised an eyebrow. 'Are you going mad? Mrs Rogers went mad, remember her, Mae? She had that sign in front of her house that said ASTEROIDS NOT WELCOME.'

'I'm not going mad.'

'Do you ever think about Mummy and Daddy?'

Mae took a breath. 'I'm still in school, aren't I?'

'Because Mum wanted you to go to college. Tell me the story again.'

'You know it.'

'They were driving. I was in Mummy's tummy. You were in the back. We were leavers.'

'Yes.'

'And then the truck,' Stella whispered.

The truck.

'You want to pray tonight, Stell?'

'When we go to church and pray, Felix said you keep your eyes open.'

Mae swallowed, all of a sudden too tired. She could've told Stella she stopped praying the day their parents died. She could not imagine a god so callous, so wanted no further reason to stare at the sky and look for answers.

'Then tell me a Saviour story,' Stella said.

'It's late.'

'Just one.'

'Which one?'

'Nine.'

'And then you'll shut up and go to sleep?'

'And then I'll shut up and go to sleep.'

Saviour 9.

Mae took Stella to the open-air cinema in Cheston.

They rode two buses to get there, then walked through the streets with an army of others.

Stella wore an old white bicycle helmet that Mae had covered in tin foil. And white pyjamas they'd glued an American flag to. A NASA logo their grandmother stitched. A jetpack made from upside-down Coke bottles.

The screen was set up in the Victoria Emery Park. Mae laid a tartan blanket down on the grass as they settled among a crowd. Some painted their faces with neon, held glowsticks aloft and sang along to a girl with a guitar and a decent voice.

A mother cradled her baby and swayed, her husband drank beer and watched them like they were the last good thing in his world.

'Will it work this time?' Stella said.

'Yeah, this time.'

'Kinetic energy,' Stella said. She sat cross-legged. 'Two spacecraft

go up. Tom and Jerry. Tom lands on Selena and sends details back to Jerry.'

'So Tom gets the dangerous job and Jerry gets the glory. Jerry arrives exactly where Tom tells him to. And Jerry slams into Selena so hard the kinetic energy sends her off course.'

There was raucous applause when the rocket launched. Mae painted every scene for her sister, in such detail that Stella gripped her hand tightly and squeezed.

Stella slept on the bus ride home.

Mae carried her up their street, her arms burning, her sister's head against her chest.

She did not pray that night, but she came close.

Tom and Jerry missed by two hundred thousand miles.

Mae lay there till her sister's breathing changed, till her own eyes grew heavy. And only then did she allow herself to think of her parents.

At first she thought it was a nightmare that woke her, maybe Abi again, but then she felt the rumble, ran from her bedroom across the hall to Stella, who did not stir.

She checked on her grandmother and saw her deep in a medicated sleep, her white hair all that poked from the sheets.

Outside, the road pulsed with the flash of car alarms. Neighbours came out into the street, pulled their robes tight and looked to the sky.

She saw Peter and Caz, Stan and Mary. They exchanged nervous smiles, looking up and then down.

Mae walked out into the centre of the road as the cars

were silenced one by one, the howling dogs quietened, front doors were closed and bedroom lights switched off.

She walked on down her street, towards the marina and the coast of fishing trawlers and sailing boats. And up the high street and past the church.

There was a sign hammered into the grass outside.

JESUS FORGIVES.

Mae knew that while he might forgive her, she'd never forgive him.

When she reached the white house she clung to the gate and wanted more than anything to see him, but she wasn't sure what she would say if he came out. Maybe she would tell him she hated him. That if he ran into the water again she would not stop him.

She heard the low hum of a generator and followed it to the Prince house, saw the gates open and stepped through. This time she skirted the house, past the swimming pool, and stopped at the edge of the hole.

'I left the back door open for you.'

She turned to see Hugo. He wore shorts and no shirt, skin tanned gold. He sat by the hole, his feet free of the edge.

'I already took everything worth stealing.'

There were lights and discarded machinery, scaffolding twisted down and disappeared. A small lift shaft, the land beside propped and held back with concrete posts so thick Mae reached out and touched one.

'Don't you care, what people say about you?' he said.

She noticed a slight slur in his voice, then saw the empty beer bottles beside him as she sat.

'Even if I did, they'd still say it.'

'You could try harder to fit. You could look like her . . . Hunter, and the rest. You carry your books in a plastic bag. Your clothes . . . life could be easier.'

He passed her a bottle. There was a lot she could have said, nothing that would have mattered.

'We started with shovels.' He lifted each bottle in turn, shaking them for beer. 'Just me and my father, digging through the night.'

There beneath that moonlight, the bruises so dark and angry, each print a reminder that no picture was clear.

'My mother. What he does to me – it used to be her.'

She could offer no words, no empty sympathy.

'We were close, me and her. It was us, and it was him.'

'She's a leaver,' Mae said.

'We're all going to leave, Mae. One day someone's there, and the next . . . Remember Mr Fullerton, taught maths. I mean he even left all that shit on his desk. Family photos. We watched the caretaker bag it. Half this street, the houses are empty.' He squinted towards the moon, raised his hand up and blocked it with his thumb. 'I didn't get a chance to . . . She was just gone. And that night he started digging. And it was survival and nothing else.' He puffed out his cheeks. 'Shit, I don't know why I'm telling you this.'

'So don't.'

Mae stared into the hole, so deep the light disappeared long before it bottomed out.

'I look for her.' He talked like Mae wasn't there. 'Sometimes I think I see her, or hear her. I'll get up in the night and come outside and think maybe she's come back, but I know –' He shrugged. 'Wherever she is, it's got to be better, right. How can it be worse? I don't even mean *here*. You see it, on the news, like those people in Paris, on the streets. It's like, they're angry, but they don't even know what they're angry about.'

'Dying,' she said, quiet. 'You try not to think about death until you have to, otherwise you realise too much that it's all too little.'

'Abi . . . hearing her voice again.'

Abi had come to her house.

She'd tried to call her three times.

Then she'd walked through the school grounds, into the woodland and jumped from the white cliff onto the rocks below.

'Hunter thought there was something going on between us. But she always thinks that.'

Mae looked at him and wondered if there was. Girls watched him the way boys did Hunter. She wondered if they even got on, or if maybe it was written in their stars, that pull to be coveted, the mutual attraction of self-satisfaction.

Behind she saw the glimmer of a Ferrari.

'It's rare,' he said. 'That car. It has a place in the bunker. He talks about driving out into a new world.'

'We'll make the same mistakes again, each and every one of them.'

'Not me.'

She glanced at the towering white house in the distance.

'Maybe Abi's lucky,' he said. 'The wait is over. Maybe they should've told us one week before. Ten years, it's like we're all serving time for a crime we didn't commit.'

'On that tape, she sounded scared.'

He stood. 'We're all scared, Mae. Some of us are just better at hiding it than others.'

'Is that why you cut yourself?'

He stared down at her and something in his eyes made her shiver.

'No. I do it because I deserve to hurt.'

10

The caretaker swept away Abi's shrine till all that remained were a couple of paper hearts he'd missed.

Mae pressed a hand to the cold metal locker and thought just how easily Abi lifted out. Not just her, James and Melissa too. Theirs had been easier to understand – that undying love would soon die. Sergeant Walters had been in, found a diary in Melissa's locker, the pages bursting with poems and drawings of another life, this one eternal. The tragedy was mitigated, they were inseparable till their shared end.

'Hey.'

Felix wore a black leather jacket, the collar upturned. Two sizes too small, the cuffs ended by his elbows, a white T-shirt hinted at the bony chest beneath.

Most days Mae was grateful for his existence.

'I don't know where to begin here,' Mae said.

'Candice rented *Grease* seven times.'

'And that's why you're so greasy?'

Felix fussed with his hair. 'No gel in the chemist so I had to use olive oil. My mother was pissed off. This shit's a commodity now. Do you think I need a signature scent to go with this look?'

'Body odour not working for you?'

He dabbed sweat from his brow. 'You try wearing pleather in this heat. I'm thinking something woody, possible side note of patchouli, that'll take her home.'

'Do you even know what you're talking about?'

'The damn trees outside her house,' he snapped.

'To keep perverts out.'

'You can just hide among them. If anything, it makes it easier to prey.'

'Save me that T-shirt, I'll wring it into a pan tonight. Stella wants bacon.'

Felix pulled a comb from his pocket. 'Danny Zuko is the ultimate ladies' man. Check it, even had my mother stud it.' He spun.

Mae frowned. 'Tirds?'

'T-Birds. The gang in the film.'

'I think the *B* has fallen off.'

He swore loudly. 'That woman can't stud for shit. I don't know why the Reverend married her.' Felix headed towards the toilet, trying to wriggle from the jacket as he went.

Mae was about to follow and laugh when she saw Jeet Patel staring into his locker.

'I think they pissed on it.' Jeet held up a sodden copy of Hamlet. 'I asked them to keep the noise down so I could read.'

'Who?'

He shrugged. 'Hugo. Liam. No use crying over spilled . . . urine,' he said. Jeet wore a blue shirt, the sleeves rolled back over thin forearms. On each wrist were white sweatbands. 'My mum says to ignore it, the way they are. Dignified silence, Mae.' He smiled.

Mae nodded, she got it, knew it was bullshit but got it.

'I remember when they did it to you,' Jeet said.

'Washing detergent.'

'For the record, I don't think your clothes smell, Mae.'

She smiled, then walked into class and took a seat at the back.

The kids in front watched a video on their phones.

Chelyabinsk, Russia.

The footage taken from the dashcam of a truck on the motorway. The bolt of light appeared in the sky and began to tail down like a rocket.

It grew larger, brighter than the sun, faster, a speeding hunk of blazing rock.

And then the noise.

And the screams.

A dozen kids had turned and run from the park because there was somewhere to run. And that was a small rock. No bigger than twenty metres.

The speaker cut her from the nightmare.

Morning prayer had been thrust upon them after Saviour 8 failed.

Mae waited for Mr Silver's smooth voice to lull them with talk of judgement and forgiveness, like the two could ever co-exist.

There's got to be more to it.

More to what?

Kids looked at each other, then up at the speaker fixed to the ceiling.

This bullshit existence. I do my schoolwork, empty the dishwasher, hit the snooze button through my weekends. I dye

my hair because the world order tells me individualism is
social suicide.

Miss Holmes was on her feet and ran out into the hallway.
Abi's voice followed from every speaker in the school, chasing
the teacher's frantic footsteps.

We're told to make a difference in a world where difference
isn't exactly tolerated. Too fat, too skinny. Too poor. Too good or
bad at something; if you straddle the margins, you're doomed.

So what should you do?

You should live life in the empty middle. You should work
hard at school so you can work hard at work. You should covet
a nine-to-five and a decent pension, and a house and a car and
holiday in the sun. And then . . .

Selena?

The problem is . . . we crave the extremes, like some fatal flaw.

Everyone stared up, like Abi's voice was a gateway to a
world they couldn't turn from, a world that was calling out
to each of them.

My parents think I'm depressed. Or maybe they just think I'm
a teenager, because if you fall into that category then your problems
are easier to dismiss, your needs are a fallacy, your beliefs change
with the wind. You're not a living, thinking, hurting person. You're
a whirlwind of unreasonable emotion, of fickle desires they'll
make sure burn out long before you're deemed worthy of opinion.

Your parents don't listen to you?

My mother searches my room, maybe for clues as to who I
really am. She's scared I'll make her mistakes, like she owns them.

Were you ever happy?

Two years ago. I stood on the beach with Mae and we created

*a new world order and it was so goddam perfect. And now I'm
just like them, I'm the nothing that makes Mae something.*

You left her behind?

Mae was numb to the sounds around her, to the tears falling
from Sally Sweeny's eyes, the ghostly pallor of Hugo Prince
as Abi's face came back to haunt him. She didn't notice the
caretaker sprinting towards the comms room. All she heard
was Abi. Her Abi.

*The exact opposite. She moved forward each day, and I did all I
could to stand still. Except I was standing in a line of ra-ra perfect
prefects, pristine emptiness and whitest lies. I've drifted through
years that couldn't matter more. I've drunk caramel macchiatos
in shopping centres and smiled my way through dressing-room
fashion shows. I've planned a future I'll never have and a future
I never wanted. I've listened to a dozen girls talk so much crap
my ears bleed with faux feminism and boys, make-up and boys,
asteroids and boys.*

Boys.

Boys.

Boys.

But when you were with Mae?

We talked about men.

Mae laughed, so abrupt it caught her by surprise. She felt
the eyes of Hunter and Lexi and Candice as they bored into
her, but for a moment she was mute to them too, mute to their
popularity and pouts, their smokey eyes and thonged arses.

Why are you crying, Abi?

*I just . . . I know things are going to get worse now. And I know I'm
not going to make it. I look just like them but I'm not what they see.*

Make it?

Wherever you all are heading. I won't be with you. I can't now. I have to do something bad. Killing yourself, is it the same as killing someone else? A life is a life, right. If we're all created equal, does that mean we all die equal, or do some people move ahead while others slip behind? I just need . . . I need to talk to Mae first. I need to tell her sorry. And that's such a bullshit word.

What are you sorry for?

I didn't back her. I stood by and watched, the way people treat her, blame her. She got caught stealing that time, from the shop in town. But they didn't get it, what she stole. It was food, for her sister, for her grandmother.

Stealing is wrong, no matter the circumstance.

I want to lie on the beach at midnight and spin the world the wrong way. You think we can rewind time like that? I want another perfect, empty night with Mae. I want to talk.

About men?

And music. And art and science and where the two meet.

Where do they meet, Abi?

In the sky above us. Plato said every soul has a companion star that it returns to upon death, so long as a just life is lived.

And how do you live a just life, Abi?

That's the thing, we finally worked it out. Me and Mae, we worked it all out.

Tell me?

You become a Forever. Only I messed that up too.

And what exactly is a Forever?

Their collective breath held.

Like they were about to be enlightened, after years adrift in the dark.

Mae could feel the excitement, the expectation that thundered around the school, around the five hundred faces trained on the voice from beyond.

And then the speaker died along with the lights and the whirr of the fan as the power was finally cut.

11

The tape ended on the kind of cliffhanger that had her called back into Mr Silver's office, where he demanded to know just what kind of sickness she'd infected Abi's mind with.

At lunch a dozen kids had sought her out, burning her with their stares and their questions. Like she and Abi had unlocked the meaning of life then swallowed the key. The rumour mill got to work and by the time the day was done they had entered into some Montague–Capulet pact, only Mae hadn't followed her over the cliff edge.

When she finally made it to her shift at West Video she was drained.

She endured for the much-needed minimum wage, a place to hang out in the evenings and as many free movies as she could watch.

Across the street, Felix whiled away the hours in West Wine, doling out fifty-pound bottles of red so people could soften the world in style.

A couple of shops were darkened. The old ice-cream parlour, once owned by an Italian named Rosa, who headed home after Saviour 7. The last day, she'd given out free ice cream. Stella had eaten so much she was sick.

She looked up to see Sally Sweeny crossing the shop floor, shoulders and head down, clothes so loose they hid the shape of her.

'Felix said you have ice cream. He's out.'

Mae pointed to the freezer.

Sally took out half a dozen tubs and piled them high on the counter. She retied her blaze of red hair, watching the ice cream intently as she handed Mae the cash.

'Are you having a party?' Mae said.

'Every day is a party, bitch.' Sally pulled at the neck of her sweatshirt, like it was cutting off the circulation. 'You got *Fifty Shades*?'

'Out.'

'It's Selena, people are either fighting or fu—'

Mae shrugged. 'If you can't get on, get off.'

Sally smiled as Mae began to bag.

'Leave one out. I'll eat it on the walk home.'

'You need a spoon?'

'I carry one.'

Mae went to hand Sally her change.

'Put it in the pot. Cancer kids or deaf dogs or whatever.'

Sally opened a tub of salted caramel, took a metal spoon from her pocket and stabbed it.

'Is it true you found her?'

Mae nodded.

'It's a long way to fall. Must've been so much blood.' Sally stared at the counter as she spoke. 'My mother said she was glad.'

Mae felt the air cool.

'Piano. It's my life. I had a chance at more . . . Abi never took it serious. She could play, but she held us back. Missed practice. Turned up late to concerts. We don't all have rich parents. Some of us need this.'

Sally picked up the bag, walked towards the door and then stopped. 'Her face . . . Was she still beautiful, or did the Abi Manton everyone saw just disappear?'

'She was dead, Sally.'

'She died the day she bowed down to Hunter Silver.'

Mae watched her leave, then she saw him.

He left West Wine with a bag, in front of him the last of the day burned off as stars edged out the sun.

Mae walked out and sat on her kerb, Felix opposite.

'That boy,' she said.

'Bought a single bottle of tequila. Means business. And that's not all he asked for. Asked if I knew a short girl, dark hair and tattoo on her wrist.'

Mae glared in the direction he'd headed. 'And do you?'

'I'm almost a Forever, right?' He pointed to the *F* on his wrist. 'Deny until you die. What did you do?'

'Saved his life.'

Felix dropped in the street and struggled to do press-ups. 'Phase three of the wooship. Candice likes Liam, and he's ripped,' he wheezed. 'I told my mother I'll only consume protein from here on.'

'I think your biceps are actually inverted.'

He stopped mid-push and slowly lost all power. His cheek gently met the pavement as a passing car sounded the horn.

'You keep looking down the road,' he said from the ground.

'Don't tell me Mae Cassidy, she of stone heart and bad attitude, has a crush on a pretty summer boy.'

She gave him the finger.

'So let me get this straight. My attraction to Candice is banal and obvious, whereas your attraction to that kid is . . .'

'Non-existent.'

'Ask him out.'

'Ask out Candice.'

'I will once I turn myself into the kind of boy she might actually notice.'

'She doesn't like Tirds?'

'I ended up in the nurse's office before she could even see it. Pleather and thirty-degree heat don't go well together.'

Mae began to laugh.

'She ended up cutting me out of it. Caught the goddam T-shirt too. I had to walk home topless.'

'I sometimes wonder why we're still friends.'

At nine Felix brought out a couple of cold beers.

Mae lit a cigarette and blew smoke towards the moon.

They toasted each other. 'To the creeps,' he said, and stared at her, waiting.

'And the weirdos,' she said, finally.

'Sometimes things feel too solid, you know? We're too strong to break apart.'

'But we're not. Superiority is an illusion.'

'I tried to pray again last night.'

'And?'

'It's my voice in my head. There's no one listening, Mae. Our real eternity is made of supernovas and black holes and –'

'Asteroids.'

Mae didn't notice the two girls until they were right beside her.

They stood hand in hand, one tall and one short.

'We're Matilda and Betty,' the taller girl said. 'The Forevers –'

'They're real and they're coming for you,' Felix called from across the street.

'We'll be waiting, Mae.' The tall girl nodded, and then they turned and headed towards the beach.

'Lesbian crew,' Felix said. 'You think they'd let me –'

'No.'

'What about if I just –'

'No.'

Felix closed his eyes and lay back on the pavement. 'Maybe in the next month we'll get answers to every question we've ever wondered about. We'll find out the meaning of life. We'll fall in love and get laid and meet the most amazing people and save a life and take a life and –'

'And maybe we'll just die an extraordinary death at the end of a life so ordinary it barely counts.'

He stood and walked into the middle of the street and held his hands up to the sky. 'I reckon I can take her.'

Mae smiled.

'You think Abi is looking down?'

'Or up.'

He looked across at her. 'She said she had to do something bad. What if it was so bad it got her killed?'

Mae looked up at the stars, trying not to feel the chill that ran down her spine.

12

At Newport she left the bus and crossed dying grass, the sun fierce above.

Most shops were closed down, most cars sat on flats. Flyers plastered a phone box, the glass shattered.

The truth will set you free.

She pressed the buzzer outside the pawnbroker's and watched the man inside look up, then release the lock and frown at the same time.

She pushed the caged door and stepped into rows of glass cabinets, people's possessions displayed crudely. Electricals to jewellery to rare books and coins.

'You again.'

She handed over the laptop and camera.

He scratched his beard and stared past her at the small television on the wall, Morales on the screen.

'Nuclear,' the man said. He wore glasses on a string, put them on briefly and studied the laptop. 'A nuclear warhead will blow her out of the sky. Morales, he'll get a prize or something, when this is done. Nobel Peace . . . for using a nuclear weapon. That's poetic.'

He placed notes on the counter.

'The laptop, it's worth more.'

'It's stolen.'

'It's not.'

'Try somewhere else.'

'You're the only place in a hundred miles.'

His laugh turned into a cough. He fished out a handkerchief and wiped a streak of blood from his mouth. 'Cancer. I used to worry about going before my time, but then I see kids like you. You come in here with that look in your eyes. Is it easier, if you can't remember before?'

She said nothing.

'Why'd you need cash?' He dabbed his mouth. 'Drugs?'

'So I can find a cure for cancer in the next month.'

Another smile, another laugh and cough. More blood. 'Are you a leaver? You know there's nowhere to go. Here is as good a place as any to die, kid.'

'I'm not –'

'Bring me gold if you want real money. It'll hold its value. In the sky, underground.' He pointed towards the window. 'They're building bunkers all over. They bring me their gold so they can pay for the work.' He reached behind the counter and pulled out a thin gold necklace with a blue stone. 'This is what I pay out for.' He held it to the light and the stone shone. 'I pay pennies on the pound. If they stop Selena I'll be rich.'

'And if they don't?'

'Then I won't care much about anything.'

Mae looked at the necklace, the shape of a half-moon. She reasoned she had a moral code, muddied but there. If it carried value beyond monetary, she left it. A laptop could be replaced, a memory couldn't.

He turned back to the screen. 'Morales. Maybe he's not even real, maybe none of this is. I mean, what proof have we seen? CGI. Damn, they make new worlds on computer systems. They faked a moon landing.'

'It is real and we will die.'

'You want a buyback price?' he said.

She shook her head.

'No one ever does.'

She stopped in Pitmann Square and listened to a man who stood atop a wooden box and slurred about eternalism and gravity. A small crowd listened.

On another box a girl with a guitar played and sang about lighting candles in a daze and Mae peeled one of the notes from the meagre stack and placed it in her case.

The council offices occupied the old courthouse.

Mae took the steps slowly and found her way to the third floor.

Files stacked by the window blocked all but the thinnest slice of sun.

Colin Hayes frowned when he saw her, went to call security but she snatched the phone from his hand.

'Every month,' he said, pinching the bridge of his nose. A lanyard hung from a thin chain around his neck. In the photo he had hair and a smile, neither of which remained that afternoon.

She sat, clutched the phone and glared at him.

'You know there's nothing I can do.' He dabbed at sweat with a paper napkin.

'You all made promises. You voted for them.'

'And they worked, until they didn't. No one is paying taxes. Your grandmother isn't the only one to lose out on her pension. There's no benefits. I get women with three children, they can't pay the rent. Or the landlord wants them out because he's selling everything he owns and heading to Spain to die in the sun.'

'How am I supposed to feed my sister?'

'Ask for help. You must have friends.'

'Charity,' she said, the word hard in her mouth. 'I can take care of my family. But we need what's ours.'

'In a month things will get better. People will have to go back to work.'

'Or they'll be dead.'

'I want to help you, but I'm drowning here.' He picked up a stack of papers. 'Sixty-four thousand, three hundred and nineteen. That's how many people have been released early over the past eighteen months. No one wants to be a prison guard, Miss Cassidy. Can you blame them? People want to be with their families, or on the beach. If you want to protect your sister, you'll keep her away from . . .' he pulled on his reading glasses, 'Lewis Cranston. Oliver Sweeny. Malcolm Banbridge.'

'Who are –'

'These are people that shouldn't be going home. These are the worst of our world, and because of extenuating circumstances they'll be coming to a town near you very soon.'

She left the office and was about to head down the stairs

when she saw him. He stood alone, eyes down and hands deep in his trouser pockets.

She took a step towards him, then stopped. She felt the crossroads, knew she should turn back because something about him seemed reckless. And she was measured, she had to be, for Stella. For the fragile ship they sailed through these last days on.

He looked up.

He didn't smile, she didn't either.

Behind him she saw a large room, a circle of chairs. A whiteboard. A man with a beard led a small group.

She looked at his shoes, his legs and arms and hair. Anywhere but into his eyes.

'I don't really feel anything any more.'

He was tall and she was small. She stood her ground but the ground was soft. Her heart beat so loud she imagined all the glass around her shattering. The letters on her wrist floated up and he looked down and noticed them.

'The girl from the tape.'

It was hot, so airless she felt sweat on her top lip, beneath her arms, down her back.

Outside in the sun, on the stone steps, he stood with his back to her.

'Sometimes I want her to come, so I won't have to do it myself.' She swallowed.

'And other times?'

'It's the last thing I can control.'

He turned and looked down and in that light he dazzled her with a smile that changed his face. And then it was gone.

'You ever miss being a kid?' he said.

She said nothing.

He stepped up onto the low wall beside, his arms out wide. 'When every wall was a tightrope. When you didn't worry about shit you couldn't change.'

She lit a cigarette, the smoke filling her lungs so totally.

He wobbled slightly. 'I feel like I've lost that balance. But I don't know if it's me, or if the world is trying to throw me off.'

'You work here?'

He nodded.

'No way you need the money.'

His eyes were light, he spoke without humour. 'I go where the judge deems fit, where I can work towards being a productive member of society and atone for past misdeeds.'

'Probation?'

'Haven't you been to church? This life is probation.'

She looked out across the town. The faded awnings shaded boarded shops. The sun beat fiercely.

She fought the urge to stop him falling.

He stepped down and she breathed.

'The idea of Selena. And death. Its existential importance. You ever think that each second, each instant is the most important moment in your life because it will never happen again? We plan and wait and hope and expect. But what if we miss it?'

'What?'

He stared at her. 'What breaks into our home.'

'What drags us into the water at night.'

'Survival is basal. Take away every luxury we've known –'

'And I'll bet you've known some.'

'And that's all we're all doing. We're fighting our endless numbered days. Where we are, there is no forward. There's an immediate. And that's a luxury in itself.'

Mae glanced at the betting shop across the square. The odds changed daily. Life or death.

Mae closed her eyes to the sun. 'It's all memories and regret. What you haven't done or what you could've done differently.'

'What haven't you done?'

'Too much to list.'

'My mother says all you need is to tell someone you love them, and for them to say it back. Everything else is secondary. Distraction.'

'Like I need some idiot boy giving me flowers, reciting poetry and thinking up some elaborate promposal. It's . . . It's not even what I haven't done. It's my sister. I want her to . . . I want her to see light.

'Religion.'

'Light, not the light. What we take for granted.'

He loosened his tie and opened three buttons. 'Maybe you're asking for too much.'

'So what should I be asking for?

'What's a Forever?'

That look again, so deep like he could see every secret she'd ever kept.

She hated that her stomach flipped.

Hated it.

She saw her bus.

He took her wrist and traced the letters with his finger and she felt his touch too deep in her bones.

'What's your name?' she said.

'Jack Sail. You can just call me Sail. Everyone does.'

'You saying that like I'm everyone, Jack?'

13

She noticed him near the front of the bus.

There was something puritanical about Theodore Sandford, sitting there blessed by the sunlight.

'I keep thinking of her,' Mae said, sliding into the seat beside him.

'Yes.'

His voice was too high, lending itself to falsetto but nothing more. Kids made jokes, but when he sang they sat there as rapt as everyone else.

He pressed himself close to the glass. 'My grandad lives in White Cove. He doesn't believe.'

'In God?'

'In Selena.'

'Not believing like that. No telescope. No watching the sky, the news. No posters of constellations. That takes its own kind of commitment.'

He shrugged.

'You haven't been to see Abi's parents.' She did not know Theodore Sandford well, but she could see he looked nervous.

'I will.' He spoke quietly. There was a practised deference to him. His hair was neatly parted to the side, his shirt tucked into his shorts and buttoned to the top. On his finger she noticed he still wore the silver purity ring.

She looked down and saw the skin raw on both his knees, the scratches bloodied and dark.

'Did you fall?'

He followed her eye. 'People keep asking you about it. How you found her. What she looked like.'

'She was dead, Theodore.'

He flinched at the word. A physical reaction.

'I think her back was broken. Maybe her leg had snapped. There was blood around her head. Her jaw looked wrong, maybe dislocated.'

He closed his eyes and she stopped.

'Hearing her voice in school . . . I didn't sleep after. I used to ask her about the tattoo,' he said.

The bus eased to a stop. No one got on and no one got off.

'We were fifteen,' Mae said.

'You can get a tattoo at fifteen. You can get alcohol and drugs, and my cousin in the city said his friend has a gun. Do you think maybe Selena is doing the universe a favour?' He spoke with a sincerity that disarmed her.

'You were together for a long time but you didn't sleep together.'

He reached down and turned the band on his finger. 'Why do people make such a thing about sex? We made a commitment. I don't expect someone like you to understand.'

Hunter had started the rumour that Mae had been with a line of boys at the beach, summer boys that lined up and

79

used her and high-fived afterward. She'd seen writing in the toilets at school.

Mae Cassidy is a slut.

Mae Cassidy will burn.

'Most boys wouldn't wait. Especially now.'

'I've spent my whole life preparing for the next one.'

'You think she jumped, Theodore?'

'Yes.'

'You sound certain.'

'Death is only hard for the living.'

The bus hit a bump, her knee hit his, he moved further from her, like sin was contagious.

'The concert, the last Sunday, we each get to choose a song. Most are going with a hymn, "Abide With Me" or something like that.'

'What did Abi choose?'

'Something about creeps and weirdos.'

Another time and she might have smiled, might have allowed Abi's death to colour her memories.

'Whenever we tried to practise, she'd cry. I mean, she'd cry so much that we had to stop.'

She watched his face as he spoke, the delicate bow of his lips. He was the kind of innocent that could be shattered. Mae couldn't imagine him with Abi, or with anyone at all. He was to be displayed at the front of a choir, to be projected as a Sacred Heart ideal.

'Where were you the night she died?'

He smiled sadly. 'Where I always am on a Sunday night, practising with Sally Sweeny. That's my life. Sometimes everything is simple. And sometimes nothing makes sense. But most things fall somewhere in between. Was it you . . . the recordings?'

Mae shook her head.

'Whoever's doing it, they need to stop now. They really need to stop before something bad happens.'

'Something bad already happened, Theodore.'

He pressed the bell as they reached the edge of town. 'If you're looking for answers, Mae, you should look to the sky.'

'I do, only it's not God I see rushing down towards us.' She stood to let him pass.

'Faith is a choice. It's not thrust upon you. You have to work hard at it. I don't think Abi ever understood that.'

She saw him as she stepped off the bus.

Behind him, purple cannoned from the water.

He carried flowers, a small bouquet of daisies that looked like they'd been torn from someone's garden.

She chewed the inside of her cheek.

He held them out.

'That's the sorriest bunch of flowers I've even seen. Did you steal them?'

'Yes.'

A group of girls passed and stared and he ignored them.

'You always dress like you're going to a funeral?' she said.

'I gave all my clothes away.'

The church bell rang loud.

'You didn't ask if you could come into my life. Now you're here.'

81

She felt his hand on her lower back, his chest against her.

'I'm not. I'm nowhere,' she said.

Their lips were close, too close.

'You're everything I hate about this town,' she said.

She walked away, back towards home, carrying her daisies. As she passed the church, she saw Theodore cross himself and head inside.

She stopped by the door.

He cried without shame, small beneath the cross.

14

They buried Abi on a day too beautiful.

Half the school littered the grounds of St Cecelia, some cross-legged on the grass, some sitting on broken gravestones. In the distance surfers carved the waves.

Reverend Baxter spoke choice words about God's need for another angel, like he wouldn't be drowning in them soon enough.

Though Abi was close to eighteen, she took her place in the children's cemetery, in a spot beneath white blossom so fragile Mae kept her eyes fixed to it as Luke Manton screamed his daughter's name, his knees in the mud, his hand on the coffin.

Abi's mother hid behind large sunglasses, separate from her husband, separate from all of them.

Maybe it hit home then, to everyone there. The kids that came because there was nothing else to do. The neighbours showing face. Death in all its finality.

'Are you okay?' Felix said.

Mae took a breath. 'She left us behind. Everything we did before. Our flawed idea of perfect.'

'My father, the people here and the god they pray to, that's flawed. Open your eyes, Mae. You'll see it again.'

When it was done they drifted towards a church hall filled to bursting.

Luke Manton took a plastic chair and a bottle of vodka and remained by his daughter's grave. No one went over, no one knew what to say. Of all the words left, not one of them fit.

'Paper plates,' Sally said, from the buffet table. 'They don't have the structural integrity for what I've got planned.'

Mae saw an empty foil serving platter and held it up.

'That's my girl,' Sally said, taking it and loading it with sandwiches.

Mae watched her, the way she went through food, sweat ran down her forehead and dripped from her nose.

'I'm surprised her ex came.' Sally air-quoted ex with her fingers, then licked barbecue sauce from them. 'You know she ditched him?'

Mae looked up, surprised.

'He's all right now he's got his little minion with him.' Sally nodded in the direction of Jeet Patel. 'It'll say understudy on his grave, you know, if he gets to have one. Theodore gets the solo, he's got the voice. Not that Jeet complains. He's like a rainbow . . . Makes you wonder what's underneath though, right?'

She gripped a bottle of wine between her knees and wrestled with the cork.

'Candice is here,' Felix said, as Sally sat down beside them.

'Candice Harper?' Sally laughed. 'You might want to pick easier prey, Javelin.'

'She likes bad boys,' Felix said. 'And they don't come badder than me.'

'Yeah, I saw the Tird incident. That was actually bad. Nothing says sexy like being cut out of a fake leather jacket by the school nurse.'

'You think Candice heard?'

Sally nodded. 'I had French with her when you strolled topless past the window. *Répugnant.*'

'The protein hadn't kicked in yet.'

Sally looked him up and down. 'I'm sure it's made a world of difference.'

'You want me to strip down and prove it?'

'Sure. The buffet table is missing a Twiglet.'

Mae left them. Outside she saw Lydia Manton standing at the far wall, watching the water in the distance. Expensive dress and heels, her hair immaculate.

Lydia took a cigarette from her purse, lit another for Mae and passed it to her. 'You think it was cold, the way she treated you.'

Mae said nothing.

'I grew up poor, Mae. I know about judgement. You don't look a certain way. We had a group in our school like Hunter's.'

'Everyone does.'

'You have to want more for your own kids. You have to want them to have an easier time.' She held the smoke deep, then blew it towards the clouds. 'The Forevers.' Lydia gripped the cigarette tightly. She wore diamond studs in each ear and the even expression born at the hands of a surgeon, forever fixed in neutral. 'You must have known you'd drift apart. Abi was practising violin and you were practising . . . giving yourself a tattoo. We could finally afford tutors. We could –'

'I get it.'

Lydia looked at her. 'When you're a teenager, you think you won't change . . . but you think the world will.' Lydia's mouth tightened and she dropped the cigarette to the ground and stubbed it out. 'Abi was supposed to be my little princess. I had this idea of her, how she'd be everything I wasn't. But she and her father were always closer . . .'

Mae watched the water. 'She loved you.'

'Abi hated me. She could never see it, the bigger picture. Girls like Hunter live nice lives, Mae. Luke doesn't believe she jumped. Thinking someone did this to her is easier than thinking she chose not to come to him with her problems. He's slurring about murder and it's not helping him, not this close to the end.'

'You think it's the end then? No one ever says that.'

'Whatever happens with Selena, this is our end. People looked at us and I saw their envy, and I liked it.'

'Everyone likes it, they just don't admit to it.'

'But what they saw wasn't real. We've all got secrets, Mae. But now, with the time we have left, it's how deep you bury them. That's all that matters.'

'They didn't check . . . how she died?'

'Lay her down, cut her open. My girl died a saint, that's all anyone needs to remember.'

She squeezed Mae's shoulder, a little too hard, then headed back inside.

Across the cemetery Mr Silver sat alone on a bench, away from Luke Manton but watching the freshly dug grave, the mountain of lilies.

'Dead people receive more flowers than the living because –'

'Regret is stronger than gratitude,' Mae said, turning to see Hunter beside her, stylish in a short black dress, her hair scraped back, her cheekbones severe.

'My mother sent me over here. She saw you by the cliff edge and feared the worst. And she hates a funeral as much as I do.'

'Showing face.'

'Like the rest. You think Sally wants to be here? Last I heard she and Abi almost clawed each other's eyes out in class. And Theodore, Abi ditched him because he wouldn't sleep with her.'

'They wore purity rings.'

'There was nothing pure about Abi Manton. She used to follow Hugo around like a bitch in heat. I only hung out with her because her mother kept stopping by to invite my parents to her pathetic parties. We used her for a while, used her mother's need to make her fit. I'd come back from the beach and Abi would be waiting for me at my house. Like, she'd been there all day, just waiting. Tragic how far some people will go just to fit in, just to be me. And I thought envy was a sin.'

'People say I'm cold.'

'Oh, you are. They'll find out for themselves soon enough.' Hunter nodded in the direction of two girls who stood hand in hand, staring at Mae. 'Like the Forevers wasn't some forever-friends club where the loser girls bitch about the popular girls.'

Hunter took the cigarette from Mae's hand, took a long

drag and flicked it to the ground. 'We have a sweepstake for who's next. I got Sullivan Reed.'

They looked over at Sullivan. He sat on the grass, a sketch pad beside him, head tilted so his hair hid the scars.

'So if you could hang on a little longer before you take your turn, that'd be great. Thanks, Mae.'

Mae drifted towards the cemetery, sat alone and watched the sunset.

They made the walk at twilight.

Two hundred filed from the church down to the beach, where chairs had been set out in neat rows before a stage wrapped with fairy lights. Flowers were arranged in stone vases as tall as Mae.

Theodore stood at the front.

Sally Sweeny took her seat behind a white piano, one last chance for Lydia Manton to paint the town green.

Service books were handed out. A sketch of Abi's smiling face took the front page, Mae saw the delicate scrawl at the bottom. Sullivan Reed was a talented artist.

The Reverend Baxter thanked Abi's friends for lending them their voices on that perfect summer night.

They played.

Theodore sang.

People cried.

Mae focused on the water, the lapping waves as night crept into the day.

It was as Sally led them into the last song, and Theodore sang about giving himself away, his hands tied, his body bruised, that they turned the last page of their book.

And then they saw it.

And two hundred heads bowed and read the last words of Abi Manton in delicate italics.

It takes a lot for Mae to cry. When her parents died I sat beside her at the church, held her hand and waited for her to break but she didn't. She kept it together for Stella. Mae held strong. And she stayed that way.

Sometimes she drinks so much I know she's trying to get away. She cares for her sister, for her bitch grandmother. That night on the beach, we were fifteen, nothing had happened, not that day, but maybe it was years of holding on that finally took their toll.

The sun set. The sky . . . that blaze of colour. You ever think maybe the world is too perfect to exist? Trillion-to-one odds. A star exploded and sparked our sun, volcanoes erupted and gave us water. Complex molecules reached a chance collision that every single one of us is born from. Oxygen. Asteroids. A chain of events so spectacular that two girls ended up on a beach drinking vodka and waiting for it all to be undone.

I didn't realise she was crying. I just looked to the side, and she was watching this perfect sunset, and she cried her heart right out of her body.

Maybe it was then Mae Cassidy appreciated just what we'll lose.

We'll lose our chance to be better.

To fix ourselves and our mistakes.

We'll lose our chance to be kind.

To be something.

To be true.

To live.

Right then Mae decided not to see Selena as a curse. She decided to see her as an opportunity. An opportunity to fast-track all the coming-of-age bullshit and become exactly who we are right now. Because deep down we all know.

All that confusion is just misplaced fear.

We don't waste time living another person's life, another person's lie. We grab hold of it right now, and we say, I am. Not I might be. Not I could be.

I am.

I am.

I am.

'So what am I?' I said as Mae passed me the bottle of vodka.

Mae smiled. She's got a great smile, but you have to be lucky to see it. 'I know what I am. I'm a creep.'

I laughed. 'And I'm a weirdo.'

Mae reached out a hand and I took it.

'What if we take back Forever?' Mae watched the stars blink out one by one as the old sky died and our new one took shape.

She looked tough, even crying, like her tears were so hot they scarred her. 'Why can't it be, for us? And I'm not talking God or some religion's version of heaven. I'm talking our own Forever.'

She held her bottle to our moon and we grabbed hold of the Forever that was stolen from us. The Forever in fairy tales, the ever-after that doesn't burn out.

It wasn't for the perfect prince and princess, it was for the girl who lost both parents when she was ten, it was for the sides of us that we keep hidden because we know the world isn't willing to accept. We rewrote the rules. We chose the Forever we dreamed of.

Tolerate, don't subjugate.

I won't ask you to live my life, so don't ask me to live yours. We made Forever for the creeps and the weirdos, the freaks and the outlaws. We decided we'd be blind to anyone that was blind to us. If I can't see your hate, it has no power.

If Selena didn't come, or even if she did, we refused to live in their world any longer. A world where beauty is objective.

Where money equals class.

Where the misshapen are beaten till they fit or disappear. You can say it was childish bullshit, naive, impossible, but you know what? This was our summer of impossible things. So while we still had stars to wish on, we chose not to die in their world.

Mae took the needle and the ink, and she branded our wrists and our souls.

We knew long before that moment that we were Forevers. A simmering storm since the day we were born. We made that pact then. If you're crying because the world has spit in your face, you don't have to cry alone. We are an army of each other, and an army of one.

That single word told you nothing and everything.

It told you we were good if you were one of us.

Bad if you weren't.

We agreed to meet at midnight on the beach each night.

We'd do it till the end and till the beginning.

We'd pass each other in school corridors, in shopping centres and bars. And we'd see the word and know.

Together we held hands and ran at the water.

Forever was always.

And it would be again.

15

As the music faded and the sun drowned, Mae got to her feet and ran from the crowd before they could turn and see her.

She sat alone on the sand and drank down the bottle of wine she'd taken from the side table.

Drank till the world began to swim.

'Are you okay?'

She looked up. 'It's been a long day, rich boy.'

'But it's almost over now. They're all almost over.' In his hand he held a service book.

'Maybe the sun won't rise tomorrow. Maybe it won't see the point.'

She drank more, determined, her face tight, like it was medicine she could not live without.

She lay flat on her back, arms and legs out.

He lay beside her and looked up.

'Are you okay?' he said, again.

'That's a shit question.'

'Why?'

'Because okay should never be enough.'

'So what is enough?'

She turned, her face in the moonlight. 'The time we have left, we strive for brilliance. Nothing less.'

'So, are you brilliant?'

'Maybe I was once but I'd just forgotten.' And then she leaned over and pressed her lips to his.

She held his face tight, and kissed him so hard and desperate, like that kiss alone could carry her away.

'Boys make everything worse.'

'Okay.'

'People were crying,' she said.

'They still are.'

'It was supposed to be joyous.'

'That's the thing about goodbyes, they rarely are.' He held out his wrist. In his other hand was a pen.

'You don't want to do this,' she said.

He stared at her with those dark eyes. 'I want my Forever.'

'There is no –'

'Tell me you didn't mean it. A place for everyone, for the people who don't fit anywhere else. Tell me you didn't mean that.'

He saw the truth in her eyes.

'A place for everyone who's ever felt alone. We'll collect them like strays and we'll give them a home.'

'I want to go home.'

'You already have a home. It's the biggest home I've ever seen.'

'It's empty rooms for empty people.' He took a syringe from his pocket and snapped the needle from it.

Mae gripped his arm, his flawless skin, and she watched the ink swim into his blood.

She knew nothing about him.

She knew enough.

16

The autumn I turned fifteen, we gathered on the beach and held hands as we stared at the screen by the sheer cliff face.

Liam had rigged the projector up.

I sat beside Felix as we watched Saviour 8 launch from the desert in Kazakhstan.

We didn't speak, not one of us, but we all felt it, that this was the one.

Morales had sold it.

The newspapers ran it daily in the boldest print.

Our planet will be saved.

I looked to the right and saw tears in Abi's eyes. And to the left, tears in Hunter Silver's.

The craft had been detailed on the television, in the newspapers, drawn on the whiteboard by Mr Starling. It would land on Selena and blast rockets from the surface. The angles would be altered, she would miss Earth by two million miles.

We shared out popcorn.

Liam and Hugo set off fireworks.

A small crowd formed on the clifftop and watched.

It was cold but we stripped off and held hands and ran into the water.

We shrieked and cried and splashed till we could no longer feel our bones.

We ran back up to the beach and huddled beneath our towels.

'Tell me about today,' Stella said.

'It came and it went.'

'Was Abi's body laid out? Did people go up and look at her dead face?'

'No.'

'Did you go to Mum and Dad's funeral?'

'Yes.'

'I was in the hospital because I was too small.'

'Yes.'

Mae remembered the night too clearly. Sitting in the hospital waiting room as dusk caved to dawn in a breath held till it hurt. People came and went, more pain and more fear, more crime, more casualties. The room in half-dark as she watched the large television screen, the sounds muffled by what she had seen, so tired the colours blurred. Nurses gathered beside a doctor in scrubs, a cluster of drunks too dizzy to focus. Together they watched as Russian rockets ripped the atmosphere over Rio, a million on the streets, bold colours, carnival sounds and dancing as they cheered on a united world. The nurses held hands, one dipped her head in prayer, then crossed herself when she was done.

'After the truck hit us they cut me from her,' Stella said. 'But I wasn't ready to come out. That's why I'm blind.'

'Yes.'

Stella had lived in a tank her first month, a creature too fragile to breathe the fleeting air. Three buses to reach her each day, Mae rode them alone and numb.

Their mother did not wake to meet her second child.

'Do you know about fate?' Stella said.

'What about it?'

'Is it real?'

At five weeks Stella was strong enough to emerge, to lie in her sister's arms as Mae gently rocked her and told her nothing of the world outside. Mae's had been the first finger Stella gripped, the first chest she pressed to.

You will be loved.

You will be loved.

You will be loved.

'We don't have control over Selena. So our destiny is to die soon.'

When she fell and cried, Mae picked her up, dusted her down. At four, Mae taught her sister to swim. Sometimes Stella said Mae was too tough. Mae knew that was okay. Sometimes Stella did not get her way and she screamed and told Mae she hated her. And Mae knew that was okay too.

The shadow in the sky was growing. They had to be tough. Mae had kept Selena from their lives until the day before Stella started school. They sat on the beach and had that conversation. No emotion, just the coldest of facts. Stella took the news with an evenness that told Mae she could not possibly understand.

'Will it hurt?' Stella said, sleepily.

'No, it won't hurt.'

'Will you read me a story?'

'You could read one to me,' Mae said. 'I love to watch you read.'

'I've read all the braille books at the library. We don't have money to buy new ones.'

Stella curled into Mae, something she did when she was worried.

'Will you tell me about Saviour 1?'

'I will. One day I will.'

Mae stayed with her till she slept.

Then she pulled on dark jeans and a black hoodie.

Mae stood across the street from the Manton house and watched. For a while she tried to imagine what it must have been like for Abi, all of a sudden thrust into the kind of life they used to laugh at. Shiny cars and plastic smiles.

She climbed the wall, stayed low and moved down the side of the house.

In the back garden she saw the large glass doors open, and inside the glow of the television lit Luke Manton's sleeping form. Slumped to the side, mirroring the empty bottle in front of him.

She entered silently and threaded her way past a tower of beer cans. Luke had commandeered the living room, the rest of the house was immaculate.

Mae climbed the stairs with care, saw one bedroom door closed and guessed Lydia Manton was on the other side of it, dead to the world, the only peace coming when she swallowed a couple of sleeping pills and escaped into her dreams.

She tried a couple of rooms before she found Abi's.

It was cold and clinical. Grey walls and carpet, the kind of achingly cool more at home in a magazine than real life.

The first thing she noticed was the artwork. Sweeping scenes on large canvases hung on each wall. Abi's initials in the bottom corner. Each showed the beach, some by day and others moonlit.

Mae recognised them at once.

In every picture there were two shapes on the beach, more shadow than anything else but Mae knew exactly what she was looking at. That perfect September day when they'd stood in front of each other and sworn their Forevers.

She sat at Abi's desk and flipped through a notebook, then tried each drawer and found nothing more interesting than paints and brushes.

It should've been taped off. The room should have been sealed till people in paper boiler suits had combed and dusted it. There should have been police all over town. A girl was dead.

In Abi's wardrobe, dresses hung with the labels still attached, the prices so eye-watering Mae could not imagine such waste.

Whatever she'd been hoping to find wasn't there. The room was ordered and immaculate.

Abi's old room had been yellow and filled to bursting. She collected everything from feathers to stones, driftwood to cheap paperweights.

Mae walked over to the bookcase and scanned the shelves, from *Anna Karenina* to *Lord of the Flies*, Faulkner to Steinbeck. Nothing stood out, until she reached the bottom. Something about the early edition of *Lolita* made her stop. Mae remembered Abi reading it on the beach, the old vicar telling her it was the devil's work.

She picked it up, started to flip the pages, when she saw it had been crudely hollowed out. Inside Mae traced a finger along the pack. Microgynon. Abi was on the pill.

She thought of Theodore Sandford, the purity rings they both wore. Maybe it really was nobody's business, or maybe the lie had come too easily to him.

Mae crept back through the house, staying silent but there was no need. Luke Manton's heavy snores drowned her footsteps.

Back out on the empty street she heard noise.

She spun, saw no one but her heart rate began to climb. She turned and walked, then heard it again.

Footsteps.

Behind her.

Mae picked up her pace but still they followed.

The shape was dark, and coming at her from the shadows.

She broke into a sprint.

He was on her fast, a sharp push sent her sprawling into a bin store. She rolled and aimed a kick that caught him hard. He stumbled and Mae moved to the side. She scrambled around wildly as he fell heavily on top of her, knocking the air from her lungs. She couldn't see his face, just a red hoodie pulled tight, the darkness swallowing his features.

And then she felt his hands moving up her thighs, stopping at her pockets as he pressed. She wished she had her knife. She'd cut him. She knew that about herself.

He grabbed her bag and began tossing the contents from it.

Her fingers brushed something cool.

Glass.

She clenched her teeth as she gripped the bottle and brought it hard against his head. It shattered in her hand, she felt the blood hot on her as he fell backwards.

Mae climbed to her feet and set off again.

This time she cut across and climbed the steep wall in front of the Prince house.

Their garden was a mess of machinery, scaffolding and tools. She looked back, stunned as the figure dropped over after her.

At the end of the garden Mae jumped down onto the track behind.

The cliff face was severe but she knew the best route down. She moved down the rocks, they evened out and eventually she came to the beach.

A fire burned in the distance and she headed towards it, then screamed when she slammed hard into someone.

'Mae.'

'Sail,' she panted, her chest on fire.

She dropped to her knees and he fell with her, keeping her level as she pressed her cheek to his chest.

'What's wrong?' He gripped her shoulders tightly.

She pointed, barely able to speak. 'Nothing. I handled it.'

The fire crackled, the smoke rose and the water broke in arcs. A large group of kids was sitting around it, still wearing their funeral clothes.

Sail read her, and then ran back the way she had come, disappearing into the darkness.

17

Felix wore a white suit, the red shirt beneath unbuttoned to his navel. '*Scarface*. She rented it twice last autumn.'

'So much nipple,' Mae said.

'I've never been more glad to be blind,' Stella said.

Felix scowled at them. 'The general theme in her favourite movies is that she likes her men rough and ready.'

'Ready for what?' Stella said.

'Rejection,' Mae said.

'And so today, my friends, I'm letting it be known that I, Felix Baxter, have moved into the narcotics trade.'

Stella frowned.

'You're going to sell drugs?' Mae said. 'You don't have drugs.'

'I raided my mother's medicine cabinet,' Felix said, coughing again. 'I might just hold the cigar, grip it between my teeth when I walk past Candice . . . you know, put out the vibe.'

'That you're an arsehole?' Mae said.

'That there's a new cat in town,' Felix said, holding the cigar away from himself and wafting the smoke with his free hand. 'And he's about to flood West with the good stuff.'

He opened his jacket and Mae glimpsed a couple of packets poking from the inside pocket.

'Benadryl?' Mae said. 'Isn't that for hay fever?'

'General allergy relief,' Stella said.

Felix took gold-rimmed sunglasses from his bag and slipped them on. 'This is just the start. By the end of the week Sacred Heart will be drowning in white. I'm talking pure fairy powder.'

'I hope it's non-bio, otherwise I might need the Benadryl,' Stella said.

As they turned onto the bay they saw a crowd. They managed to get close enough to see the graffiti on the town sign.

Bold red.

THE FOREVERS.

Mrs Abbott stared at Mae like she had red paint on her hands.

Sergeant Walters crossed the street as Mae told Felix she'd catch them up.

'You should've given a statement.' He squinted towards the bay, dark circled his eyes. 'Might've been someone from out of town. You shouldn't walk at night.'

'Because you can't keep us safe? When's the Chief coming back?'

He drew breath at that, dipped his head a little and looked at the town sign. 'This thing . . . the Forevers, do I need to be worried about it?'

'You need to be worried about finding out what happened to Abi.'

He ran a thumb over his badge. 'Every crime gets punished. I am my father's son.'

They watched Mitch Travers, the newsagent, haul out the advertising board.

Everyone watched.

For a moment no one breathed.

'Twenty-three days,' Sergeant Walters said.

'She didn't jump.'

'You can't believe all that Forevers stuff.'

Mae looked him in the eye. 'If you're not with us, you're against us.'

At school, crowds parted for her.

Heads turned. She heard whispers, noticed girls looking down at her wrist. Teachers regarded her with cold stares. Hunter's group openly laughed.

The class fell silent when she walked in. Mae moved down the centre aisle and took Abi's old seat at the back.

Mr Starling began, 'The shockwave and fireball killed every living thing in a thousand-mile radius. Chunks of rock flew back up into space, turned molten then rained back through the atmosphere and pounded the earth.'

Behind him were a series of whiteboards decorated with colour, belts, the dawn of the solar system, the channel between Mars and Jupiter.

'Asteroid means star-like,' he said it slow, meeting some of their eyes, trying to hold some kind of interest.

'Every month you tell us that,' Liam said.

To her left Mae noticed Sullivan Reed leaning over a pad, his hair forward to cover himself.

'The difference between a comet and an asteroid. You see, comets are partially made from ice –'

'We know all this shit. Everyone knows everything about asteroids. We've grown up with them. You make us take science, like we give a crap. We're all wasting our time here. We should be getting high, or getting laid.' Liam held up a hand for Hugo to slap.

Mr Starling turned and looked at the boards behind. He'd tracked other large asteroids and drawn detailed paths, immense pressure was shown with blue waves, acceleration in red. 'The Torino scale rates asteroid impact risk from one to ten. Before Selena the highest rating ever given was a four. Apophis.'

'What's Selena then?' Lexi asked, running a hand through her hair.

'She's a ten.'

'A perfect ten,' Candice said.

'Just like you,' Felix said under his breath.

'Did you say something?' Liam glared, then looked Felix up and down, from his black boots to the ill-fitting suit to the cigar poking from his pocket. Liam shook his head. 'Absolute weirdo.'

'A perfect ten,' Mr Starling said. 'A perfect chance of striking us with a perfect chance of catastrophic consequences. Tens are predicted to come along no more than once every hundred thousand years.'

'I want to see her.'

They turned to the back of the class, where Sally Sweeny sat.

'I want to look up at the sky and see her. She's just pictures in newspapers, and graphics on a computer screen, she's not real. If she's going to kill me, I want to look her in the eye first.'

Sally spoke quietly but everyone listened.

Mr Starling took his glasses off. 'Light pollution gets in the way. There's people journeying to Chad, in central Africa. To Madagascar. They'll see her first.'

Liam was up then, drawing laughs as he stooped himself over and waved his arms in the manner of the teacher. He affected the quiet way Mr Starling spoke. *More than one million asteroids have the potential to hit Earth, but only one will in our lifetime.*

Jeet Patel raised his hand.

As he began to speak, Liam continued to mock Mr Starling.

'Shut up, Liam,' Mr Starling shouted, the words landing like dynamite.

'Why didn't the two ships work?' Jeet Patel said.

Mae tuned it out. She knew how it ended, the solar storm that took out Adam, the detail Eve sent back not nearly enough. There were other projects, an international agency was formed, Mr Starling grew animated when he talked of the Chinese effort that exploded on the launch pad. A billion-dollar failure.

'What can we do?' They all turned to look at Felix. 'Tell us what we can do.'

Mr Starling smiled sadly. 'We can put our faith in science. Or we can put our faith in God. Either way I'm afraid there's some praying involved.'

Felix closed his eyes. 'But –'

'We can just live out our last days doing whatever the hell we want,' Liam said.

'So fatso can eat herself to death,' Lexi said, as she turned and pouted at Sally, who gave her the finger, 'and Mae can whore herself to death.'

'I didn't hear your father complaining last night,' Mae said.

'Lexi's father is dead,' Hunter said, glaring.

'I wondered why he didn't seem that into it.'

'Right now I don't want to be here,' Liam said. And with that he stood.

There was a moment when he faced Mr Starling, and then the old teacher walked over to the door and held it open. Liam walked out, slamming into Mr Starling as he passed.

'That's Abi's seat,' Sullivan Reed said.

Mae looked at him and caught a glimpse of the page. The sketch was of a girl, she looked like Hunter Silver.

'You drew the picture in Abi's service book,' Mae said.

Sullivan stood quickly. He walked with a slight limp, half dragging his right foot across the floor. She noticed a deep scratch on the side of his head as he followed Liam out the door.

'Can we get on with the lesson now?'

Mae tracked the voice to Jeet Patel and she flinched inwardly as Hugo got to his feet.

Mr Starling tried to step between them, but not before Hugo reached over and shoved Jeet from his chair.

'The animals are growing restless,' Sally said. She wore her customary jeans and sweatshirt, despite the heat. 'The Forevers. It's like the start of the uprising or something. You know someone stuck those service sheets all over town. My mother asked me if I was a Forever this morning. Like it's some kind of disease.'

'What did you tell her?'

'No. But she checked my wrist anyway.'

Mae looked to the door again. 'Did Sullivan know Abi?'

'They took art together.'

'That scratch on his head.'

Sally laughed through her nose. 'His cat. He spends all lesson drawing pictures of the thing.'

Mae frowned.

'Pussy addiction,' Sally said, opening her bag and reaching for a chocolate bar. 'It afflicts most boys in this school.'

'Did someone say pussy?' Felix said, spinning around.

'Calm down, lamp post, we're talking four legs and a tail.'

Mae absentmindedly ran a hand across the desk, then looked down when she felt the scratched letters, carved deep into the wood.

A heart.

The initials in it.

AM

TS

She might not have paid it mind, had Theodore Sandford's initials not been scored out a dozen times.

The cafeteria fell silent as Mae crossed the floor.

She took a seat alone at a table at the head of the room.

She thought of Abi, what she'd found in her room, that she'd scratched Theodore out. There was an easy leap to make. They'd slept together and then Theodore had ditched her. Maybe she was depressed enough to do something drastic.

She caught glances from a group of younger girls. They took it in turns to look her way and smile.

Hunter sat at a table with Hugo, Liam, Candice and Lexi. Her army around her.

Heads turned again, this time it was when Jack Sail walked into the room. The whispers were loud, she saw Liam fix him with a hard stare.

Hunter Silver kicked out the chair opposite her.

It played like theatre. Everyone watched. Hunter didn't invite anyone to sit at her table.

Sail stopped by the chair, looked up at the girls who all smiled his way. Lexi teased her hair, Hunter crossed her legs, her skirt riding up her thigh.

Then he saw Mae, and walked over.

'Can I sit?'

'You're about to commit social suicide.'

'I could try, but I have a feeling someone might step in and save me.'

Mae kicked out the chair, mimicking Hunter, who seethed as he sat down. She caught the eye of Sally Sweeny, who winked at her, then turned back to her food.

'Last night, I looked –'

'I know.'

'No announcement today. No voice from above,' he said.

'Threat of expulsion now, maybe they lost their nerve. They're looking at the service sheets. They were printed in town but the guy swears the page wasn't in there when they were collected.'

Felix slumped down at the end of the table. 'I tried to attract Candice's attention in the library. I lit the cigar and sent over a bad-boy smoke vibe.'

'And?'

'It triggered the fire alarm. I'm in serious shit with Mr Silver.'

'Who's Candice?' Sail said.

Felix finally noticed she wasn't sitting alone. 'Summer boy?'

Sail extended a hand, which Felix tried to bump with his fist.

'Candice is Felix's –'

'Goddess,' Felix said, head in his hands. 'I need a grand gesture. An overture. A way to halt my inexorable agony.'

'Felix wants to ask Candice to the Final,' Mae said.

'I've seen the posters,' Sail said.

'But I have two problems,' Felix began. 'One of them of them is sitting next to her.'

Sail turned in his seat. 'The one with the painful-looking cheekbones?'

'That's Hunter.'

'The one with the hair?'

'Lexi. She's never cut it. Apparently it gives her special bitch powers.'

His eyes settled on Candice, and then Liam. 'Steroids. It's likely to have shrunk his –'

'It hasn't,' Felix sighed. 'He was windmilling in the showers. Pretty sure that thing could power a small town.'

'Second problem?' Sail cut in. 'Because it's clearly not style. That suit . . . that shirt . . .' He nodded in appreciation.

'She doesn't know I exist. But that's about to change. Tonight. I may need some help though.'

Sail picked an apple from his tray and bit into it.

'Church at midnight,' Felix said.

'Sounds sacrificial. I'm in.'

'How's the drug dealing going?' Mae said.

Felix shook his head. 'It was going well. Miss Lock bought two paracetamol. Then Becky Lane tried to order Calpol from me. Lexi overheard so it's only a matter of time before it gets back to Candice.'

'So technically you're a drug dealer,' Mae reasoned.

Felix rolled his eyes. 'More like a pharmacist.' And then he clocked the tattoo on Sail's wrist and raised an eyebrow at Mae.

'I pledge allegiance to the fantastic Forevers,' Sail said.

'And yet your sleeve is down.' Mae held her bare arm aloft. 'Uncool by association isn't enough. You need to shame yourself down to our level.'

With that Sail stood on his chair, then climbed onto the table. He held Mae's eye as he rolled up the sleeve of his jacket. Talk died as heads craned to see the word printed on his wrist.

'I hereby declare myself a Forever. And though there is no official leader, if you want in, you need to speak to Mae . . .'

'Cassidy,' Felix said, grinning.

'Mae Cassidy. If you're not with us . . .'

'Okay, arsehole,' Mae said.

Sail winked at her, then hopped down and walked out of the room, eating his apple.

'He seems . . . nice,' Felix said.

Mae shrugged.

Felix grinned.

'What?'

'You like him too.'

'He's pretty and rich and soft. And I've got bigger things on,' she said.

'Abi?'

'I'm going to find out what happened to her.'

'Sergeant Walters didn't get too far, so where do we start?'

Mae glanced across the cafeteria. 'It's usually the boyfriend, right?'

111

18

She saw the girls outside the church.

They stood together, hand in hand, their backs to the entrance.

The tall girl was the first to speak. 'I'm Matilda.'

'And you're Betty,' Mae said.

Betty smiled but took a step back into the shadow cast by the cross.

'Reverend Baxter thinks we'll burn,' Matilda said. Her hair was dark, pixie short.

Betty was surfer blonde, softer, shy. 'We'll be at the beach. Every night. We'll be there.'

Mae watched them leave.

She found Theodore inside.

The air cooled, the heat of summer edged off beneath the towering stone and painted glass.

Mae took a seat at the back, alone, only a handful of others were scattered around as Sally Sweeny played the old organ.

Mae watched them sing, their voices one, till Theodore stepped forward and stole all the light in that quiet way he did. His voice soared, filled the cavernous space and brought tears to the eyes of Miss Holmes, the music teacher, who sat there and watched Theodore like she'd caught a glimpse of heaven and realised death was nothing to fear.

'*Laudate dominum . . .*'

'The boy can sing,' Reverend Baxter said, as he settled in beside Mae.

'That's what they say.'

She looked at Felix's father, his kind eyes and the way he tapped his foot slightly, like a tremor was shaking the floor beneath him.

'I've been hearing things, Mae.'

She watched the flickering candles.

He cleared his throat. 'What Abi said, it . . . it was powerful in its way. I don't like the idea of us and them.'

'There are those who believe, and those who don't. You should know that better than anyone.'

'I spent a long time shadowing the old vicar before I took over. There's room for questions, even for doubt. I speak of forgiveness and that's –'

'Some things are unforgivable.'

He looked sad then, but managed to nod. There was a lot she could have told him, maybe asked him why God could forgive repenting murderers but he himself could not forgive his son's lack of belief.

'I do worry about him,' he said, quiet, reading her.

'You should.'

'He was always a strong-willed child.'

'He's still strong. Did you see what he wore to school today?'

'I know he'll be happier when he finds God.'

'They say faith is blind.'

'Do you pray for Abi?'

'Do you?'

'Of course. And I pray for you, Mae. Do you ever visit your parents' grave? I think it might help you. I know that you've struggled. I'm here for you.'

'I know where I belong, Reverend Baxter.'

He smiled again, touched her hand and moved off.

She spotted Sullivan Reed sitting in the far corner, his head bowed. Maybe this was where they came, those who didn't fit.

'Isn't Theodore sublime?' Jeet Patel said, as he stopped beside Mae.

Sally's words came back to her, Jeet Patel being the eternal understudy.

'The Forevers – that was beautiful, Mae. I can only dream of a world like that.' He smiled again and moved to the front as the Sacreds filed out.

Only Theodore remained.

He didn't notice her, sitting beside the arch, so small she paled into the stone. She was about to walk over when he dropped to the stone floor so hard she heard the crack of his knees echo. She thought of the bruises, the cuts across them that day on the bus.

He bowed his head low, clenched his eyes closed in a prayer she could almost feel.

Something about the desperation, the pleading, made her think of Abi. Theodore was atoning.

Mae waited for him to finish.

Blood trickled down his shins but he made no move to

wipe it. He took a seat beside her, before the heavy cross, the depictions.

'Hunter said you didn't want to sleep with Abi. But I think you did.'

'You're back to this?' he said.

'I'm just getting started.'

'You don't understand.'

'Then make me.'

'My parents liked her. They liked that I had a girlfriend. And that she was in the choir. Abi . . . she was everything. We used to play church songs, she got us into Nirvana.'

Mae almost smiled.

'I loved Abi. People didn't get it, and that's all right, but I saw something in her that I needed. And she gave it to me. And you want to make it about sex, but it was so much more than that. It was something real to us, in a world where kindness is getting lost.'

She watched him speak, the way he looked at the cross.

'Sex . . . we didn't have sex. We're seventeen, Mae. We are capable of something different.'

She thought about what she'd found in Abi's room, the way Abi had scored out Theodore's initials in the desk.

'You broke up.'

'I think she was seeing someone else.'

She heard the faintest trace of something harder before he caught it, reined it in.

'There's no hatred, we don't marry the people we're with at school. It's fine.'

'No one wants to be rejected, Theodore.'

He took a breath. 'There's a bigger picture. What we desire in this life –'

'Who was she seeing?'

'I didn't ask. Does it even matter? She changed, she lost her . . . she was just lost. I tried to help her but she . . . she was quiet. She drank more.'

Above them the church bell shook the building.

'You know she saw you on the beach, Mae. She'd walk to the window in her new bedroom and see you sitting down there alone.'

For a year she waited for her friend to come back to her, waited by the dark water, some nights in the rain, the howling wind, the biting snow.

He stood, the blood on his knees had dried dark. 'Those girls outside, they never come in.'

'Your god doesn't make them feel welcome.'

He smiled, like she'd disappointed him, then walked away.

'Theodore.'

He turned by the door.

'What were you praying for?'

'The same thing everyone is. Forgiveness.'

19

Sail stopped by the big door, like he didn't want to take another step.

Mae watched him, the careful way he moved.

The floor was stone, the mourners had lit candles. He glanced up and around. 'This town, everything is so beautiful.'

His eyes dropped to hers, his pupils large.

Maybe she wanted to kiss him as the saints frowned down on them and the floor opened to fire.

Felix wore a hooded top, his face so drawn it was like he'd already crossed over.

Sail stood at the top of the pulpit as Mae took a bottle of communion wine and a silver goblet.

She stared at the cross. 'Forgive me, Father, for I have sinned, and am likely to again.'

Mae passed the goblet to Sail, who drank liberally. 'AD 30, that was a vintage year.'

'You need to sleep,' Mae said, glancing at Felix.

Felix rubbed his eyes on cue. 'Two hundred and sixty-four hours – that's the record. I'm closing in on sixty.'

'At least take a drink.'

'Can't mix it with the pills. Damn near shat the bed last time.'

'Felix is trying to stay awake long enough to learn everything. And I mean everything,' Mae said to Sail.

'Knowledge is power,' Sail said into the microphone, then raised a fist.

'At the moment I'm just looking for a way to get Candice to notice me.'

'I thought we were Forevers,' Sail said. 'We're not invisible anymore. Tell us the plan.'

'*Ten Things I Hate About You*. Three years ago Candice rented that movie and kept it for six weeks, racking up a decent fine. You know what that tells me?'

'That she lost it?' Mae swirled the goblet.

'It tells me she wants a grand gesture, an all-singing, all-dancing promposal spectacular.'

'Shame you can't sing or dance.'

'Firstly, I've been listening to Barry White since I was a kid. The Walrus of Love is inside me.'

'Jesus,' Mae said.

'And, secondly . . .' Felix stood and began to gyrate.

Sail nodded.

'She also rented *Dante's Inferno* and *Backdraft*. You know what *that* tells me?' Felix said. 'The girl likes fire.'

They emptied into the graveyard, dodging the gravestones as night fell. Above they heard the steady buzz of electricity lines.

Felix led them to Ocean Drive, where Sail headed into the white house alone.

Mae and Felix leaned against the wall.

'This kid's richer than God,' Felix said. 'You chose well.'

'I didn't choose –'

'You know it's okay to actually like a boy, Mae.'

'I don't do boyfriends.'

'You just do boys.'

'Meaningless sex.'

'That's an oxymoron.'

'Spoken like a true girl.'

He looked at the sky. 'People are still working. We're still at school.'

'What's the alternative?'

He shrugged. 'It's like we're stuck in some alternate reality. One day the world is turning, and then next . . . damn. Why don't I feel anything? When I go to church . . .' Felix swallowed. 'Why can't I tap into the higher power. Maybe I'm too young. I'm emotionally retarded.'

'You cry every time you read a book.'

'I fell in love like you fall asleep.'

'In forty-five minute bursts?' Mae said.

'Petrol, just like you ordered.' Sail said, an apparition in the dark, he carried a small plastic jug. It sloshed as he walked.

'You want to tell us the plan now?' Mae said.

The smaller gate was open and Felix led them down the side of the large house and into the garden behind.

'That's her window,' Felix said, and pointed.

'I'm afraid to ask how you know that,' Mae said.

Felix got to work. He pulled out a crumpled piece of paper and gripped a small penlight between his teeth. Then he set about carefully pouring the petrol over designated patches of grass.

'What the hell are you doing?' Mae said, as the rich smell of petrol filled the air.

'I saw it online. Fire writing. Candice comes to her window and sees our names flickering beneath the stars.'

'And then she runs out screaming as fire rushes towards her house.'

Felix waved her off. 'Controlled burn. When she comes down I'll drop to my knee and give her the flowers. Sound good?'

'You don't have flowers,' Mae said.

Sail looked around, saw a rose bush and snapped it at the base. He handed the plant to Felix, who took a deep breath and nodded.

Mae and Sail crouched together, side by side, his arm touching hers.

She looked at the shape of his face, knew without question he fit.

Matches flared against the dark.

The letters ignited as Candice appeared at her window, mouth slightly open as her face glowed in the flame light.

'She'll see him now,' Sail said.

'Seeing him and actually –' Mae stopped as she noticed the smell, kind of chemical, and then smoke, darker than she had ever seen. She bent down and touched the grass.

'This isn't grass.'

'What?'

'It's fake grass.'

She felt the heat as sweat began to run into her eyes.

Felix glanced back at them.

'It's spreading,' Mae said.

Flames grew high and gathered like a wall. A light breeze sent them rushing towards a timber summer house, which ignited in seconds.

'Controlled burn,' Mae said.

Felix puffed his cheeks out, a slight puzzled frown on his face.

Fire crawled and spread and thundered, thick smoke billowed, black against ink sky, the smother so thick not even moonlight could make it through.

They walked over to where Felix stood, the rose bush limp in his hand.

'What do we do now?' Felix said, panic creeping into his voice.

Sail surveyed the blazing shed. 'We run, man. We run.'

They sprinted out into the street and separated. Felix and Sail headed back up Ocean Drive while Mae cut into the small copse outside another towering mansion.

Before long gates began to open as neighbours came out into the street and clustered around Candice's house.

She could hear the crackle of the fire as people gasped. A dog ran by her, spooked as it bolted into the street behind.

She saw Hugo there in board shorts, the bruises on his body expertly hidden.

Mae watched as Luke Manton staggered up the street holding a half-empty bottle.

She watched in shock as he caught sight of someone in the crowd and began to shout. There was a struggle, and he dropped the bottle.

He looked wild, screaming and cursing.

A couple of guys held him back, but Hugo remained rooted to the spot.

'If I see you again, I'll kill you,' Luke Manton said, as he was slowly led away.

It was only as the distant call of sirens was heard that the group thinned a little and Mae could see the person Luke had attacked.

He stood there, unflustered, his eyes locked on Luke as he trailed into the distance.

Jon Prince.

Hugo's father.

20

Mae woke to the smell of burning, raced from her bed and down the stairs.

She caught it just in time, the flames licking the edge of a pan as she took it into the garden and dumped it on the stone path.

She doused it with the hose, watched it sizzle and die before she realised it was bacon, the pack still sealed, the plastic warped and blackened.

Then she searched for her grandmother, in her bedroom, the living room and even the crumbling garage beside their house.

Mae checked Stella, saw her sleeping so made the decision to head out to the end of the street.

It was early, West slept. Mae scanned the road; her grandmother had not left the house in months.

Down through town, shops still shuttered, fishing boats crept from the marina, men standing on the deck as they headed towards the horizon.

Mae cursed under her breath.

And then she heard laughter coming from the beach. She ran down the slope, crossed the sand and saw a cluster of kids seated around a dying fire, empty beer bottles, a radio playing as Mae followed their eyes to the old woman, waist deep in the water and staring at the sky.

The sea was cold as it filled Mae's shoes and crept up her jeans.

'Grandma.'

'Is it true, Margaret?'

Mae heard more laughter, closed it off and gently placed an arm around her grandmother's shoulder.

'It's cold, Grandma. You're shivering.'

'But is it true? . . . Is there something bad in the sky? I was watching the news this morning, and they said . . . Well, I won't tell you what they said because I don't want to upset you.'

Mae watched the last of the trawlers.

'I can make us eggs for breakfast.' Mae gently led her back towards the shore.

Her grandmother snatched her hand away, Mae caught a rock and fell heavily, for a moment the water covered her face before she climbed to her feet.

The laughter grew, but then Mae saw one of the group splinter and head towards her.

Hugo stood there, his skin golden in the first light.

Behind him Hunter lay on the beach and smirked.

'Are you okay?' he said.

She turned her back on him, the water dripping from her hair as she followed her grandmother up the beach.

Stella still slept, the smallest mercy as Mae helped dry her grandmother and get her back into bed.

Mae made eggs and when Stella came down they ate them in the garden beneath an apple tree their father had planted when Mae was six years old.

'I need to take in a baby photo, for the memory capsule. We're going to bury it and in a million years the new people will find it.'

'New people?'

'Miss Hart told us about evolution. It happened once, it can happen again.'

'Is she the one that smells of wine?'

'Mae,' Stella said, quietly, 'some of the other kids, their parents are going to dress up for the show. Like they're going to the ball.'

'Eat your toast.'

'Miss Hart said it would be special.'

'And your egg.'

Stella wore denim dungarees with a flower on the pocket and hockey socks pulled up high over them.

'I know you wear black but –'

'You want me to wear all pink and spend my last day looking like an actual arsehole?'

Stella turned back to her egg.

Mae didn't notice the side gate was open till the dog walked in.

Skinny, with large patches of fur missing.

'What's that?' Stella said, turning her head.

Mae swallowed. 'Nothing.' She stared at the dog, willing it to turn and leave.

'I can hear something,' Stella said.

'Squirrel.'

'Paint what you can see.'

'No.'

'You never say no. It's not fair.'

Mae sighed heavily. 'I see the apple tree and it's too bright and the apples are blue today. And the house is purple and the sky is burnt.'

Stella set her fork down and listened. 'And?'

Mae closed her eyes because she knew what would come. 'And there's a dog and it's the ugliest dog I have ever seen and I think it has mange and possibly ticks and fleas and might well die in the next few minutes.'

Stella's mouth dropped open as she whispered, 'Jesus. Oh, sweet Jesus.'

Mae hissed at the dog, who ignored her and went on sniffing the ground.

Stella attempted a clicking sound, then a small bark. The dog ignored her too.

'Is it pedigree?'

'It's barely breathing.'

'Should we feed it?'

'No.'

'Stroke it?'

'No.'

'Bathe it?'

'I'll turn the hose on it if you want.'

Stella placed a hand on her chest. 'How long have I wanted a dog, Mae?'

Mae ignored her, thinking of the times they'd applied, the rundown charities that no longer answered their phones.

Mae hissed, then clapped her hands loudly. 'Eff off.'

'You can't say that to a dog.'

'Eat your egg and stop talking.'

'She sounds hungry.'

Raggedy tail in the air, it tracked the ground all the way to an old crab apple long since rotten. A single lick and then it went on.

Mae was so distracted she didn't notice the egg sail past her head till it splattered on the ground.

She turned slowly.

Stella kept her eyes down on the empty plate.

'Stella, what just happened?'

'Sounds like an egg fell from a nest. Poor mother bird must be saddened.'

'Stella . . .'

The dog began to eat the egg.

'Can we keep her?'

'What do you think?'

'I think yes.'

'It's not even a bitch.'

'Stop swearing in front of the dog.' Stella was up on her feet and instinctively found her way to the dog and began to stroke its bony head.

'You look nice,' Stella said to the dog. 'Do you have a name?'

Their grandmother appeared by the kitchen door, glanced at the sky then stepped away. 'I need you to pick up bread and milk. Do you think you can manage that?'

Mae nodded.

'We can't keep that dog. We barely have enough food as it is. I suppose you two ate the bacon.'

Mae took a breath and nodded again.

'I'll share with her,' Stella said, petting the dog so hard its eyes began to bulge. 'Her name is Lady.'

'More like the tramp,' Mae said.

Stella covered the dog's ears with her hands.

The dog followed them to school. Mae did all she could to dissuade it, shouted and threatened and made to kick the thing, but still it followed.

Eight thirty and her shirt clung to her, the heat so thick she could barely breathe.

'Tracy Kent is a leaver,' Stella said.

'Where?'

'Scotland. They have a house by a loch. She said she saw the monster once.'

Sometimes the dog forged ahead, sometimes stopped to sniff the air and raise a single paw.

'Is she tracking?' Stella said. 'She might have bloodhound ancestry. Probably worked for the police at some stage. What is it, girl? A bomb?'

The dog pissed on a tree then moved on.

Down Ocean Drive.

Sail stood by the white-house gates.

'Who is it?' Stella said to Mae.

'No one, Stella. Just a boy I hate.'

'Boys make everything worse.'

Sail clutched his heart, then dropped to his knee and carefully took Stella's hand. 'Nice sunglasses.'

'They hide my blind eyes.'

'Well, you look very cool.'

Stella pulled Mae down 'Paint him for me,' she whispered.

Mae reluctantly whispered back.

Stella raised an eyebrow. 'I can see why you hate this one.'

Mae watched the water.

'This is my new dog,' Stella said.

'New?' Sail regarded it. 'He's beautiful.'

Stella smiled. 'She's called Lady.'

Sail scratched his head, glanced at Mae and mouthed, 'The balls on it.'

He walked with them.

'So you live in the white house?' Stella said, as she took his hand.

Stella did not take people's hands. Not the dinner lady who chaperoned them across the street each morning, not their grandmother.

'Yeah, you can come see it . . .' Sail caught himself then, looked so distraught that Mae fought the urge to tell him it happened all the time.

'You can paint it for me,' Stella said.

'Paint it?'

'Mae paints the world for me, except sometimes I know she makes it more fun.'

'I'd be honoured to paint it for you, Stella.'

'So you're not a vampire?' Stella said, mildly disappointed.

'Afraid not.'

'So what are you, Jack Sail?'

Sail dropped to his knees again, this time in full view of the morning mothers sipping their coffees and frowning at him.

'I'm just a boy, kneeling in front of a girl, asking her not to hate him.'

Stella grinned at Mae, who shepherded her sister through the gate.

'What about Lady?' Stella said.

Mae looked down at the dog, who sprawled out by the gate. 'She'll be fine.'

It took a lot to make Stella cry, but right then Mae saw the tears brim in her sister's eyes.

'I'll watch her,' Sail said.

Stella hugged him tightly.

'That was stupid,' Mae said, as they walked towards Sacred Heart, the dog trailing them, glancing back now and then like it was looking for Stella.

'So . . . I'm stuck with your dog?'

'Stella's dog. And you better look after it, or you'll break a blind girl's heart.'

Sail looked back as the dog headed towards the beach.

'Don't be late,' Mae called.

In science Liam stood at the front of the class. 'Listen up. Someone damn near burned my girl's house down last night.' He pointed at Candice. 'She says she thinks it was some boy wanting to ask her to the Final.'

Mae glanced at Felix, who slumped low in his seat.

Liam held up a muscled arm and pointed it around the room. 'I will find out who did it. Her mum had drawings and shit in there.'

'Paintings,' Candice said. 'The summer house was where she painted. Some of the paintings were of me as a child. They meant a lot to her.'

'And your bush,' Liam said. 'He desecrated your bush.'

Mae raised an eyebrow.

Candice nodded sadly. 'The rose bush in my garden.'

'Ah, that bush,' Sally said.

'My grandmother's ashes were scattered under that rose bush.'

Felix looked desperately at Mae, his eyes wide.

'Whoever did this is dead. And I don't mean that . . . like, I'll beat on them.'

'Gross,' Sally said, wrinkling her nose in displeasure.

'Shut up, fatso,' Lexi said.

'Fatso is so retro I kind of like it,' Sally said.

'I mean actually dead. Dead,' Liam said.

'*Dead* dead?' Felix said.

'Dead isn't dead enough,' Sally added.

'Selena dead,' Liam said for clarification, then took his seat as Mr Starling walked into class. Before he could begin, the speaker above told Mae to head to Counsellor Jane.

As she walked down the school hallway she ignored the posters on the walls: the Final, an art project depicting a new civilisation, a couple of papers looking at the best of mankind's creations.

Mae stopped at the door, pressed her head against the cool wood and closed her eyes.

How are you feeling?

Is there anything you're worried about?

What do you think happens when you die?

She sat, ignored the flicker of the candles and tried not to gag on the incense. It was then she looked up, and saw the mess that was Counsellor Jane. She was pale, her eyes shot with blood, heavy bags beneath them. Instead of the beige suit, she wore an old T-shirt and faded jeans.

Mae could smell cheap wine.

They sat in silence for ten minutes.

Counsellor Jane broke first. 'You should know that these sessions are no longer being recorded.'

Mae looked over at the empty space where the tape recorder once sat.

Counsellor Jane coughed. 'Being scared is natural. After Abi Manton, and the two other children who sadly left –'

'James and Melissa. To hang like that though, it takes a level of forethought that makes me feel something. Sad, despairing, I don't know. Whatever.'

'You can talk here, Mae. That's what these meetings are for.'

'I thought they were to keep us from freaking out. So the teachers can maintain some semblance of control.'

'You think the teachers have lost control?'

'I don't think we should be here.'

'So where should you all be? On the streets? Causing more trouble? If they do what they say, if they stop Selena –'

'Then we'll just carry on. If I wake up on July twenty-first, will I be happy? Does anyone really want to die? I mean, people want to stop living, like when they're depressed or sick or old. But there's a fundamental difference between wanting to die and not wanting to live.'

'And what is that difference?'

Mae looked at the clock and imagined the constant second hand, the ticking so loud it shattered the glass windows and let the sea air in.

'Passivity,' Mae said. 'We could all choose to die, any of us, there's a hundred ways we could end it. But . . . no one chooses life. It's thrust upon us like some godawful responsibility. Make your life count. How about I make my death count?'

Counsellor Jane had taken to making notes on index cards, shorthand, like their feelings could be summarised so succinctly.

Depressed.

Anxious.

Rebellious.

'How do you make death count? You tattoo a word on your wrist and hope that others do the same? And then you won't die alone?'

'You don't get it.'

'I spoke to Sergeant Walters. He's worried about the Forevers.'

'There is no Forever. Haven't you heard?'

'Everyone in town has read it. Someone posted it online. It's noble but . . . Mr Silver wants you to calm things down. I have students in here talking about getting tattoos. Young girls.'

'I don't know how we got where we are. Looks, gender, sexual preference. Race. We want total blindness. Total acceptance.'

'It's not that simple.'

'It is. On this it is. Enlightenment is empowerment. I simply choose not to live in your world. I'm as blind to you as you are to us.'

They sat in uneasy silence.

'A lot of the students that come in here, they want to talk about Abi Manton,' Counsellor Jane said. 'They're scared.'

'Last I heard, suicide isn't contagious.'

'And yet three children are dead'

Mae looked up at the clock. 'Self-absorption. Self-pity. Self-flagellation. I talk and you listen. There's an imbalance.'

Jane opened her eyes again, like she'd forgotten where she was. She sniffed. 'I don't know what I'm doing here. We should stop.'

'Are you okay?'

She shook her head. 'I thought I could help . . . I don't know . . . the responsibility. I don't sleep. It was supposed to be a favour to Mr Silver, but Abi . . . now . . . I think I'm done here.'

Mae glanced at the clock again, tried not to roll her eyes as she spoke. 'There's a boy.'

Jane breathed, finally on familiar ground. 'You like him?'

'No.'

'But?'

'He doesn't look at the sky. He just looks at me.'

'And how does that make you feel?'

'Like I'm seen.'

'And that's a good thing?'

'No.'

'Do you think that's why Abi did it? And James and Melissa? Because they wanted to be seen.'

'No, I think they wanted to be forgotten.'

Counsellor Jane looked like she was searching for something to say when they heard the shouting.

She was up and over to the door. In the corridor Mae saw two boys about to go at it.

'You're dead,' Felix said, and then he pushed Sail.

Sail pushed him back.

Felix looked like he was about to swing a punch when Jane stepped between them.

Mae crossed the office quickly, flipped open Counsellor Jane's notepad and fired off a dozen shots with her phone. She didn't know what exactly she was looking for but guessed Abi Manton would be the trending topic over the past few days.

When it was done Mae met them outside, by the old chapel. 'You took your time. I had to bare my soul in there.'

'Did you get it?' Sail said.

'I'll look over it tonight and then report back tomorrow,' she said.

'What's tomorrow?' Sail said.

Felix deflated. 'My birthday party.'

21

'They made me wear a goddam tie,' Felix said.

He stood in his back garden. A barbecue smoked away in the corner. Balloons hung from string draped between two trees. Plastic tablecloths, crêpe paper decor, a home-made banner tacked to the back of the house.

HAPPY SWEET EIGHTEEN FELIX.

'Sweet eighteen? There's no such goddam thing.'

Mae stood there and held a small gift in her hand.

He snatched it from her. 'I see you went all out this year. Is it wrapped in tin foil?'

She grabbed a beer from a paddling pool filled with ice cubes and popped the cap with her teeth.

'Cufflinks?'

Mae nodded. 'What do you get for the boy who'll be dead in a month?'

'Anything but cufflinks, I'd imagine. You know I don't actually own a proper shirt.' He studied the cufflinks carefully. 'I'm sure I've seen Mr Silver wearing these exact ones.'

'A popular choice in these parts.' She avoided his eye,

instead focusing on the colourful piñata hanging from the oak at the bottom of the garden.

'Please don't tell me you stole these from the head teacher?'

Mae shrugged. 'I've spent a lot of time in his office lately.'

A cluster of elderly women emerged through the side gate and charged at Felix.

Mae took a step backwards and watched as Felix's great-aunts smothered him with lipstick kisses while he scowled from the centre of them.

The cluster drifted towards the food as Felix pawed the prints from his face.

'Happy birthday, Felix.'

Mae turned to see Sail, who held out a gift, expertly wrapped.

Felix hugged him, taking Sail by surprise.

'He's had a glass of Jesus's blood,' Mae said.

Felix unwrapped the present. 'A sleep mask. *Très amusant.*'

They took their plates to the bottom of the garden and sat side by side on the grass. Behind, the sounds of music and laughter drifted through the warm summer air.

'I heard my mother on the phone,' Felix said. 'She told the family there's to be no mention of Selena today.'

There were games set out on the grass. Mae saw Stella playing chess with Felix's grandfather, the old man grinning as Stella manoeuvred each piece carefully, locked in straight-faced concentration. The girl played to win.

'You ever have a day where you forget?' Felix said, watching Stella.

'Some days I wake up and it's normal, for a few seconds. And then I remember. But those seconds . . .' Sail said.

Felix raised his beer.

Mae nodded. 'I had it before . . . you know?'

He nodded. He always knew. Mae didn't speak of her parents and Felix didn't ask. He'd come to the funeral, sat alone at the back and didn't speak to her the whole day.

'My father hasn't said it. Happy birthday, he hasn't said it. You ever wonder when that point is, when you stop being a kid and turn into a . . . I don't want to say an adult. When I was a kid he'd say it, he'd see me and . . .' He swallowed, then loosened his tie. 'My Auntie Nia is drunk.'

They looked over and saw a big lady dancing alone, holding a hot dog and staring longingly at it.

'Her husband's a leaver, didn't take her with him. She prays for him every Sunday at church. I know we don't talk about it, especially not today, but you ever think about all the things we'll miss out on?'

Mae smiled into her bottle. 'Never.'

Felix laughed and clinked her glass. 'The fantastic Forevers, too strong for all this self-reflection bullshit.'

'I can finish that off for you,' Mae said, looking down at Felix's wrist.

'You know what, I'm still trying to figure out exactly who I am, Mae.'

'You're brilliant as you are,' Sail said.

Felix smiled. 'You want to tell my father that?' He stood, offered Mae and Sail a hand each and pulled them to their feet. Together they walked slowly back.

'You know all these kids?'

'The Reverend invited the Sacreds,' Felix said. 'Let's hope this party doesn't get too wild.'

Sally Sweeny sat at a picnic table. In front of her was a mountain of food. Burgers, hotdogs, steak, pork chops. She ate like she was possessed.

'I remember the old Sally,' Felix said.

'What was she like?' Sail said.

'Like Hunter, like Lexi. Like all the rest.'

'Candice,' Mae said.

Felix shook his head. 'Candice isn't like those girls, she's got a mind of her own.'

'No, I meant Candice Harper is standing over there.'

'Bullshit, why the –' He stopped mid-sentence when he saw her, deep in conversation with Mrs Harries from the church. 'Jesus Christ.'

'I thought you didn't believe?'

'I'd convert for her. Is she my present or something?'

'Go and talk to her,' Sail said.

Felix nodded, then began to pace. He pulled at his collar, then loosened the tie and slowly began to hyperventilate. 'I can't go over. She likes a bad boy. What do I say? I'm normally the master of this shit. Remember that time I asked Sasha James to the cinema, and she was two years older. Smoking, Sail. This girl was, like . . .'

'And you took her out?' Sail said, impressed.

'He actually told her he had free tickets. She thanked him and went with Hugo Prince,' Mae said.

'I'm going over,' Felix said.

'Do it,' Sail said.

'What do I –'

'Thank her for coming. Then ask if she wants a drink,' Mae said.

'Perfect,' Sail said.

Felix took a shot of sherry from a nearby glass. Mae raised a hand in apology to the old lady who glared at them.

'Thank her for coming, ask if she wants a drink,' Felix repeated under his breath.

Sail and Mae followed behind.

Felix approached, took a deep breath and smiled at Candice.

Candice smiled back, so dazzling even Mae felt her stomach flip for him.

'Hi,' Felix said, his voice shaking. 'Thanks for drinking. Would you like to come?'

Candice stared at him, suitably horrified.

'Jesus,' Mae said, under her breath.

Felix looked at Sail, tears forming in his eyes. Sail led him away, back into the group of aunts. 'He's drunk,' Sail called, over his shoulder.

Mae caught up with them. 'That was awesome.'

'This might just be the worst day of my life.'

And then the Reverend opened the patio doors and shepherded Sally towards the old piano in the lounge.

'Sally and Theodore are going to perform something for us.'

'Yeah,' Felix said. 'Worst day of my life.'

'Drink through it,' Mae said, stealing another glass of wine.

Theodore channelled Ben E. King.

Sally stopped eating, Auntie Nia stopped dancing and Felix forgot about what he'd just said to the hottest girl in school.

Mae felt someone brush against her, looked down and saw Stella entranced by the boy with the beautiful voice.

Jeet Patel sat on the grass in front of them, looking up at Theodore with something like wonder in his eyes.

As late afternoon drifted to early evening, Mae drank more beer, found herself alone at the end of the long garden and lit a cigarette.

'Hey,' Mae said. She offered Sally a cigarette as she approached.

'No, thanks. I'm on a health kick.' Sweat blistered from every pore, a chocolate stain sank into the front of her jeans.

Mae glanced down at Sally's hands, the knuckles buried. Her red hair was wild. 'A couple of girls in my English class wrote Forever on their wrists in biro. You see it?'

Mae shook her head.

Sally kept her eyes down. 'Abi talked about you. Sometimes after practice we'd sit around in the chapel. Jeet's dad has a wine cellar so he'd take a bottle now and then and we'd share it.'

Mae smiled.

'I mean, his dad gave it. Not like he'd steal.'

Mae looked over at Jeet, who was busy helping Mrs Baxter clear the plates and glasses away.

'I'd had a shitty day. I hate PE, right,' Sally said, looking down at her body. 'Those shorts . . . with these legs. When I was in the shower Lexi stole my clothes. The crap they've got in lost property.' Sally laughed but Mae could see the hurt.

141

'I had to walk home in this skirt, might as well have been a belt. Lexi, she filmed it all, put it online, racked up the hits.'

'They'll die like this,' Mae said. 'It's like . . . most people get to look back at the way they were and know they were dicks at some point. But . . . this is it, Sally. For them, this is it.'

'You and Abi, if half that stuff was true then you're all we've got now. All I've got. The Forevers. What if you look like I do – can you still join?'

'The Forevers was a thing, but a long time ago. And I know people are talking about it, and looking to me, but I –'

'But you meant it. About everyone having a place? About having someone you can call, no matter what you've said, what you've done? No judgement?'

Mae breathed smoke deep. 'We meant it.'

'And if shit happens, you've got my back, Mae?'

'Sure, Sally.'

'I mean it. If I need you . . .'

'And if I need you?' Mae said.

'You want me to mess up Hunter Silver? I'll eat her for breakfast. And then I'll go back and eat her breakfast. Probably some soya-milk bullshit but I'll swallow it down for you.'

Mae smiled.

Sally dabbed the sweat from her face. 'Abi died alone. I just . . . I don't want to be like her. You've opened the door to all of us creeps and weirdos.'

'You think about dying?'

'There's a science to it. Ten and a half cups of sugar in one sitting can end the life of an average man. Me, I'd need closer to thirteen. Nutmeg. That can do it in five teaspoons. A skinny thing like you, maybe less.'

'You're trying to eat yourself to death, Sally?'

'Everyone looks at me and sees a giant question mark. My mum's friends, I hear them, they talk about me and say, *Such a shame what happened to Sally*. They preferred me when I hitched my skirt up and dyed my hair and existed in my ditzy look-how-endearingly-dumb-I-am bubble.'

'So you did it to break away?'

'Abi Manton. I looked at her and it was like seeing the girl I used to be. Everything I'm not now.'

Mae heard a trace of resentment in her voice. 'Why did you fight?'

'Abi came back from a meeting with Mr Silver. I guess it was about her grades slipping because she looked so sad. And then we played. "The Swan". It's too beautiful, you know?'

Mae had heard them play it before.

'She played it too fast. I told her she didn't take it seriously, that she didn't care enough. Girls like Hunter and her group, they don't know how easy their world is. They don't need to try. Abi just lost it, she screamed and swore and stormed out.'

The heat rose another notch and thickened the air between them.

Sally watched the sky. 'I thought it would be nuclear war, or climate change, maybe some kind of pandemic. But this, no erosion, no survival of the fittest, just erasing us all . . . it's so beautiful. And so goddam final. I can do it, Mae. And it won't mean shit.'

'Do what?'

'I can do the most awful things I've dreamed about.'

Mae looked at her. 'I'm not sure what you mean.'

They heard a noise, turned and saw Mrs Baxter with a relic of a video camera mounted on her shoulder as she handed Felix a small bat.

Felix shot Mae a desperate look, and then he glanced at Candice and hung his head in sad resignation as a great-aunt tied a blindfold around his head and gave him a nudge.

'This is the best party I've ever been to,' Sail said.

No one was prepared for the ferocity with which Felix attacked the piñata.

He dropped the bat, ripped the thing from its cord and landed heavily on top of it. And then the punches rained down, till a neighbour girl began to cry.

Maybe it was the frustration of turning eighteen and knowing death was already at the door, maybe it was the fact that the only piñata Mrs Baxter had been able to get was a pink unicorn.

As Felix tried for a headbutt Sail gently pulled him from the pieces. 'It's over now.'

Mae applauded furiously.

Jeet Patel pushed past them, carrying the cake. 'Can I get you guys a slice?'

Sally took the whole thing from him and retreated towards the shed.

Things got worse when a circle formed around Felix as his mother handed Mae the video camera and asked her to capture the magic of Felix opening gifts.

'This one's from Mrs Fairbanks,' the Reverend said, handing Felix a small parcel.

Mae recognised Mrs Fairbanks from church. Late eighties, blue rinse.

Felix unwrapped the small leather journal, then flipped it open and sighed heavily. 'It's a five-year diary.' Mae zoomed in close as he shook his head, then looked directly at Mrs Fairbanks. 'Is this some kind of sick joke? What the hell is wrong with you?'

Auntie Nia led Mrs Fairbanks away to console her.

'Can I stop filming now? I'm losing sensation in my shoulder,' Mae said.

There were calls for Felix to make a speech.

He stood at the front and said a brief thank you. And then his father stood beside him.

'I wondered if you wanted to lead us in prayer?' the Reverend said, no smile.

His family implored, Mae could feel the energy directed at Felix. She wondered if it wouldn't have been easier just to go with it, never would a lie have been so white.

Felix gently shook his head, and then his father turned his back and went back over to the barbecue.

'Are you ready for our gift, son?' Mrs Baxter said.

Felix was about to quit when they heard it.

The sound of a car horn rang out a dozen times.

Felix's mouth dropped open. 'You didn't. You've bought me a Benz.'

Mrs Baxter grinned as Felix jumped to his feet and ran around to the front of the house. Mae and Sail followed along with everyone else.

The car.

Small.

Rusting.

Orange.

The Fiat Panda smoked as one of Felix's cousins gunned the engine and pulled to a stop on the driveway.

'What the hell have you done?' Felix whispered, his face fraught with horror.

'Check the number plate,' Mae said, zoomed in close, then quickly back to Felix's face.

K1TT3N

'Came with the car,' Mrs Baxter said, a trace of pride creeping into her voice. 'Your father drives a hard bargain.'

Felix swallowed.

'Oh, son,' Mrs Baxter said, as the first tear escaped from Felix's eye. 'He's too choked up to speak.'

'Kitten,' was all Felix could manage.

22

It was close to midnight by the time she made it to the bay front.

A fire burned high.

Driftwood twisted like horns. The float of voices and laughter, she stayed far enough from them.

She lay back on the sand and watched the stars, tried to pick out clusters Stella had spoken of, but could not place a single one.

'The last Forever.' Hunter came over, she wore denim cut-offs and a vest. She dropped her sandals to the sand. 'That stunt you pulled at Abi's funeral. You know you're wasting your –'

'Take the night off, Hunter. It's been a long day.'

They sat in silence for a moment.

'Did you even care when you heard?'

For a moment Hunter quietened, her voice lost its edge. 'Time is condensed, right. Each day is a year of our lives. So I gave Abi one night. And the next day . . .' She snapped her fingers.

'If we're saved, there'll be an army of girls with deep frown lines. I don't intend to be one of them.'

Mae frowned.

'You see, Mae Cassidy, you'll be their wrinkled queen.'

They heard lapping waves and the crackle of fire.

Hunter opened her bag and pulled out a bottle of wine. 'Lafite-Rothschild. I think it was an anniversary present.'

Hunter drank, then lay back, her head beside Mae's. 'What if this is the end?'

'Then we should be thankful for this.'

'We're each our own devil, and we make this world our hell.'

The two girls came towards them.

'You came,' Matilda said.

Hunter sighed heavily.

Betty looked at Mae. 'Hunter calls us the dykes. And she says we'll burn.'

'And she calls me a scrubber because my mum cleans her house,' Matilda said, with a smile.

Hunter raised the bottle to them.

'At first it was just us two, and then the next night there was Adam, Casey, Mehmet and Bryony. And tonight there's five more of us.' Matilda stood tall, her pixie cut framed large, smoked eyes.

Betty's lips were painted bold red against her golden skin, she knelt in the sand. 'Make us Forevers, Mae. We'll follow you into hell.'

'Don't you mean heaven?' Hunter said.

Betty stared at her intently. 'Not the way we're going to spend the next weeks.'

They clustered around Mae.

'Stick and poke, right,' Matilda said, producing a needle and pen.

Mae stalled for a moment, then saw the way they looked at her, like she was all they needed.

She got to work as others drifted over.

Hugo and two of his friends, more of Hunter's group, the girls and their silver hair.

Their beach was too perfect, it drew the crowds, even at night kids drove in from neighbouring towns.

Behind the pastel houses loomed.

They clustered together, printed each other and drank cheap wine and smoked cigarettes.

When she was done Matilda hugged her tightly. 'Our perfect Forever. If you ever want us to kill Hunter for you . . .'

Mae smiled but Matilda just stared.

Betty nodded alongside her. 'We'll disappear the body. No trace. We watch CSI every night before bed.'

'Thank you,' Mae said, then puffed out her cheeks.

They passed around warm beer. Mae smelled weed.

'You can see it now. With a telescope you can see the station on the moon,' Hugo said. 'There's people living up there.'

'They're not living. They're waiting,' someone said. 'They're still building, I saw it on that show. It's like . . . a holding pen or something.'

'I heard there's a hotel up there, for the rich, and restaurants and bars and you can go get wasted on the moon. And here we are, stuck on a beach, close to nowhere.'

The fire began to die, the moon and stars did enough, but still, the voices came from shadows.

They debated, cooked up facts, verbatim regurgitation, they

talked about life and history and everything they would not know.

That night the Forevers grew to a handful. Kids that would spend their days hiding their wrists from parents and teachers, and their nights on the beach.

At midnight Sail came and sat beside her.

She wondered where he'd been, why he hadn't been at school. She wondered who he was, who she was.

'You reached people. What you said, it means something in a world of nothings.'

'Maybe they just think it's cool to walk round with a tattoo.'

'Maybe, but sometimes the closer you look, the less you see.'

'And that means?'

'Take a step back. People believe in your words, that's all.'

They walked up to the bay front, climbed the hill and crossed into the cemetery. Mae glanced at Abi's grave, saw a dozen teddy bears had been left, and a sprawl of flowers that shamed the graves beside.

'These ones,' Mae said, stopping beside them, side by side and still so new. Too new.

'James. Melissa,' Sail said, reading their names.

She noticed he touched the stone.

'A cemetery for lost souls. I try and wonder where they are,' Mae said. 'I try to see them some place light and bright and safe.'

Sail stared at the gold lettering, so ornate, like it had taken a million years to carve.

'Why do we have to rest in peace?' he said. 'At our age the last thing we want to do is be resting.'

'Go wild in peace?'

'Better.'

She led him deeper, the moonlight their guide as they brushed past the limbs of a willow tree and found a bench behind the crumbling stone wall and the long drop to the water below.

'Jesus, this town,' he said, like maybe his parents had really found the perfect place to die.

'This spot, it's kind of hidden,' Mae said.

Along the coast were other towns that cast their glows, black between making each an island.

'Are we closer to the stars here?' he said.

'I need to know something about you,' she said. 'Because now you know I have a sister. And that's too much. The balance . . .'

'I was in Chicago,' he said. 'There's a place there, and if you're sick then you go there and you talk to this doctor. He takes people, people that everyone thinks are broken, and he tries to put them back together again.'

She looked over and wondered how someone like him could ever be broken.

'So I was there and I looked out the window, and I was like forty floors up and I'm watching this sea of ants. And then it starts raining but I couldn't smell it.

'I had to get outside. But the windows don't open, so I sneak out and I take the stairs. Forty flights. And I run into the street. There's steam on the street and yellow taxis and businessmen with black umbrellas.'

Mae could feel it.

'And I ran down the sidewalk, and I was wearing these slippers they make you wear and they're soaked through. And the rain got heavier so I headed into this museum. Big stone steps and arches and flags. And people are looking at me like I'm crazy in my gown.

'This painting. It's like, there's this perfect summer scene. The lake and the canoe and sailing boats, and the Victorian ladies. And I stepped closer, so close a guard started walking over. And that's when I saw it.'

'What did you see?'

'That up close, it's just colours. Just strokes. And that's us, Mae. Up close, alone, we're so nothing, so perfectly nothing.' He stood, his eyes still on the sky. 'And you can lift out a single dot of colour, a single person, and no one really notices. Because it's still a masterpiece. And I'm happy I got to be part of it. Happy I got to sit in one perfect still of an imperfect world.'

'But . . . ?'

'But if you're not alone, if you matter too much, to too many people, then you don't just lift out, because you drag them with you.'

He stepped close to the edge, the slightest breeze and he'd drop.

'Sometimes breathing . . . if you focus on it. Because you have to do it, it becomes something too hard.'

She thought about kissing him. 'I still hate you.'

'You don't know anything about me,' he said.

'I know enough.'

'I don't know anything about you.'

'You know too much.'

'I know Abi was a Forever.'

From her bag she took out her phone and together they looked through Counsellor Jane's notes.

152

There were names at the top, traits at the bottom. The fear was cold, the talk of Selena, of both believing and not really believing they would die.

Mae smiled at Jeet Patel's card, the single word, HAPPY, bold against the angst.

Only one stood out.

Sullivan Reed. There were some shorthand notes, and then, at the bottom, the name Abi Manton, with a question mark.

'I think I want to die here in this spot,' Mae said.

'Okay.'

They sat in silence and felt the universe shrink a little. She did not tell him that the headstone beside that bench belonged to her parents.

23

In West Groceries she bought food for Stella and their grandmother. The shelves had been bare for a long time. Things vanished, things Mae could no longer recall.

'Hey.'

Mae looked up, confused to see Candice working behind the counter.

Candice read the look. 'My parents are making me pay for the summer house that burned down. They said it was, like, my fault that boys get obsessed with me. I won't even have time to work it off if Selena hits us. So what's the point?'

Mae placed the groceries on the counter.

'Are you going to the Final?'

Mae shook her head. 'You?'

'I guess. Liam hasn't asked, he just assumes we'll go together.'

'Everyone does what's expected of them.'

'Except for the Forevers.'

Mae said nothing.

'Sometimes it's just easier being in than being out. You're cool though, Mae. What you said, what you had with Abi, it was cool.'

'Stop being . . . nice, the world's messed up enough already.'

Candice held a tin up and inspected it. 'Hotdogs in a can. Gross.'

'That's better.'

Mae handed her cash.

'It's short. You need another pound.'

Mae searched her pockets, the heat finding her cheeks as Candice watched her. Mae picked up a chocolate bar she'd got for Stella. 'Can I put this back?'

Candice shoved it in the bag. 'We'll be dead by the time they do stock check.'

Mae nodded.

Candice turned back to the small TV behind the counter, leaned back on her stool and chewed her gum.

Down the high street people were drinking coffee outside Lou's.

She gazed in every window, and then she stopped when she saw it.

West Fine Art.

The kind of place that opened when the summer people started building and the money flowed into West.

When she opened the door and stepped inside she was hit by a blast of ice-cold air that prickled her skin.

It was empty, museum quiet. Polished wood floor, the windows small and arched. She gazed at a couple of paintings, abstract washes of colour, white skies and white water.

And then she thumbed through prints. Familiar scenes, waterlilies and pearl earrings. She stopped when she came to The Nightmare, the darkness pulled her back to Mr Silver's office.

'Henry Fuseli.'

Mae turned.

The man had a thin moustache, glanced her up and down, then turned back to his newspaper, speaking without looking at her. 'A few years before he painted it, Fuseli fell for the niece of a friend. He was infatuated. Obsessed. She is mine. I am hers.'

'What happened?' Mae said, her throat suddenly dry.

'Her father didn't approve. She married someone else and Fuseli poured his feelings into this painting. People say it's about sex, I see only lost love.'

'That painting in the window, the beach scene,' she said.

He sighed through his nose. 'Ghastly, isn't it?'

'Where did you get it?'

'You think I'd hang something like that?'

'It's important.'

He bristled, looked at her again and decided he could do without the battle. 'Our Saturday boy. He has the . . .' He motioned to his cheek. 'I can only assume he has a thing for the artist, because he badgered me relentlessly for a month till I agreed to stock it. And then he said the girl had died and now it's in the window. We might actually make some money from it. Nothing hikes value like death.'

'Sullivan Reed?' she said.

He nodded. Mae felt the adrenaline kick then. 'Can I talk to him?'

That nasal sigh again. 'He works weekends. What day is it today?'

'Do you know where I can find him?'

'I can't give out his home address.'

'I'll stay here till you do.'

The Reed house sat at the end of an overgrown lane. Towering high but seriously rundown, the whitewashed weatherboard was rotten in several places. Mae looked up at the roof and saw several slates missing.

Outside was a rusting truck, each tyre flat, the windscreen cracked. She stepped up onto the creaking deck and knocked on the door.

At the side window the net curtain twitched, and then Mae found herself face to face with a large woman with a hard face. She had rollers in her hair and wore a yellowed dressing gown.

'What do you want?'

'I'm here to see Sullivan.'

The woman's face transformed into a wide smile, her eyes lighting up.

She clutched Mae's arm and shepherded her into the house.

The smell hit her first. A mix of damp and some kind of chemical.

Mae brought a hand to her mouth.

'Ammonia,' the woman said. 'And citric acid. You get used to it.'

Mae looked at the torn wallpaper. Dark swathes of mould oozed from the ceiling and ran down the door frames.

A heavy grandfather clock ticked away.

'Sullivan's my boy. I'm Suze.'

Suze wore white Crocs and scratched at a line of nicotine patches that ran up her arm. 'Cravings. Sullivan's always on at me to stop.'

She opened a door and Mae gasped as she stepped inside. Every wall, and the ceiling, was lined with paper. Even the windows had been blocked.

'The only thing that'll stop her. We sit in here for a while, maybe even a week. I got the cans.' Suze pointed to the far corner, where Mae saw a sorry collection of tinned prunes.

'So you must be her,' Suze said, beaming wide. Two front teeth missing, the rest brown and yellow. She dabbed at her mouth with a handkerchief, the drool appearing every time she spoke.

'Who?'

'His mystery girl. He doesn't say much, sly one, that boy. But I know he's courting. Lovesick. Always locked away in his bedroom. He won't even let me in there now, keeps the door locked and takes the key with him. Says he's working on his art.'

'His art?'

'He takes photographs. Old-fashioned camera, used to belong to his father. God rest his soul.' Suze crossed herself as she sank into a foil-wrapped armchair.

'Is he here?'

'No. You can wait though,' she said quickly.

Mae heard the loneliness then.

'He never stays out too late. Afraid of the night. You have to be now, all these kids drawn to the darkness. I walked through town and saw two girls holding hands. Lesbianism.'

Mae nodded like she got it.

'Playing with fire this close to the end. Leviticus. Chapter eighteen, verse twenty-two.'

Mae looked at the walls, at the pages and pages of paper.

Up close she almost gasped when she realised they were pages from the Bible.

'It doesn't bother you then?' Suze said.

'Excuse me?'

'Sullivan's cheek. He grows his hair all long like a girl to cover it. He should be proud, you know. He earned it.'

'Earned it?'

Suze smiled. 'Lost his way a while back. I caught him . . . those magazines.' She shook her head. 'Well, he had to show he was sorry.'

Mae felt a draught on the back of her neck. 'How?' she said, quietly.

'And the great dragon was thrown down. Satan. And his angels.' Suze smiled. 'He won't make it to this house. Selena, his form, she'll burn up at the windows and we'll watch and we'll rejoice. Because the heathens, those sinners, they'll –'

'Could I please use the toilet?'

Suze flinched a little, then nodded. 'Use the spray after. You'll find a bottle in there. I make it myself. Sullivan has allergies, we have to keep the house clean.'

Mae left the room.

'Upstairs. Second door,' Suze called.

Mae climbed the creaking stairs. She saw the bathroom straight in front, looked inside the doors beside and saw stacks of empty boxes. She tried the door at the end and found it locked.

Sullivan's room.

She took her bobby pin and got to work, eased the lock and gently opened the door.

The room lay in total darkness, the only window blocked by a heavy sheet.

Mae almost screamed when a cat shot past her.

She fumbled around for a light switch, and when she found it the room was plunged into red.

Her breath caught as she took in the scene.

Wires criss-crossed the ceiling, and on them dozens of photographs were pegged. There was a mattress on the floor, the bedding clean and neat.

Mae looked at the photos. Most were of West. The beach. The water. Trees and leaves.

She sat down at his desk. There was a large sketchpad, and she flipped the pages, the building horror caught in her throat. Abi's smiling face. Some of them colour, all of them beautiful.

A dozen of Abi and Theodore.

The last drawing showed Abi at the bottom of the cliff, her body twisted, exactly as Mae had found her, her soul floating free towards the sky.

She could picture it. Sullivan getting knocked back, Abi getting knocked over.

As she went to leave the room she saw it hanging on the back of the door.

A red hoodie.

She ran out of the room and down the stairs, breathless as she made it to the door.

And there stood Suze, blocking her way.

'I made you tea.' Suze held a mug, the contents dark.

Mae held up a hand. 'I have to go.'

'But Sullivan should be back soon. He'll be so sorry he missed you.'

Mae tried to keep her smile casual. 'Maybe I can come by later. I have to get back for my sister.'

'You'll come for dinner?'

'Sure.'

'I'll make something special. Pigeon.'

Mae felt the bile rising up in her throat but managed to keep that smile there.

'Do you know where Sullivan is now?'

'Oh, he'll be taking his photos. He's documenting the world as it is in these times. So we don't forget.'

'Where exactly?'

'His favourite place. He likes the lighting, the noise. The woods. By the school.'

24

She sprinted past the old truck and back down the overgrown lane, cursing when she realised she'd left her shopping bag in the house.

At the end she slowed and panted, glanced back and saw Suze watching her, no smile, just watching.

Mae ran to the police station, breathless and sweating. She found the door locked, cursed loudly, drawing a shake of the head from an old lady walking past.

She pressed her face to the glass but the blinds were closed.

She knew she should wait, maybe for Sail, maybe for Felix.

And then she saw the sign, *Forever*, written across in bold red.

Mae had to know, time was running out.

By the time she made it to the school the place was deserted.

Mae crossed the sports field and stood at the shadowed line of trees.

She wondered if this was where Abi had stood, if someone had lured her into the woodland or if she'd set off with grim determination to end her own life.

Maybe Sullivan Reed was in there now, lying in the leaves,

his camera aimed at the trees. Mae felt a chill when she thought of his bedroom, that red light and all those pictures of Abi.

And then she heard it.

A scream.

Her blood began to pump fast.

Mae turned towards the sound.

Another girl. She looked back at the school building, a long way, even if she ran.

She cursed, then moved quickly, beat back the fear by breaking into a run, the adrenaline coursing.

At the edge she slowed.

She began to creep, keeping herself low and covered by dense branches.

The girl was leaning back against the wide face of an oak tree, knees pulled to her chest.

Hunter Silver.

And there, facing her, was Sullivan Reed.

Mae moved nearer.

'I need you to see what you are, Hunter,' he said.

Mae looked around, reached for a stick long and thick enough and then moved slowly and carefully.

'They tell you to confess your sins, but it isn't enough. You have to pay for them.'

Hunter shook her head.

'Selena, she's the leveller we've been waiting for. Kids like me. Kids you step on every day without noticing. She's coming down and we'll end up in the same place. We'll be the same.'

He took a step nearer.

'Leave me alone.'

'You take girls like Abi, and you make them like you.'

Hunter pushed herself back further, hard against the tree. 'What do you want?'

'I just want you to see, Hunter.'

Mae moved from the shadow.

She cut between trees, there and then not, keeping herself directly behind as Sullivan turned and glanced around.

Mae froze, her muscles tensed as she thought of Stella and the kind of world they existed in. She could still go, drop her stick and melt back into the shadows, leave behind Hunter Silver.

It was Stella that kept her from doing that. She told her sister they were fighters, that the world could be broken down into two groups, as simple as good and bad, no longer room for the shades of grey.

'Please,' Hunter said.

Mae thought of all the times Hunter had got on her. Made up lies, told people she was a slut. She could stand there and let it happen, or turn and walk away, let Hunter's screams send her off to sleep each night.

She looked at the word on her wrist and thought of Abi and everything they'd believed in.

Mae moved.

Sullivan was quick to turn, but slow to move his feet.

Mae brought the stick down hard across his head.

The noise was ugly.

Heavy and dull.

He fell back to sitting, for a moment his eyes rolled back into his head, and then blood seeped down his face. He slumped to his side, face in the leaves as Mae stood ready, the stick held high in case he moved again.

Hunter got to her feet. She spat on Sullivan. 'Freak.' And then she aimed a kick at his ribs.

Then another.

Mae put a hand around her waist and pulled her back.

'Enough now. It's over.'

Hunter stood there panting, hair wild, eyes wild. Her make-up had run.

'I need my shoe,' Hunter said.

Mae looked down and saw Hunter's bare foot in the leaves.

'Fendi slides. I'm not leaving it' She spoke calmly, like the tears, the screams, it had all been an act.

They found it beside Sullivan.

'You think he's dead?' Hunter said, staring at Sullivan's sprawled body.

Mae saw the slight rise and fall of his chest and shook her head.

'Maybe call Sergeant Walters when you get home, but leave my name out of it.'

Hunter nodded.

They began to walk back towards the clearing.

'He followed me. I just . . . I wanted to be alone. You ever feel like that?'

Mae said nothing, just glanced at the gunmetal sky as the breeze picked up.

'He was going to rape me. Or try. What the hell is going on in this town?'

'It's not just this town.'

'I've never even spoken to that kid.'

'I think that was the problem.'

'You could've left me,' Hunter said.

'I could have.'

'I would have totally left you. Or maybe hidden and filmed it.'

They moved on in silence, till the trees began to thin. Hunter stopped, bent over and retched, fighting for air as reality came at her. Mae stopped, reluctantly moved back and joined her.

'I think I twisted it.' She wiped sweat from her head with the back of her arm, then gritted her teeth as she studied her ankle.

Mae took a breath, then hauled her up.

They moved on together, Hunter limping, Mae taking her weight.

They made it to the field as sunlight punctured the clouds.

A group of kids were playing football. Some boys looked over.

Hunter wiped the tears from her cheeks and pulled a pocket mirror from her bag. 'They won't see me weak.'

By the bay they stopped and sat on a bench. Hunter needed a break.

'How come you were there?'

'Long story,' Mae said. She lit a cigarette and held the smoke deep. Hunter held out a hand and Mae passed it to her.

Hunter inspected the tear in her shirt. 'You ever wonder why I hate you so much?'

'No.'

'You could be one of us. But you think you're better.'

'I am.'

Hunter smiled at that. 'That's what I mean. You're fearless. And I'd rather you weren't. You talk to me like I'm nothing. You do it in front of other kids.'

Mae wondered if that were true.

'You don't know about pressure, Mae. You don't know about living perfect, and dying perfect. The all-perfect Silver family. My father will bury this.' She picked at the blood on her hand. 'He'll tell Sergeant Walters and it'll be swept under. Parents have enough to worry about. It'll be his first thought, when I tell him. He'll think about Sacred Heart.'

Mae thought about the toll of looking after Stella. Her existence was basal. She was an extension of her sister.

'This doesn't make us friends,' Mae said.

'Hell, no.'

Hunter hugged her then, so unexpected Mae did not even push her away.

'Thanks, bitch.' Hunter limped off towards her side of town.

25

The blow came from behind, so hard she fell against the fridge, caught her head, her knee bouncing from the metal door.

'Where's the food, Margaret? You had money for food. Now what am I going to feed your sister?'

Mae thought of the night before, Hunter and Sullivan and all that had happened. She bent down and rubbed the pain away. 'I'm sorry. I got –'

'I can't trust you to do a simple thing.'

'I'll sort it.'

Her grandmother shook her head, then noticed the tattoo on Mae's wrist. 'What have you done to yourself?'

'You've seen it before.'

'Wash it off.'

Stella walked into the kitchen, trailed by the dog.

Mae straightened quickly and smiled.

'Don't worry, Grandma, it's temporary. They only last a month.' Stella said, attempting a wink in Mae's direction.

Outside they found Felix waiting at the end of the path, a high-pitched whining shattered the morning quiet.

'What the hell,' Mae said, clamping her hands over Stella's ears as Felix nodded to Kitten, idling behind him.

'I'd rather walk,' Mae said.

Felix climbed into the driver's seat and revved the engine.

'What is that? Is an animal in distress?' Stella said.

Mae helped her into the back and fastened her belt.

The seats were pink, fluffy dice hung from the rear-view mirror and Mae saw a dozen perfume bottles in the door card. 'Was Kitten a madam in a previous life?'

'What's a madam?' Stella said from the back seat.

'Duck down,' Felix hissed.

Mae saw Candice up ahead.

'Please, Mae. I don't want Candice to think we're together.'

'I'm not sure there's a person alive that would think we're together.'

'Just do it. Felix needs us,' Stella said.

'So you're embarrassed of a blind girl too?' Mae said.

Felix shook his head. 'She'll see me with Stella and think I'm all charitable and shit. Heart of gold.'

'Exactly,' Stella said, as Mae sighed heavily and ducked low.

Felix slowed the car a long way short of Candice. 'Roll the window down for me. She'll think it's electric if she can't see you.'

Mae swore at him but slowly rolled the window down.

'I need her to notice me.'

'In this thing?'

'A cat with wheels . . .'

'A kitten,' Stella said.

'. . . I'll be blipping on her radar, for sure.'

'Oh, for sure. Maybe some music?' Stella said, as Mae scowled at both of them.

Felix pressed a button on the antique radio. The music was deafening.

'What the hell is going on?' Felix screamed, desperately fiddling with the dial. 'It won't change. It won't turn off.'

'Why is it raining men?' Stella said.

Kitten crept towards Candice, who stood there, hand on hip, frowning as the music thundered.

'Shut the window,' Felix hissed at Mae.

Mae tried. 'I can't get the angle.'

'Quickly.'

'Just . . . be cool. Nod your head or something,' Stella said.

Felix began to nod as Mae frantically wound the window.

'She can see your arm,' Felix said through his teeth.

Candice took a step back to the safety of her driveway as the freak show rolled past.

Felix clutched his head in his hands as they dropped Stella at school.

'Why does nothing ever go right for me?'

Mae squeezed his shoulder. 'You ever think maybe you don't need to change for someone else?'

He smiled sadly. 'Look at me, Mae. You know how it works – better than anyone you get it. That's why you and Abi . . .'

Mae told him what she'd found in Sullivan's bedroom.

'You think he did it?'

She'd lain awake all night asking herself that same question.

'Yeah.'

'Shit.'

'I tried to reason it, maybe he tried to stop her jumping or something.'

'But then he would've gone straight to the police. Or told someone.'

She nodded.

Kitten died on Ocean Drive. Felix tipped his head towards the sky and swore. Every curse word he knew as steam smoked from the bonnet.

'We need to water her,' he said, then set off up the long driveway towards the white house.

They stood in front of the towering white door.

Felix pressed the bell a couple of times.

They were about to turn and leave when the door opened.

A maid stood there, smiled briefly then disappeared inside.

'Sail,' Felix called out as they stepped into the cool, cavernous hallway. 'We need water.'

'Let's just go,' Mae said.

Felix walked through as Mae cursed under her breath. Acres of white marble and glass. Through the back they saw a colonnaded pool house, a collection of gleaming cars and a dozen trees standing to attention in neat lines.

The house was too quiet, a museum in the making. Polished floors so clean they bounced light into Mae's eyes.

Before she could stop him, Felix climbed the marble stairs.

She ran after him.

'Sail,' he called again.

'This place is too white,' Felix said, as he opened door after door. 'Where's all the colour?'

Mae was about to drag him back downstairs when they found it.

The colour.

The room was pink. There was a small sleigh bed, an army of soft toys and a doll's house so beautiful Mae smiled at it. A toy chest sat in the corner, a tutu hung from the wardrobe door. A small desk and chair, pink lace curtains, and letters in an arc above the headboard.

ALICE

They heard a noise at the end of the hallway, backed out of the room and saw the maid again. She frowned at them.

Outside Felix watched her carefully. 'You've got a bruise coming up.'

Mae touched her head.

'I heard your grandmother,' he said.

'Yeah.'

'She's tough.'

'I deserve it. Whatever she says, I've deserved it over the years.'

'You know that's bullshit.'

Sergeant Walters walked from the station and stopped them, told Felix to go on and Mae would catch him up.

'Hunter Silver,' he said. 'Mrs Abbott saw you walking her back. Sullivan Reed took a nasty hit to the head.'

She said nothing and he nodded, like it was okay. 'I went to the Reed house. His mother . . .'

Her mind ran to Suze, the bible pages and Sullivan's dark room.

'How did you find him?' Sergeant Walters said.

'Cosmic forces. Does it even matter now?' She thought of breaking into Abi's room, seeing her painting.

'I've seen his house, his bedroom.' Sergeant Walters rubbed his eyes, like he was trying to rid himself of the memory. 'Obsessive. I'll search properly. I know the tapes are there, he was mumbling something about showing the world the real Abi. The real Hunter. Maybe some closure for the Mantons. Who knows?'

Mae thought of growing up in that house and what it might do to a person.

'Sullivan won't speak. I've got him locked up in one of the holding cells in the basement. Not designed for long-term use, but I can't get him transferred right now. Maybe I will in a couple of weeks. He's eighteen.'

'So he'll die down there?'

'We'll stop –'

'He will.'

'I uphold the law, Mae. It's always black and white. Always.' He looked down at his shoes. 'School, it's getting rough there. The suicides, now this thing with Hunter. You know my mother taught history? She was everyone's favourite. You have any teachers that really care?'

She thought of Mr Starling, how he asked after her grandmother, her sister. How he took the time to check she was okay. When she handed homework in late he didn't question her.

'It wasn't what this is now,' he said.

'You sound like you're surprised. Maybe everyone knew it except for you and your father.'

'The service book. That talk of the Forevers. Someone copied more of them . . . they're everywhere. The public toilets. The noticeboard outside the church hall. The pharmacy window. Hell, they even put them through people's doors.' He placed a hand on the metal gate, like he was steadying himself.

'I remember my father talking about your dad. They went to school together. Said he was good.'

'He was.'

'And he said your grandmother can't care for you. He always knew that, even back then. You'll be eighteen soon though.'

'I won't.'

'The end. Maybe. The nearer we get, the more I think about it. I have the law, Mae. It's what keeps us decent, it's what keeps our world worth protecting. So when Jon Prince blocks his driveway so building control can't inspect the bunker, it's me that writes the fine. And when Barbara Sweeny calls me because she can't get her daughter to stop eating, it's me that mediates.'

'So eating is a crime now?'

He shrugged.

'There'll come a point when you can't protect us.'

Sergeant Walters smiled sadly. 'Maybe, but until then . . . My father spent his life preserving this town, keeping it safe. I will do the same. No exceptions.'

Mae watched a group of girls pass. Matilda and Betty nodded towards her.

'So if I find out you've done anything –'

'I haven't.' She thought of the houses she'd broken into, the things she'd stolen.

'You should get to class, Mae.'

At school she saw Hugo and Liam, by the steps, sprawled out in matching white vests.

Jeet Patel headed down and Hugo stuck out a leg. The fall looked painful but Jeet climbed to his feet quickly and walked towards the maths block, not looking back. She wondered at his life, what fresh hell each day brought. He just went about his business, and for some reason that became other people's business.

'The United States, the European Space Agency, Russia, China, India and Japan,' Mr Starling said. 'They're the only ones with launch capabilities. Selena, if she was much smaller, we could nudge her. West is safer. We break her up and send part of her to the desert. People would die –'

'But not western people,' Liam said. He looked to Hugo for a high five but Hugo was busy staring out the window.

'So we send her away from us,' Liam went on. 'To a weaker country. We evacuate some of them, but the rest . . .'

'You're talking about Lexi's family,' Hunter said.

Lexi frowned. 'But my mother is from –'

'So now we're onto space wars,' Mr Starling said. 'And I'd rather not get into this again after last time.' He smiled at Amy Harris, who'd been slapped by Sofia Diaz after she suggested aiming Selena at South America.

'Now, can anyone tell me what the smallest are called, less than a metre across?' Mr Starling asked.

Liam talked over him, mimicking, holding court in the ugly way that drew idiot laughter.

'Meteoroids,' Mae said, loud enough for Liam to momentarily quiet.

Mr Starling smiled a smile of such gratitude she had to look away.

'And what is a meteoroid made of?'

Liam stood, played to the laughs and mimicked everything Mr Starling did.

Mr Starling put his hand in his pocket. Liam did the same.

Mr Starling sighed.

Liam sighed.

'I feel bad for him.'

Mae glanced sideways as Hunter settled into Sullivan Reed's seat, hooked her bag carefully over the back then took a small mirror from her pocket and began fussing with her hair. She pouted, applied lip gloss, oblivious to the stares of a dozen boys around. Or maybe not oblivious.

'Where's fatty today?' Hunter said, looking over to Sally's seat.

Lexi turned around in her chair. 'She was crying in the toilets just now. Too funny.'

Mae thought of Sally, how tough she looked, how much it would've taken to make her cry. She thought of Lexi stealing Sally's clothes.

Up front, Liam went back to his act, Mr Starling carried on behind, drowned out but still he went through motions. For his part Liam grew louder, reached for a metre stick and used it as a makeshift cane, hobbling around desks till the laughter grew.

Mae looked at the three boards, the progression and decline. And beside that the word map that stretched from ceiling to floor, heavy canvas, as wide as a car. Stella fixated on lost art, made Mae read her books from the library that referenced statues and mausoleums, pyramids and temples. Seven wonders flattened, a billion years of progress not stalled but rewound.

Mr Starling moved on to 2011 MD and NASA's plan to capture an asteroid. Mae strained to listen but could not hear much above Liam, who was now just shouting random words.

Mining.

Habitats.

Robotics.

Each came a second after Mr Starling spoke it.

Mae stared at Liam, red-faced and sweating from the exertion. This was what lessons were reduced to. Some teachers kept control, maybe through distance. Shakespeare, fractions, the structure of a symphony. They stayed in their boxes. But Mr Starling, each and every lesson brought them closer to the sky.

'951 Gaspra. Vesta. Eros.' Mr Starling spoke louder, desperately looking out to see if he was reaching any of them.

'Just sit, Liam,' Jeet Patel said.

It earned him a hard slap to the back of the head from Hugo. Most eyes were on Liam, wondering what he'd do next. He grinned, then moved down between chairs and snatched the glasses from the top pocket of Mr Starling's jacket. The laughter grew as he put them on, then peered over his nose and wagged a finger at a cluster of his friends.

'Liam, please.' They startled when they heard a clap. A single clap of the hands by Mr Starling. Silence as Liam turned towards him.

'Take your seat now. That's enough for today.' Mr Starling spoke quietly again, not meeting the boy's eye.

Sally Sweeny entered and walked across the room, her eyes still red as she took her seat.

'Are you okay?' Mae said.

Lexi turned again. 'What's the matter, Sally. Did the bakery close down?'

'Shut up, Lexi,' Mae said.

Liam stood up again. 'I'm bored of this class. You need to teach us something new.' And with that he strode towards the front, picked up a board eraser and slowly dragged it across a month's worth of painstaking detail. Asteroids smeared, the detail lost as he trailed from one to the next. When he was done, he walked back to Mr Starling, stood directly in front of him and dropped the eraser to the floor.

They stood face to face. Liam taller, imposing, smirking.

They sensed something would happen.

But no one was truly prepared for the punch.

It echoed.

The sound of Mr Starling's fist colliding with Liam's chin. Liam's eyes rolled as his knees weakened and he folded to the floor.

Out cold.

They watched open-mouthed as Mr Starling turned back to the board and slowly began to fix the diagrams.

Among all the chaos, no one noticed Sally Sweeny take the scissors from the drawer beside her.

And no one noticed her gently take hold of Lexi's waist-length plait.

But as Sally cut it free and tossed it out the window, Lexi's scream could be heard echoing out across the whole school.

26

She found the collar caught on the side gate, the lead still attached.

In the back garden Stella petted the dog.

Mae slipped the collar over its head.

'What's going on?' Stella said.

'I'm taking the dog back.'

Stella shook her head, the tears filling her eyes. She tried to take Mae's hand.

'Please,' she said.

'It's not ours, Stella.'

'No, Mae. Please let me keep her. There's not long, they don't even miss her.'

Mae said nothing.

'I put up posters,' Stella said, desperately. 'Mrs Baxter took me out after the party and we put up posters. I did what you said, but no one has come for her.'

Their grandmother stood in the doorway. 'There's not long, Margaret.'

'You want to pay to feed it?' Mae fired back. She pulled on the lead. The dog got up but tried to pull back towards Stella.

'I hate you,' Stella said. 'You're mean and everyone knows it and that's why no one asked you to the Final and that's why Abi moved away.'

Their grandmother leaned down and held on to Stella as she sobbed.

Mae walked in silence, the dog pulling back, her muscles burned, the last days had taken a toll.

The collar gave an address on Parade Hill, at the top of Ocean.

She stopped as a truck rolled through the gates of the Prince house.

She saw Hugo directing it, met his eye and he waved her over. She tied the dog to the gate.

'You all right?' he said.

She nodded.

'Can't believe you saved her like that.'

'Neither can I,' Mae said.

She followed him down the side of the house. Past the glass garage that housed the rare Ferrari, and the swimming pool, lit from beneath, the blue so heavenly Mae fought an urge to dive straight in, sink to the bottom and wait out the next weeks.

The hole was cavernous now. Hugo lifted a barrier and stepped onto the metal plinth, motioned and she stood beside him.

He pressed a green button and they gripped the rail tightly as the lift groaned and creaked. It took them down, past packed earth, dense rock torn by mechanical hands. Lights had been punched into the stone and shone out eerily.

It stopped far below and Mae craned her neck to see sunlight.

The bunker.

Steel like a vault.

A heavy door was propped open. Metal walls, secondary power from generators as tall as Hugo. They walked through the entranceway and it opened out to a sprawl of harried workmen, electricians with clipboards, an architect with measuring tape.

'Looks expensive,' Mae said.

'I heard my dad talking about trying to offload the chalet in St Moritz.'

'Jesus, no,' Mae said, a hand to her mouth.

Ahead they came to a small group. Hugo walked over to his father, who stood with other men but dismissed them when he saw his son.

'You've been with Hunter this morning? You weren't home,' Jon Prince said.

'Gym.'

His father nodded at that, then glanced over at Mae. 'You just bringing girls down here, Hugo? Remember what I said.' He gripped Hugo's arm and squeezed it so hard she saw Hugo flinch. And then Jon Prince seemed to remember they weren't alone. He aimed a tight smile at Mae. 'I suppose it wouldn't hurt, there's no way planning can stop me now.'

He was taller than his son, perma-tanned, his hair pulled back into a tight ponytail. He pressed a hand to Mae's lower back, must have felt her tense but didn't move it.

He spoke of secondary air, a year's worth of supplies, the ability to compost, the infrastructure to be self-sufficient.

'I think we'll stop her. But if we don't, we're prepared.' They looked at the kitchen, pared-back stainless steel, elegant. Survival would not be basic.

'How many people can you fit in here?' Mae asked.

'It depends on how long you want the air supply to last,' Jon Prince said. 'The less inside, the better.'

'What's that room?' She pointed.

'That's for the Ferrari. It'll likely be the only one left in the world soon enough. Of course there's others building underground. The Chinese government. The Russians. Basically anyone with the means. But that car. They only built a handful.'

'It won't save you,' Mae said, and the men around stopped, Hugo and his father watched her, the noise cut to dead silence. 'It won't even buy you time.'

A moment passed till Jon Prince laughed. And then the other men joined him as Hugo wandered towards the lift.

As Mae turned to follow, Jon Prince stopped her. 'You were the one with Hugo when . . . the Manton girl.'

Mae nodded.

Up close he was even bigger, his eyes even colder. Something about the way he looked at her left her fighting a shiver.

'You were friends with her?'

Mae did not answer.

'But she didn't say anything beforehand? She didn't mention any names, people she thought might have upset her?'

He stood so close Mae took a step backwards and found herself pressed against the steel wall.

'You see, Mae. Sometimes girls your age, they see things that aren't really there.'

'Pretty sure girls my age see just fine.'

He looked over at Hugo, something passed between them.

Maybe Jon Prince could see the look on her face, because he stepped back and smiled.

Hugo walked her back to the gate.

'Your father,' Mae said, 'does he know Abi's dad?'

'Who do you think is building the bunker?'

She watched him head back in, then turned and walked the dog along Parade Hill.

The steady hiss of sprinklers.

At first she didn't know if she imagined the music, so beautiful she stopped still and moved towards the kerb.

It floated from the open window of the pretty cottage behind. Mae sat down on the kerb, closed her eyes and breathed deep. Some nights she could barely breathe. She thought of her parents, wondered if they would be proud of her but knew deep down they would not. She was not a girl to be proud of. In her bag was a small bottle of vodka she had stolen from the supermarket in Newport. The woman at the checkout had been too old and too trusting, like the world was still good, like it had ever been good.

The music died. She smelled barbecue smoke.

Mae turned when she heard the gate open and watched as Sally Sweeny heaved a bin out in front of the house.

'Hey,' she said.

Sally startled, like she'd never had another kid so close to her home.

'Mae,' Sally said. 'Is that Benjy?'

Sally knelt and stroked the dog.

'I found him.'

'He belongs to my neighbour Mr Leonard. He ran away during the fire at Candice's house, must've got scared. I kind of hoped he wouldn't come back. Mr Leonard is one of those people that takes out his problems on his dog.'

'That music, what was it?'

'Prelude in E minor. Chopin.'

'It kind of broke my heart.'

Sally smiled sadly. 'It'll do that, Chopin. They played it at his funeral. He requested it.'

'He had his own music played at his funeral. Badass.'

'Who's your friend?'

Mae saw Sally's father at the door.

The cottage was beautiful. The roof thatched, the grass neat. Mae opened the white gate and walked up the path, the sun hot on her neck.

There was a cross-stitch.

BLESS THIS HOUSE.

The man was short, his blonde hair parted neatly at the side.

'I'm Sally's stepfather, Oliver. Please come in.'

Inside, white walls and floral curtains, dark beams crossed the ceiling. She smelled apple pie.

Sally's mother appeared in the kitchen doorway and stroked the dog, gave it a bowl of something and watched it curl up. She wore a red apron and a smile that matched her husband's. 'I'm Barbara, but everyone calls me Barbie.'

Looking at her perfectly styled hair and make-up, Mae could believe it.

She followed them through the kitchen.

More signs on the walls.

AS WE FORGIVE THOSE WHO TRESPASS AGAINST US.

FORGIVENESS IS THE GREATEST GIFT.

LOVE. COMPASSION. FORGIVENESS. ACCEPTANCE.

The garden sprawled with flowers, so many Mae was dizzy with the colours. Across was a tall maple tree, a swing hung from the branch. Mae followed Sally over.

'They suspended you then,' Mae said.

'Totally worth it.'

Through the bushes she caught sight of the neighbour's kids, running through a sprinkler and laughing.

'Are you here to convert me, Mae?'

'Yes.'

Sally smiled, squinting into the sun. 'This swing, it's been here since I was small. You ever wish you didn't have to grow up?'

'It was a race when we were young, to be the first to go with a boy, drink, smoke. Now we want time to stop.'

'Maybe it has. Maybe it stopped ten years ago. I heard about Sullivan Reed.'

'Yeah. You think it was him?'

'It doesn't look good.'

Barbie and Oliver beckoned them over.

They'd already laid a place at the table for Mae. She couldn't say no. Oliver stood by the barbecue, flipping burgers.

Mae sat beside Sally and watched her parents. It was orchestrated, a picture-perfect snapshot of family life.

Barbie brought out sides, steaming potatoes, salad and buns. She touched her husband's back each time she passed him. Mae wondered about intimacy, how it could endure, how they could be so content. It was like they hadn't heard, or didn't want to know.

Pork chops. Sausages and burgers. Chicken legs and great hunks of steak.

Sally filled her plate before her parents had poured the wine. Started eating before Barbie bowed her head to say grace.

Mae sat and watched as Sally methodically worked her way through the food. Ketchup spilled down her chin, mayonnaise streaked down one cheek.

Sally's parents exchanged looks but neither said anything.

Barbie tucked a napkin into her top and nibbled on a rib.

'I saw the posters in town,' Barbie said. 'This dance then . . .' Sally shovelled in a mouthful of potato. Barbie waited, watching, patient.

'Have you got a date yet, Sally?' Oliver said.

Sally ignored him, reached for a third burger and washed it down with a glass of Coke.

'The school will still let her go, despite what she did to that poor girl's hair,' Barbie said.

'The boys at school are arseholes,' Mae said.

Sally aimed a grateful smile at her.

'You're still beautiful,' Barbie said.

Sally worked on her third pork chop.

'Maybe go easy on the food, we have company.'

'Doesn't bother me,' Mae said.

Barbie stared at her daughter. 'Gluttony is a sin.'

Sally stared right back as she bit a sausage in half.

'I worry about you. You know she can barely sit behind the piano now. Has to stretch herself. Such talent and she's intent on wasting it.'

Mae glanced at Sally, who looked about ready for Selena to hit.

'You know I used to wake her at four, seven days a week. People think it's a gift, to be able to play piano like that, to sing like Theodore does. But it's earned, Mae.'

Mae watched Barbie as she spoke. She looked delicate but Mae could sense a toughness beneath. And Oliver, for his part, he sat there mute, like the conversation wasn't happening.

'Everyone's talking about Sullivan Reed,' Barbie said, shaking her head. 'Did you know him, Mae? So sad what these kids are doing now. The drugs. All the alcohol. I heard about what happens at the beach at night. I'm just glad my Sally has her head screwed on right. Of course she's too large to be invited out now.'

'Actually,' Mae said. 'That's why I came over. I was going to ask Sally to come over to my house to watch a movie tonight.'

'Oh,' Barbie said. 'That would be nice, right, Sally? Sally doesn't like to go out in the evening. Not even to church. Those kids by the beach, they can be so cruel if you're . . .' she dropped her voice to a whisper, 'a bit fat.'

Sally stared through her mother.

'You know, I bought a painting from Sullivan Reed once,' Barbie said.

'The beach scene?' Oliver said. 'I did wonder where that had come from. But then I wondered about everything when I came home. I barely recognised Sally. But I know she's still in there.'

'Sullivan was actually very sweet. He was over the moon when I bought it.'

'He works on commission,' Sally said, her mouth full of coleslaw.

'No. I think he was excited for the artist. It's rare for people to care that much now. For someone to want to help someone else.'

'He's a murderer,' Mae said.

Barbie took it in her stride. 'Their sins and lawless acts will be forgotten. He's a merciful God, Mae.'

Sally put down her food. 'You know what else God said? An eye for an eye.'

27

They walked slow.

Mae stopped off to let the dog into the old house, watched it climb the stairs and take its place at the foot of her sister's bed. She imagined Stella's face when she woke, her smile reaching Mae's.

Every now and then Sally stopped and caught her breath. Tourists stood outside the Rose and Crown and drank. Mae caught snippets of conversation, talk of their last weeks, talk of Selena. One man raised a glass to the sky, spilled most of the contents down his arm and then began to cry. His wife slipped an arm around him.

'Goddam summer people,' Sally said.

'Your stepfather, he said something about not recognising the house when he came back. Was he a leaver?'

'Yeah,' Sally said. 'But he came back. I didn't expect to see him again, but then we got a letter out of the blue, and then another.'

'People make mistakes.'

'Forgiveness takes strength. But it also takes strength to hold a grudge. I mean really hold it, so tight you worry it'll break you.'

As they rounded the curve they saw the beach fire.

This time there were twenty of them.

And that night the new Forevers of West told their stories. They passed around a bottle of champagne, stolen from Hannah Lewis's parents. It was a special bottle they were saving for their twentieth wedding anniversary. Mae treated it with the appropriate respect.

'Jesus, pass it on,' Betty said as Mae chugged.

Most stories had been told before, but no one interrupted, no one dared take anything from the person holding the bottle. There were no rules, you could speak about anything, but for those fleeting moments you had an audience that listened, you got to feel like you had a voice in a deafening world.

Mehmet Ceyhan took the bottle and he told them how he cheated in his exams, and that his parents found out but they kept it from the school.

Becky Lane stood, so far from the fire all Mae could see was the dark of her hair, and she slurred and held the bottle like a microphone.

'When Selena comes, in that last moment, I'm going to go up to my bedroom and I'm going to get off and I'm going to have the world's biggest orgasm because the world . . . it'll be small, right?'

There was laughter, applause and cheers as she curtsied and passed the bottle along.

Sail lay beside her.

She hadn't seen him arrive, he just drifted across the beach and settled with the group.

Matilda stood. She said some nights she was so afraid of dying she crept across the hallway and climbed into bed with her parents. On another day she might have been mocked, but everyone there understood that fear too well.

It came back to Mae and she did not stand, instead drank some more and passed it to Sail.

'I don't like public speaking,' he said, a slight slur.

'Say anything,' came a voice from the darkness.

Mae saw the profile of his face beneath the moonlight.

'My Selena story.'

A couple of people encouraged. Everyone liked to hear these stories, it took them back to when it began, and maybe to before.

'I had a sister.'

Mae saw a slight shake in his hand.

'Alice, and she was five and she was sick. I mean, the kind of sick you don't get better from. We knew that when she was born. We knew she'd die. They said that, everyone said that she'd die like that would somehow lessen her life. I couldn't breathe. I thought I'd die too.'

Silence fell then, the kind Mae had not heard at the beach before.

'My parents ... we went to a hospital in Switzerland because that's where this doctor was, but even he couldn't do anything. Money, it gets you so far, but there's always things that you can't ...'

He glanced down at Mae.

'So, she died in the morning. And I sat at the hospital, in one of those rooms where there's a TV and games. They wouldn't

191

let me see her, they said she was gone. But we stayed there the whole day. And when we were driving back I saw cars pulled over to the side of the road, some just stopped dead. And they were broadcasting it on every radio station. People climbed out and stood on the motorway and stared at the sky.'

He drank again. 'When I look back now, there's something beautiful in that. But I don't know exactly why. The uniformity . . . everyone reduced to human. Kind of like we were Forevers.

'My parents don't have photos of her. Or rather they have them, they just don't put them out on display. And they don't like to talk about her. I think they died that day, I think we all did. My house is a mausoleum, we exist in our own tombs. Sometimes we pass each other by, we might nod or smile, but we're nothing to each other. We're nothing without Alice.'

He held their attention with his words.

'I have photos on my laptop, every picture I could find, I scanned them and sometimes when I hear about Selena, I go to my bedroom and I check in with Alice. And I feel better. You know, live or die, whatever happens. If there's somewhere, after, then I'll see her again, and if not then I'll just go through whatever she went through. If it's dark, that's all right. Alice went there, and I'd follow her into hell.'

He passed the bottle.

Mae got to her feet and ran from them, from the Forevers calling her back, from the boy who'd finally let her see the part of his life that broke him.

He ran after her.

Up the curve of Ocean Drive, the mansions nothing now, the cars and the pools.

192

She slowed a little when they reached his house. And then finally she turned to face him.

'The laptop I took.'

He smiled like it was nothing.

The pain in her stomach, catching her out, the dryness in her throat. Sometimes she laboured under the illusion she was a good person dealt a losing hand. She knew right from wrong, her heart was in the right place. But right then, standing before him, beneath the harsh lights of his world, she saw herself.

He tried to say something, maybe he read her, the look on her face.

'I'm nothing good,' she said.

He tried to take her hand but she slipped it from him. 'I need to go and you need to stay here,' she said. 'And that's how it will be.'

He watched her walk away.

She knew he couldn't really see her, because she was never really there.

On the edge of the bay she heard footsteps, only this time she didn't run.

She was shoved hard, fell forward, hitting the ground. She turned over and looked up to see Hunter standing above her, fists clenched.

Mae didn't wait to find out what Hunter wanted, instead she grabbed a fistful of sand and threw it up into Hunter's eyes.

Hunter stepped back, and in that time Mae was up and on her. She knocked the other girl off her feet and came to land heavily on top of her. She pinned Hunter's hands down and straddled her.

'Get off of me,' Hunter said, blinking back sand. She tried to heave herself up but Mae kept her pinned.

'Calm down,' Mae said.

'Fuck you.'

'In a minute I'll let you up. And then you can tell me what you're so mad about. But if you come at me again I'll knock your perfect teeth out. Tell me you understand.'

Hunter stared into her eyes, that fire burning so hot Mae didn't know how it would go.

She got off, let Hunter up and took a single step backwards to give her some room. They were far enough from the crowd that no one saw the fight.

'You stole my necklace,' Hunter said.

Mae frowned.

'I want it for the Final. My father gave it to me. Everyone knows you're a thief, Mae.'

'I don't know what you're talking about.'

'Bullshit. I thought I'd lost it, but I always keep it in a jewellery box hidden in the back of my wardrobe. And then I found out from Hugo that you broke into his house. And I realised it was you, you broke into my pool house. You're a thief.'

'You think I'm dumb enough to break into the headmaster's house?'

The fight left Hunter as quick as it arrived. 'It's special. Look, if you took it, even if you sold it, I'll give you the money and you can get it back. I won't even say anything to Sergeant Walters.'

'I didn't take your necklace. I never take anything special. I take shit that can be replaced. Nothing sentimental.'

Hunter shook her head.

Mae gripped the gold cross she wore. 'My mother gave me this. It can't be replaced. I'd never steal someone else's memories.'

Hunter sat down on the sand.

Mae sat beside her.

'He's going to kill me. He thinks I don't like it because I never wear it. But it's too special to wear, that's what he doesn't realise. Everyone has a Selena story, right?'

Mae nodded.

'It was Saviour 3 when I got it. You remember that one?'

'We were ten. It was autumn.'

'That was the first time I understood it. Before it was just some fairy tale. The big bad monster in the sky. But Saviour 3, when it failed I saw it in their faces. You see my parents, they're, like, perfect. They've got their shit together. I watched it unravel that night.' Hunter swallowed.

Mae said nothing, just watched her.

'They put me first, they protect me from everything bad. That's what parents should do, but how many of them actually do it? How many of them would live their whole life solely for their children?'

Mae might have believed most would, but that was before.

'But this was something they couldn't protect me from. I repay them every day, Mae. I'm so sickly sweet sometimes I gag. My mother's idea of her perfect little girl. We go to church, shit, we knit together. I bake. I wear a goddam apron and bake cupcakes for old ladies. I'm head girl. I counsel, I give speeches, I even take the mail to the post office since the secretary declared herself a leaver.'

Mae watched her then, the shift, so slight others might not have noticed. The veneer didn't slip, but maybe dulled a shade.

'How I am, to you, to others. How I can be behind their backs. If I don't do that I might explode. I'll smile one last sickly smile and then my body will blow into a million pieces. I'll splatter my perfect pink bedroom with brains and guts.'

Mae let the warm sand run through her fingers as she watched a couple of Forevers slow-dancing on the beach.

'It hit him hard. When he realised he couldn't save me from this. He gave me the necklace and told me to hold on to it when I get scared. It's shaped like the moon. It's everything.'

Mae felt her pulse quicken. 'The stone. What colour is it?'

'Blue. He said it matched my eyes.'

28

Stella woke in the night.

Mae heard her and crossed the hallway to climb into bed with her.

'Lady is here. Am I dreaming?'

'No.'

Stella touched the sleeping dog's head.

'I had that dream again. Everything was black . . . not everyday black, this was too black. I couldn't even sense you. Not at all. What if that's what it's like?'

Mae pressed a hand to her sister's head. 'It's not. I promise.'

'Will Mummy and Daddy be there?'

'Yes.'

'How will I know them?'

Mae closed her eyes.

Saviour 2 launched on a Saturday evening.

Mae's parents had taken her to London to see an opera.

Rigoletto.

When the world was still round and the future unblemished. Mae had worn a new dress. Her father looked handsome in a dinner suit and black tie, while her mother shone in her emerald ballgown.

Mae did not know what an opera was, did not know the beauty of sacrifice or the power music could have.

She had cried when Gilda was revealed.

Her mother had taken her hand and told her it wasn't real, but that wasn't what she needed to hear.

It would take two months to discover that Saviour 2 had failed.

'Will they mind that I can't see them?'

'They won't mind.'

Stella found her hand. 'What I said before –'

'I know.'

'Will you sleep here tonight?'

'Yes.'

She caught the first bus of the day, sat alone, now and then the driver caught her eye and smiled.

'Not long,' he said.

She nodded.

'Thirty years I've driven this route. My wife wants me to stop. What the hell else would I do?'

'Talk to her?'

He laughed so hard the bus veered.

At Newport she sat outside the pawnbroker's for an hour before the lights flickered on and the man unbolted the door.

He frowned when he saw her, coughed and held up a hand. 'No more stolen laptops. I had the police here the other day. Think they'd have something better to do, what with the world going to shit.'

'The laptop. I need it back,' she said.

'Five hundred.'

She looked at him like he was joking. 'You gave me fifty.'

He said nothing when she pleaded, even when she swallowed her dignity and begged. He simply looked past her at the television as Morales talked. 'He's trying to stop a tank by tossing marbles at it. We're doomed.'

'That necklace you showed me last time,' she said.

He shrugged.

'Blue stone, looked like a moon.'

He pointed to the window, where she saw it on display. No doubt it was Hunter's. It was too unusual, too unique to be anything but.

'How much is it?'

'You can't afford it.'

She kept her eyes on the stone. 'Try me.'

'A thousand.'

'How much did you pay for it?'

He didn't even bother replying.

'You said a girl brought it in.'

He shrugged, like he'd said nothing like that.

She walked over to the counter and stared at him, unflinching. He didn't look like the kind of man who could be intimated.

'What did she look like?'

He looked up at the TV screen behind. 'I don't remember.'

She reached into her bag and pulled out a stack of notes.

That got his attention. And she pulled out the photo Luke Manton had given her and showed it to him.

He put on a pair of reading glasses and studied the photo.

'Yeah.'

'Are you sure?'

'Believe it or not, we don't get many teenage girls coming in here. Especially not with a memorable piece like that.'

She looked at the photo, at Abi's smiling face, and felt that familiar stab in her gut. 'Did she say anything?'

He snorted, then met her eye and maybe he could see the pain because he softened. 'She took less.'

'What do you mean?'

He looked down. 'I said I didn't have much cash on the premises, that she'd have to come back. It's an old trick. People see through it.'

'But she didn't?'

'It was clear she was desperate.'

Mae watched him. 'And?'

He sighed. 'The eyes. I've got nieces, you know when they've been crying, even if they try to hide it.'

'You didn't ask?'

'Do I look like a counsellor? You don't come in unless you're desperate, and with Selena, everybody's desperate.'

Mae walked into the council building, up the stone steps to the first floor and looked for him. She tried offices. It was Saturday but the place was busy. A mother stood with three children, the youngest screaming herself raw. Their belongings were stacked in the corner, two suitcases and a cardboard box.

He kicked us out.

We're going to die on the street.

Mae sat for a while, and then she remembered the room she'd met him outside.

Another flight of stairs before she found it.

And then she saw him.

He sat on a chair. For a moment she watched him, the way he looked down at his shoes. It was like he didn't know what he looked like, what he had. She wondered about privilege and class, what they meant in a dying world.

Mae stepped closer, the door was closed but she looked through the window and saw the circle he sat in.

'Are you coming in?' The man was older, maybe forty, he had long hair and a beard and the kind of eyes that told Mae he'd seen a lot.

She shook her head.

'It's not too late, you know,' he said.

'It is. Whatever's in there, it's too late.'

He smiled sadly. 'I'd tell you the first step is the hardest, but to be honest they're all hard.'

He placed a hand on her shoulder. And then led her into the room.

Sail didn't react when he saw her.

She sat three down from him, took in the group, a mix of ages and genders.

People talked, listened. Sail watched her the whole time.

She wanted to go over, take his hand and tell him she was sorry. She wanted to tell him he could get his laptop back, that she knew where it was and that the cost was nothing to someone like him.

Instead she sat mute as he stood.

'I'm Jack, and I've been clean for eleven months.'

They chorused 'Hi, Jack.'

'Don't say that on a plane,' Sail said.

Mae closed her eyes for a moment, and then stood, and walked away from Jack Sail.

29

She watched Mr Starling struggle from the building.

He carried a box.

Inside she saw a framed photograph, a mug, keepsakes from his desk and a stack of notes from past students.

'What's going on?' Mae said.

Sunlight bounced from the rusting bonnet of his car. 'You're a good student, Mae. I always said that. I know what you have at home, I know how difficult it must be.'

'You're leaving us?'

He looked past her, back to the old school building.

'This is because of what you did?'

'I know my place, my role. I've been here thirty years.' He said it with a smile. 'I taught some of your parents. I've watched this school go from a struggling secondary in a small coastal town to one of the finest in the county.'

'They should have let you stay till the end.'

'I struck a student.'

'Not hard enough.'

He opened the boot of his old VW and set the box down inside, took a last look at the school. His wife had died three years before, the day after the funeral Mr Starling had sat down and told them about cancer. That day no one had messed around, just sat and listened as their teacher bared a part of himself they were quite unused to seeing. People said Selena humanised. Mae had not known what that meant until then.

'What will you do now?' she said.

'I have an old boat. I've spent a lifetime trying to make her new again.'

She nodded.

'There's been so much tragedy.' His voice caught. 'I think of James, Melissa and Abi. I know we failed, all of us who played the slightest part in their lives.'

Mae looked down, his pain hard to witness as he started the engine and drove.

She turned, feeling the heat in her cheeks as she pushed through a group of younger kids.

She passed the empty reception desk and opened the door to Mr Silver's office. She found him on the sofa, his eyes lost in the painting, so dark and threatening.

'I saw Mr Starling,' she said.

Mr Silver wore his shirt open two buttons, the sleeves rolled over tan forearms, a Swiss watch on his wrist.

'You must have known this would come, Mae.'

'He was here thirty years.'

'He was.'

'He's a good teacher.'

'He was.'

'Couldn't you just . . . ?' She felt foolish then.

'I know the student. I know he would've provoked him.'

He smiled at her, perfect teeth too white, then he walked over to the window and lifted the blinds. 'I deny it. I tell students it's a test of their faith.'

'You believe though.'

'Some days I want to tell you all not to come in. To go lie on the beach or go into the city. See things. Feel things. What's tangible, while it still is.'

'But you don't.'

'I can't. The government, we avoid the chaos. You know they're burning churches now. All across the world. Like this is proof of nothing, proof we're on our own and always have been.'

'We all know, deep down, doubt is what makes us human. It's our ability to ignore it. Evolution is a four-letter word in this school.'

'It's a test, Mae.'

'I'd rather fail.'

'You saved my daughter.'

'She didn't. I had it totally under control.' Hunter stood in the doorway.

Mae left them, walked back through halls now empty, just the click of her shoes and their echo. Out into the sunlight.

At the edge of the woods Hunter caught up with her. 'You skipping?'

Mae nodded.

'Can I come?'

'No.'

Hunter opened her bag, showed Mae the bottle of whisky.

'Okay, you can come.'

* * *

They lay flat on the sand, shoes off, the water touched their feet and retreated, leaving them with goosebumps.

Mae drained a quarter of the bottle, then sat up and passed it to Hunter, who drank liberally.

'You stole this from your father?'

'He gave it to me, told me to go find you and take the day off. He's cool, you know, not like people think.'

It was ten o'clock on a Monday morning and she was drinking with the headmaster's perfect daughter. The world must be about to end.

'Sometimes I think I can see it coming. Some days it's angry, full of fire and metals and all that shit. And other days it's just a dull rock, grey and too nothing to ever take us out,' Hunter said.

The sun rose high, the heat getting up but a breeze cooled them off. It was worse in the cities, the newspapers said London was burning. A last hurrah, a wild summer before eternal dark.

'Can I ask you something?' Hunter said, taking the bottle like she needed the courage.

'Your hair looks fine.'

Hunter looked to the waves. 'What did she look like?'

'Everyone wants to know that.' Mae's mind turned slow, the alcohol clouding over her thoughts. 'Like Abi, but not. She was just . . . empty.'

Hunter tipped the bottle onto the sand, and then reached for her bag and pulled out a pad and pen. She started to write.

'Anything you want to say, Mae?'

Mae lay back. 'Fuck me, Selena.'

'Poetic.' Hunter wrote it, then rolled the paper and slotted it into the bottle. She stood, unsteady as she screwed the cap back on, and then threw the bottle far out to the water.

'I wonder where it'll go. I mean, how it will end. Will it smash in the middle of the ocean? Or will it boil till it melts? Will anything live?'

They stretched out, arms and legs like starfish. Seventeen, young enough to clutch at the girls they had been, old enough to see the women waiting for them.

They let the world spin for an hour, the booze and the sun reddened their cheeks. They felt the faint rumble of the town behind them, this time it was less, more a slight protest than a roar of discontent. A car alarm in the distance, no one noticed, no one cared. They waded knee deep and watched the small fish through water too clear, the waves died and the ocean turned into a lake.

For a while they talked about nothing much at all, the drink still softening their words as they smiled towards the sun.

'Have you thought about what you'll do at the end?' Hunter said.

'I'll get so wasted I won't even be afraid. Then I'll grab hold of you and maybe I'll sneak my way in upstairs.'

Hunter laughed again, so loud and hard Mae couldn't help but smile.

'You going to the Final?'

Mae looked at Hunter, no emotion, nothing said.

'Fair enough then. There's a romance to it, like it really is the final dance or something.'

'It really is the final dance.'

'Then you should go. I'd lend you a dress but you're so short . . . and it'd gape at the chest and –'

'We could do each other's hair?'

Hunter glared at her, incredulous. 'Like I'd let you touch my hair.'

Mae almost smiled at that one.

'Go with the hot rich boy. For some reason he wants to risk it with you . . . STDs and everything.'

She thought of Sail. 'I messed things up. I mean, he's messed up. Together we'd be . . .'

Hunter motioned for her to continue.

Mae took a breath. 'I took something from him and it's all I see when I look at him. And he pretends it's all right and . . .' She stopped. 'I don't know why I'm telling you this.'

'The thing you took. Give it back.'

'There's a bigger picture. And anyway, I don't think I can get it back. Not on my own.'

Hunter watched the gentle water. 'I suppose I owe you a favour.'

30

'Ayisha said the postman was in her mummy's bed,' Stella said.

Mae puffed out her cheeks. 'Making a delivery, I guess.'

'What was he delivering?'

'His package,' Felix said.

Mae aimed an elbow at him.

'I think Selena has made people crazy,' Sail said.

'Or maybe she's set them free,' Felix said. 'Like now, take what I'm about to do. I'd never have had the balls to do it before. I mean, if we weren't going to die in the next –'

'I'm just glad it doesn't involve fire this time,' Mae said.

'But it does involve Felix dressed up like a zombie?' Sail said, a question in his tone.

Felix shrugged. 'She rented the *Walking Dead* box set.' Mae sighed. 'If that doesn't imply a deep attraction to zombies, then I don't know what does.'

She had helped with the costume. They'd taken a pair of scissors to Felix's best shirt and trousers while Stella helped paint his face, using her fingers, tracing the lines.

'So this is what it feels like to be white,' Felix said, looking at his reflection in the window of a parked car.

'How does it feel?' Mae asked.

'Entitled. Even as a zombie.'

Mae handed Stella a bottle of ketchup.

'More by the mouth,' Mae said.

'Not in the mouth,' Felix said, coughing.

When they were done he led them up Ocean Drive.

'Is he doing the walk?' Stella said.

'Afraid so,' Mae replied.

Felix limped, one shoulder dipped, his left foot dragging behind him.

'He should do the noise.'

Felix groaned.

They stopped by the open gates at the end of Candice's driveway. Mae handed Felix the sign.

CANDICE, USE YOUR BRAINS

GO TO THE FINAL WITH ME.

'I'm scared,' Felix said.

Sail cupped Felix's face in his hands and spoke to him, nose to nose. 'This is it. Two weeks to fulfil your destiny. I know you're nervous, it's natural. But you're the Reverend's son. When he talks, you can see the housewives stirring. The apple and the tree, Felix. His blood is coursing your veins. So channel him, lurch down that driveway and groan your heart out. And when she hears that beautiful mating call, she'll march out and finish ripping those clothes from your body.' He planted a gentle kiss on Felix's forehead and then nodded.

Felix nodded back.

'So romantic,' Stella said, clapping her hands.

'You really think this will work?'

'I've never been more certain of anything in my life,' Sail said, wiping his hands on his jeans.

They stood there, fingers crossed, nervous for him as he walked down her driveway and disappeared from sight.

And then they heard the scream.

Followed by the deafening sound of a rape alarm.

The zombie came sprinting from the drive. 'Liam's got a gun. He's got an actual gun.'

'She had to chase him with her brother's airgun. Zombie rape, man. I tell you, there's some terrifying people in this town,' Hunter said.

'Are you sure he was trying to rape her?' Mae said.

'No doubt. He was making weird sex groans.'

It was midnight.

Hunter wore black jeans and a dark hooded top. She'd tied her hair back. On her feet were monochrome black Converse and beneath each eye was a streak of warpaint. Mae had laughed so hard Hunter almost turned and left her.

'After this we're even,' Hunter said.

'Okay, commando.'

They walked up Ocean Drive in silence and stopped by the Prince house. The gates had been taken down to make room for more machinery.

The house lay in darkness, Hugo and his father in the city. 'We'll take the Range Rover,' Hunter said. 'I can handle an auto no problem.'

They walked up to the front door of the house and Mae

took the coat hanger from her bag, straightened it and twisted the end into a hook.

Hunter kept watch.

Mae dropped to her knees and pushed the wire through the letterbox. The keys were on the side table, right where they'd been the night she broke in.

'Hurry up,' Hunter hissed.

It took five attempts before she knocked everything to the floor.

'Like a cat burglar,' Hunter said.

Mae pulled the wire carefully from the door, then grinned when she saw the keys hooked to the end.

They walked over to the black Range Rover and Hunter pressed the key fob.

Lights flashed behind them.

Mae glanced at Hunter.

Hunter glanced at Mae.

And there in front of them, in the glass-walled garage, they saw the gleaming red Ferrari.

'No way,' Hunter said. 'He would kill us. I mean actually kill us dead. That thing is going in the bunker.'

'We could take your father's car?'

'Even worse.'

'We've come this far.'

'Did you not hear me? That car is going in the bunker instead of the dozen family members he could fit in there instead.'

'I saved your life.'

Hunter gritted her teeth. 'You can't ever use that again.'

'Agreed.'

212

They walked over to it.

'It looks scary. I don't know if I can drive it.'

Mae shrugged. 'It's just a car. How hard can it be?'

The engine screamed as Hunter crunched into second and they shuddered along the driveway.

'You sure you know how to drive?' Mae said.

'Sixty-five lessons,' Hunter said, as she stalled. 'The instructor said that was some kind of record, considering my age.'

From West they took B-roads. Hunter activated the wipers and couldn't switch them off again.

'Can't believe we stole a car from Jon Prince,' Hunter said. 'He's got that look in his eye, you know, like crazy. And he's a total perv, always checking me out.'

'Who isn't?' Mae said, face locked straight.

'I know, right.'

'Did you know Hugo's mum?'

'She was cool. Kind of timid, and I could tell, you know. Some days she wore heavy make-up, and it hid the bruises but not the look in her eyes.'

'And then she left.'

'And Hugo's been searching for her ever since. She took a bag, but left her only child behind.'

'She was desperate.'

'Maybe she'll come back for him, but the days . . .'

Mae watched dark fields pass by. When she was a girl they'd spilled with rapeseed, so bright, like a million fallen suns. Now they were fallow, all of them, nothing but mud baked hard by neglect and the relentless summer.

Hunter crossed the centre lines while she fussed with her hair in the rear-view mirror. Mae grabbed the wheel and kept them headed straight.

'You see all that shit in America? That space centre. I get why they stormed it, but tearing it apart like that . . .' Hunter found fourth.

'They're levelling.'

'Some people are rich enough to keep living, maybe not for long, but they've got a chance if they leave this planet.'

'You think that's fair?'

'Murder for principle, I'm not sure that's a defence.'

'But when there's no one left to judge –'

'We can only judge ourselves,' Hunter said, watching the road.

They made it to Newport as the moon edged out a cloud and finally lit the sky.

Mae pointed and Hunter stopped in the middle of the road.

'That's it?'

Mae nodded. 'That's it.'

Hunter pulled her hood up.

The pawnshop sat in darkness, but for the small red light of a security camera. Mae pressed her face against the window and looked inside.

Front and centre, with the electrical equipment, was Sail's laptop.

'Can't he just buy it back?' Hunter said, keeping an eye on the deserted street.

Mae picked up a rock. 'I have to do this myself. I took it, I get it back. Go start the car and be ready.'

Mae threw the rock as the engine fired.

The door was glass, she expected it to crack and shatter.

The rock bounced back.

She tried again, hurled it with a run-up. It thundered against the glass but didn't leave a mark.

'It's reinforced,' Hunter called.

'Thank you, I didn't realise.'

'Such a bitch.'

She tried again, this time when it cannoned back it nearly hit her.

Hunter laughed and clapped her hands, like Mae was performing a skit for her.

And then they heard the shout as the lights from the flat above came on.

The window opened and Mae recognised the owner.

He was bare-chested, and he swore at her and then, to her horror, she saw him raise a gun and point it down. And it didn't look like an airgun.

'Shit,' Hunter screamed.

Mae sprinted for the car, yanked the door open and dived into the passenger seat.

'Go,' she yelled.

Hunter slammed her foot down on the accelerator.

The car lunged violently backwards.

'You're in reverse,' Mae shouted.

Hunter screamed again and wrestled with the steering wheel.

The car swerved as they mounted the pavement and ploughed straight into the front of the shop.

The windows caved.

Glass rained down and a cloud of dust smoked into the street.

The alarm was shrill and jarring and Mae opened the door and climbed out into the wreckage.

'What the hell are you doing?'

Mae grabbed the laptop, and then headed to the other window and took the necklace from the display.

She climbed back in just as Hunter found first and they tore into the road.

Hunter screamed the whole way down the high street.

The tyre blew out as they reached the edge of West.

They opened both doors and pushed, Hunter with one hand in the car to steer. It was slow going. The streets were dead.

'Maybe he's got breakdown cover,' Hunter said, then climbed into the car and fished through the glove box.

'You know we can't actually call.'

Hunter held up a small silver hip flask. She drank, smacked her lips and passed it to Mae, who did the same.

'Ten nights,' Hunter said, and toasted the sky.

Hunter kicked her heels off and threw them into the car. Barefoot, her hair matted down with sweat, she looked over at Mae.

'I read that they did a survey once. They asked people what they'd do if they found out an asteroid was coming the very next day,' Hunter said. 'Like, if instead of giving us ten years they gave us twenty-four hours.'

'I saw it. Two-thirds said they'd get drunk.'

'Everyone knows that. But they never said what the other third would do.'

'Who gives a shit, we'd be too drunk to notice.'

Hunter laughed so hard she let go of the wheel on the corner of Hooper Avenue and Cedar Road.

They watched through their fingers as it smashed into a lamp post.

'That ought to do it,' Hunter said.

Mae drank some more, then passed the flask to Hunter.

'We could just dump it here,' Hunter said.

'There's cameras. Better leave it where we found it, he'll just think it's kids. Vandals or something.'

It took half an hour to get it moving again.

They were sweating by the time they turned onto Ocean Drive.

'You think the radio still works?' Hunter said. 'A night this wild needs a soundtrack.'

She slid into the seat, turned the radio on and cranked it up, despite Mae telling her to keep the noise down.

'"Tuesday's Gone",' Hunter said, closing her eyes.

'But we're here, right now, to see it off.'

Hunter smiled.

They pushed the car onto the driveway, stood back and surveyed the damage. The rear bumper caved in. The windscreen shattered and the bonnet folded back on itself.

'You think he'll notice?' Hunter said.

'If he's anything like his son, maybe not.'

Hunter smiled sadly. 'Hugo, he's not who you see.'

'People rarely are.'

'He's more. He's everything.'

Mae gripped the laptop tightly.

They walked back down the street.

'Thanks, Hunter,' Mae said, quietly. 'I didn't think you had all that in you.'

'There's a lot you don't know about me. And I guess there's a lot I don't know about you.'

'I still think you're a bitch.'

'I still think you're a slut.'

Mae smiled.

Hunter smiled. 'Epic night.'

'Totally.'

31

At the white house Mae climbed in through the window, placed the laptop back on the desk and let the tired wash over her.

That night, their kiss coming back to her. She almost smiled, and was about to turn and leave when she heard shouting.

Mae eased into the towering hallway, silent along the marble floor.

She saw them in the kitchen. Sail's mother was tall, might once have been striking but looked as though the slightest breeze would knock her down.

She was making coffee, her wrists so thin the dressing gown she wore fell at one shoulder and Mae could see her bones standing proud.

'You think I don't know it's her birthday tomorrow?' she said.

Sail sat at the counter. Mae could not see his face but he sounded tired.

'It's today,' he said.

She looked at the big clock above an open fireplace, logs piled high beside it. 'There's not long now. Do you think we could just let today pass?'

Sail nodded.

'Tell me, Jack. Tell me we won't have trouble today. That you won't make today about you and everything you do wrong.'

'I'm not doing it for –'

'Your father might call and –'

'He's not coming back.'

'He'll be back for the end.'

'That's too late.'

'I'm tired, Jack. I'm tired of this life we don't live. I thought it would be safer here, because you can't get yourself into trouble like in the city.'

'That's the thing about trouble, it tends to follow no matter how bad you want to leave it behind.'

'We all make mistakes.'

'I don't. I've never regretted a single thing I've done.'

She smiled. 'I know you miss her.'

His mother crossed the floor and hugged him tightly.

He was limp in her arms, his head on her shoulder.

Mae watched the unfurling tragedy, so tired for them all, for herself and her sister, for Sail and his.

It was hard to watch him, so when his shoulders shook and his mother closed her eyes Mae turned and left them, the haunt of his cries following her from their grand house and their small lives.

She went to the beach and watched the sunrise over the water.

Cool breeze gave clarity to her thoughts. Abi had stolen Hunter's necklace, ridden the same bus Mae took every month to the small town of Newport and sold it. The Mantons weren't short of money, and they gave their daughter everything she asked for. It was clear Abi was keeping something from her parents and her friends. Whatever it was it had likely died with her. Mae reasoned that everyone was entitled to a side of themselves they kept from the world.

'The best time of day.' The Reverend walked over and stood beside her.

'Yeah.'

'You look tired, Mae. Like my son. He never sleeps, you know. He watches movies all night. He thinks he's expanding his mind.'

'He isn't?'

'The more he reads about Selena, the further it pushes him from God.'

Mae looked at the Reverend then. He looked older, the skin sagged beneath his kind eyes. 'He thinks you don't see him.'

'I know that.'

'He needs proof there's a God. He's looking for divine intervention.'

The Reverend picked up a stone and skimmed it across the water. 'Felix comes into the church and he helps. He'll lay out the chairs and help with the flowers. But he doesn't see beyond. It's a test of faith, to believe in what you can't see, what you can't prove.'

'And that gets you someplace better after this. How about if I tell you every bad thing I've ever done?'

He smiled. 'We've all done bad things, Mae.'

'Even you?'

He nodded and she wondered if he knew he was failing at being a parent, at loving his son without such weighty conditions.

'Stella, she asks about my parents. I don't tell her.'

'Because it hurts.'

She said nothing.

'That pain, it's what makes us –'

'I know.'

'Kids come to see me, worried about the way the town shakes beneath our feet. People come to check and can't work out why.'

'Don't tell me it's because of God.'

He squinted towards the sun. 'Feeling is the most reliable sense. The earth shaking deep in our bones, we feel that. And that's what religion is to me, Mae.'

'Did Abi come and see you?' She held her breath for a moment.

'She came. She sat and talked to me, and every day since I've questioned myself. What I told her. What she told me.'

'How do you know you're doing the right thing?' Mae said.

'You ask yourself if it comes from a good place.'

He touched her shoulder, and then began to walk away.

'Felix needs you,' she said.

He stopped. 'He can come to me, Mae. When he's ready.'

'He doesn't feel like he belongs. A lot of the kids don't.'

'Not just kids.'

'Betty and Matilda, you know them?'

He nodded.

'They don't feel like they belong, because the old vicar said –'

'The church, it's a safe place for everyone.'

Mae smiled. 'Maybe you should tell them that.'

'I do. Selena, she's pushed a lot of people back, but she's also freed people. My sister, Nia –'

'Felix said that her husband left her. She prays each Sunday that he'll come back.'

He smiled. 'She left him, Mae. She lives with Miss Jackson now.'

Mae frowned. 'Miss Jackson, she's the deacon?'

'Yes, and she's a very good deacon. And she makes my sister happy. And that makes me happy, no matter what some of the congregation might think.'

She carried her sandals and strolled along the sand. Further up were clusters of summer people. They came and went now, a steady conveyor belt of couples and families that wanted a last taste of sea air.

He stood with his back to her, tall and broad, his shirt lay on the sand beside him as he watched boats cross the horizon. There was a surfboard by his feet.

'Hey,' she said.

'I used to think they were running away,' Hugo said.

'Who?'

He pointed at a white yacht carving the water.

'I used to be angry about it, like they should stay and work in their shops and paint their houses and cut their grass. West is beautiful, right? People always said that, but I didn't see it.'

'And now you do?'

He finally turned.

'Shit, Hugo. Jesus.'

One eye swollen shut, his bottom lip split. A neat footprint, bruised onto his chest.

'We shouldn't take these for granted. It's getting rare, each sunrise and sunset. Each passing day . . .'

'What happened?' She could have guessed.

'I remember the day he bought that car. We watched the auction online, and the money was getting crazy. I used to be proud. I used to like that we had so much, like it meant somehow I'd earned it, or I was worth more.'

'It was me,' she said, her breath catching. 'The car. Last night I –'

'I know.'

'Hunter told you?'

'You think we actually talk to each other?'

Mae tucked her hair into her hood as a light breeze blew in. 'So how . . . ?'

'The video. You don't have a car like that without CCTV, Mae.'

'So . . .'

'I watched it. I recognised you and Hunter straight off, kind of made me smile watching the two of you together.'

'And?' She thought of Sergeant Walters. He would take her in. She would see out the days beside Sullivan Reed as they waited for judgement that would never come.

'I wiped it.'

'You wiped it?'

'I told him I'd forgotten to set it before we left.'

She let that sit for a while. Nothing about Hugo made sense, nothing fit. Why his father hated him so much, why he'd lied for them. For her. Why he acted the way he did at school.

'You need to tell Sergeant Walters about your father. He'll kill you one of these days.'

'The days are running out.'

'That doesn't make it right.'

'Do you think I'm brave, Mae?' He turned to look at her. His hair was wet from the water, his skin baked gold from the summer of sun.

He had so much.

He had nothing at all.

'I see you. Everyone sees you. But I see what you do to Jeet, the way you talk about girls. I see you with Liam and the others, and you all blur together.'

'I kept the paper, from Abi's funeral. I read it every night and I want it to be true but we both know it can't be.'

She could tell him the world was what he made it, that you get back what you put in, but she knew that wasn't true either.

'I like to think in a million years we'll start over, and someone will find that paper, like in one of those memory capsules, and they'll do it all different.'

He sat on the sand.

She sat down beside him.

'They'll see your face at school,' Mae said. 'Maybe Mr Silver will –'

'My mother showed me when I was young. I watched her paint her bruises away. I know how to do it, Mae.'

She glanced over at him but he didn't look at her. 'Maybe I'm good at it.' He shrugged. 'Maybe I like it. Maybe that's who I want to be. I like looking in the mirror and seeing someone else, maybe someone who hasn't seen the things I've seen. I think I could help other people do that.'

'What are you trying to say, Hugo?'

He finally broke a smile. 'I guess I'm trying to say . . . if you're a creep. Then I'm a weirdo.'

She reached out and took his hand.

'I don't belong here.'

'You do. You belong with us.'

She opened up her bag and took his wrist.

There was no grand declaration to change, but she saw in his eyes that he wanted to be better, kinder, more. Less. And that was enough. It wasn't for her to decide who belonged and who didn't.

When she was done he studied the letters carefully.

'Hunter will kill you when she sees that. You've gone over to the dark side.'

'Nah, I think maybe I've just seen the light.'

In RE Miss Lock walked down each aisle of chairs and separated them into good and evil. Predictably the division saw Hunter and her group sitting on the good side. Mae glanced at Hugo. The black eye expertly hidden. The tattoo masked by his wristwatch.

Each student held a small placard.

MARRIAGE.

FAMILY.

KINDNESS.

FAITH.

Miss Lock talked about the concept of rapture and the instant elevation of the believers. 'End time,' she said, and pointed towards the evil.

Mae looked down at her own sign.

FORNICATION.

She held it aloft to raucous applause from the Forevers. Hugo wouldn't meet her eye but she could see he was trying not to laugh.

Miss Lock quietened them down. RE was compulsory, as was belief.

'We stand by idle and close our eyes and wait for our place in heaven. It doesn't work like that.'

'What if there is no heaven?' Candice said. 'Then we'll have wasted our lives preparing for something that doesn't exist. I'd rather do what I want now, then just say sorry at the gates. He's a forgiving God, right?'

Miss Lock took CHASTITY from her and sent Candice over to the evil side.

'The Forevers,' she said to Mae. 'I want in. Lexi does too.'

'Hunter will kill you. So will Liam. And Callum.'

'And so will Selena.'

Mae smiled, then looked over to Sail's empty seat.

She asked Miss Lock where he was, as the others debated whether sex before marriage was good or evil.

'I haven't seen him.'

She might not have worried had she not known what day it was. And so Mae felt the blood drain from her, the panic building so quick and sharp it drove her from the classroom and the school.

She hammered on the door to the white house, pressed her face to the window but saw nothing inside.

It took a while for Sail's mother to answer the door.

She wore the white dressing gown, pulled it tight around her and rubbed her eyes. Behind her the hallway was cavernous, the polished marble reflected light so hard Mae squinted.

Beautiful but faded, more shadow than person.

'I need to see Jack.'

'He's at school.'

'He's not.'

Sail's mother looked confused but not concerned. Mae wondered what medication she took, what drug had enough of a kick to deaden her to the world.

'I know it's Alice's birthday,' Mae said.

His mother closed her eyes then. 'I need . . . I have to sleep today. I don't know where he is. Wherever it is, it won't be good.'

By the garage Mae saw a couple of cars. A convertible Mercedes had the keys in the ignition. She thought of Sergeant Walters, what he'd do if she got in any more trouble. And then she thought of Sail.

She drove the automatic with two feet, each time she touched the brake she slammed forward into the seat belt. The sun shone down on her as she drove down every road in West. She stopped on the bay front and checked the beach.

She called his phone a dozen times, left the kind of frantic message she hoped would see him call her straight back, tell her not to worry, that he just needed some time out.

Mae slammed the steering wheel, then drove up and along the cliff face and back into town.

And then the big clock chimed, and Mae felt it, like the Reverend Baxter had told her, she felt it.

She knew he was there.

Through the cemetery towards the willow, she found the laptop on the bench.

It was open to a montage of photos.

Sail and his sister.

She was cute like Stella, and she had that look in her eye that showed she was taking everything in. Hair so blonde it touched white, the same blue eyes Sail had, the same delicate features. A photo of them by a rocket. Cape Canaveral. Theme parks.

The photos changed, the light in her eyes dimmed.

She looked thin, paler, she lost her hair. She lost everything.

A photo of Sail lying beside her, the two sleeping. Tubes ran into her arm, a canula in the back of her hand.

He shaved his head. His father did too.

The three of them grinned, defiant, his mother stood beside, and through her smile Mae could see the cracks.

The last photo was a single shot of Alice, in the green hospital gardens, her eyes closed to the sunshine.

And then the funeral. Mae recognised the suit, smaller, but the same cut. The same white shirt, the same black tie.

Each day was a funeral for Jack Sail, and that last photo made sure he would not forget that.

Mae found him near the edge.

The belt was tied tightly around his arm, the empty syringe on the leaves beside him.

He was pale. He was gone.

'Sail.' She slapped his face, then hit his chest. 'Shit, Sail.' She pressed her head down to him, felt the faintest breath and tried to call for an ambulance. She screamed at the man as he told her it would be hours.

Mae grunted as she dragged Sail, leaned into it as her muscles burned.

She cursed and heaved and got him close to the road, cried hard as she managed to haul him into the passenger seat, where he slumped back.

On the opposite side a line of cars backed up for a mile. Inside them she saw kids with sun hats, boots filled with picnic hampers and buckets and spades.

She reached the A road, got the hang of the pedals as she floored it away from the water. Mae passed sleeping towns, a mirror of West, boarded windows on homes too new, graffiti that spoke of eternal damnation. She saw a woman sitting in a garden chair in front of her house. As she approached she held up a sign:

WE SHOULD HAVE BEEN MORE.

A petrol station, a police car seemingly abandoned on the forecourt. They roared along the motorway, the nearer hospitals long since closed, Mae followed signs for the city.

She saw the blinking skyline in the distance as they were joined by more cars. They met tall buildings, a sense of life going on, despite what she had seen on the news.

She saw people on the streets, smiling students spilling from bars, the homeless in tents, discarded placards, some kind of protest on soaring climate, too little too late.

She kept a hand on Sail's, talked to him about everything and nothing, told him he was dumb, that she would kill him if he didn't die.

At the hospital she double-parked and ran inside.

A porter helped get Sail onto a stretcher.

Then a doctor came, a nurse and others. They took him from her like he was hers to give away.

A security guard stopped her following, no matter how much she kicked and fought. He pointed in the direction of the waiting room and promised someone would come and see her.

She stood there numb.

Above her, strip lights flickered. The place was quiet, only a handful sat spaced around. An elderly couple. A homeless girl not much older than her.

'Mae.'

She turned to see Felix. 'What are you doing here?' she said.

'The Reverend, he had a heart attack.'

She shook her head.

He held up a hand. 'He'll be all right.'

Together they sat on plastic chairs as she told him about Sail.

'Shit, Mae. It's all going to shit.'

'We're strong,' she said, but she did not feel strong.

'I'm struggling to be normal.'

'You've always struggled with that. But I think maybe normal is overrated. Think of every great person that ever lived. Normal is average, average is middle.'

'And middle is?'

'Middle is settling. If you don't reach . . .'

'You won't fall.'

Mae smiled.

'I'm guessing that's why I'm not a Forever,' Felix said, pushing his glasses up his nose.

'You really are, Felix.'

'I'm kind of running out of time to work out who I am. And I'm still worried I'll die a virgin.'

'I'd say that's a certainty.'

'There's a place in the city. You can pay for it. One hundred pounds.'

'Like you'd do that.'

'Never. On a separate note, I was wondering if I could borrow one hundred pounds?'

Mae watched a doctor hurry through. That he was still there, working, that they were all still there.

'I thought I'd feel something, now that I know what happened to her. Sullivan Reed. He wanted what he couldn't have. That's the story of every bad thing ever done.'

'They want me to be a priest. Not actually to be one, because they know, deep down they know. So they just want me to want to be one. Like that's enough for them, enough for me to get into their version of heaven. I see a pattern, Mae. Every parent in this town leans so hard on their kids because they're unfulfilled. They've reached the end and realised everything they missed out on. And they don't get it's worse for us.'

'They do. People are innately selfish.'

'People are innately good.'

'Maybe nothing is innate. We're products of genetic code . . . but that has nothing to do with personality.'

'Hugo is a dick and his father is a dick.'

'Self-hatred is the most powerful kind.'

'Hugo loves himself totally. Like Liam does. It has to be easier if you look like them, if you're good at something, if

232

you find someone to marry and have children with. And that person should be the opposite sex, the same race, a similar age.'

'Three and half billion years of devolution.'

'And now we've run out of time.'

Mae watched a woman with her son. The boy was small and he pressed his cheek to her chest and slept.

'The Forevers wasn't supposed to be about rebellion. It was about scrapping the idea of normal, and everything that goes with it.'

Felix smiled. 'That's a big ask.'

'But if we don't ask it now?'

As it grew dark Felix placed an arm around her. Mae closed her eyes and leaned on her friend.

'I've never seen you cry before,' he said.

'I wish I could say the same.'

32

He lay in the bed, a line running into his arm.

Beside were other people with other problems. She heard the steady beep of a dozen machines, helping to make sure they stayed alive for the coming days.

Sail opened his eyes.

'Every day you dress for Alice's funeral.'

He shook his head. 'I dress for mine.'

She sat on the end of the bed, reached up, his hand felt cold in hers. Everyone around them slept. A nurse sat at her station, a dim lamp beside her as she looked over paperwork.

'How many times have you done this before?' she said.

'Too many. Not enough.'

'It's not fair.'

'There is no fair, Mae. The attribution of dues. There's no equality, no proportionality. No accrued merit. There's the things we do and the things we don't do. There are no mistakes or regrets. There isn't time for them.' He looked towards the window, his head on the pillow. 'You've saved my life twice.'

She nodded.

'I would be dead if you hadn't broken into my house.'

'How's that for cosmic forces?'

He smiled and she felt her heart beat in her ears.

Felix waited for her. Together they walked outside, the Mercedes right where she left it.

She opened the door and got into the driver's seat.

'You drive now?' Felix said.

'Ish.'

'Can I do that thing where I jump over the door, cop style?'

'Okay.'

He caught his trailing foot and landed upside down. Righted himself and slipped his belt on. 'Stolen?'

'Borrowed.'

They drove from the city. Sail would discharge himself in the morning. His mother would send a car, and they'd go on like it hadn't happened.

'You didn't have to wait,' she said.

'Hot nurses. Armageddon. You think they'd be desperate for –'

'And?'

'I'm starting to think porn has been lying to me all these years.'

She dropped him home, ran out of petrol at the top of Ocean Drive so abandoned the Mercedes at the side of the road.

Mae was about to head home when she heard music floating from the church.

She walked up the path and found him at the front.

He sang from the bench, the music accompanied him from the large speakers the Reverend used to project to the masses each Sunday.

She listened, so heavenly she cried for the second time that day. There was no anger at Sail and his mother, her parents for leaving her, Selena for coming. Instead Mae heard what everyone else did when Theodore Sandford sang.

'What does "Ave Maria" mean,' she said.

'A prayer to the Virgin Mary.'

She sat on the bench beside him. Theodore wore his finest shirt, she saw the customary blood on his knees.

'I know you lied,' Mae said, her words echoed around the church.

Theodore did not look at her, just breathed, like he'd been waiting.

'Sullivan Reed. Sergeant Walters is sure, and it fits, you know?'

He swallowed.

'He doesn't have an alibi for that night. When I asked you where you were, you said you were practising with Sally. Only Sally doesn't go out at night. She watches movies with her mother. Sergeant Walters didn't check?'

He said nothing, and then Mae got it.

Still the music played on loop, the piano of Sally Sweeny.

'Man, it's beautiful,' Mae said. 'I never got it. All these years when I came to church, I resented the waste of time, like it was my time. And then Selena, and now everyone comes. Everyone's thinking there's more. There has to be more, Theodore.'

'There is.'

Mae didn't breathe for the longest time. It was coming, whatever it was, she'd been waiting a long time for it. 'Sally lied for you.'

'If we confess our sins . . .'

'What did you do, Theodore?'

'Sullivan Reed didn't kill Abi.'

Mae felt her shoulders drop.

'He was with me.'

She read him, at last she understood why the angel of West prayed so hard, why he bloodied his knees and begged for atonement.

'How does Abi fit?'

'She caught us once. Her and Sally. After practice. You know there's an office at the back of the school chapel. I was . . . undressed. And then we heard Hannah Lewis. Sullivan and Sally hid, and Abi . . . she took off her shirt.'

Mae thought of Abi, her brave Forever.

'So Hannah came in and she saw Abi standing there in her bra. With me. And Hannah . . . It was halfway around the school after that.'

'Abi kept your secret. And made life better for you.'

'Yes,' Theodore said. 'And then I caught Liam talking about her, calling her a slut. So I bought her the ring, and I wore one, and no one called her that again. It was simple.'

'She could've broken things off with you.'

'The names, the rumours, it all stopped because of her. Even in a church town, you talk like I do, you sing in a choir. People aren't tolerant.'

'You're not tolerant of yourself, Theodore.'

'You don't understand. People weren't accepting before, Mae. And now Selena, we follow the rules so devoutly because this is it. My parents didn't even like me seeing

237

Abi till we wore the rings. Lust. There is no margin, it's right and wrong.'

'Love the sinner, hate the sin –'

'Matilda and Betty, you know how they feel? Like they're not welcome, because people are afraid they'll burn by association. And Reverend Baxter, he can preach unity, but it means nothing to some of the people sitting before him. I'm not . . . I have no strength for this fight because it's a no contest now. It's over.'

'Betty and Matilda, they do have a place now.' She glanced up at the paintings, the history. 'And Sullivan?'

'He loves . . . We love each other.'

'I saw the photos in his room.'

'He loved Abi. He saw in her what you did. She stood up for us, gave us a place where we could be.'

She thought about that. There was a purity that couldn't exist any more.

'He should tell Sergeant Walters,' Mae said. 'He was with you that night.'

He cried then. Silently and painfully. 'It would come out. Sullivan, he's stronger than me. He doesn't believe. He doesn't know the fear.' He closed his eyes, like it was all too much. 'I'm scared.'

She reached over and took his hand. 'Are you a good person, Theodore?'

'I thought I was. I did.'

'At the end of this, that's all that matters. It's all you should be judged on. And any god that doesn't see that isn't our god.'

'Our god?'

'We've got you, Theodore. You don't need to be afraid. Abi said it herself. We are an army of each other.'

He didn't turn his back on God, she didn't want him to. 'When you're ready, come and find me. Take back your Forever.'

33

Mae found Stella sitting beside the television screen.

'*So it's basically Armageddon,*' the reporter said. '*We've spent billions, and the next step is something Bruce Willis taught us about twenty years ago.*'

Morales smiled but Mae could see the tired in his eyes.

He'd said he was hopeful.

He'd said he was sorry.

'*The . . . machine, let's call it a drill-shaped machine. It hits Selena head on and drives a deep hole into her core. Mere seconds later the nuclear bomb arrives in the hole. And –*'

'*Boom.*'

The audience cheered.

The host held up a hand which Morales reluctantly high-fived.

'Boom,' Mae said, as she reached for the remote and switched the TV off.

She took Stella's hand and squeezed tightly. 'Don't watch that stuff. Nobody knows what will happen.'

Outside she found Sail. He carried a bunch of flowers, handed them to Stella and leaned down to kiss her head.

'Are you ready for the show?' he said.

'I don't know my lines off by heart,' Stella said.

'If you forget, just make them up.'

Stella hugged him, then took the dog and slowly walked a step ahead of them.

'Are you okay?' Mae said.

'I thought okay was never enough.'

'I think it's the best you can hope for the morning after you overdose.'

They dropped Stella at West Primary. For once she lingered and did not want to let go when Mae saw her off.

Felix joined them on the high street, told them his father was doing better, that he'd be home before the end.

They stopped at the bay.

'You see it?' Felix said, grinning.

Mae looked at the town sign.

WELCOME TO WILD WEST.

Mae saw cars backed up a mile. 'What's going on?

Sergeant Walters was directing summer people to turn around.

'They're closing the road into town,' Felix said. 'My mother heard about it last night. The deliveries, the food, the restaurants and coffee shops, nothing came yesterday.'

Mae saw angry faces as drivers leaned on their horns. Two men got out and made to fight, Sergeant Walters cooled them with the threat of handcuffing them in front of their children.

'Go home,' he said. 'It's time to go home.'

Mae thought it would a good time for the Chief to return, the kid looked beaten.

She didn't tell Felix and Sail about Theodore and Sullivan.

241

She'd guard their secrets the way Abi had. They weren't hers to tell.

They left the noise behind.

They passed Mrs Harries from the church.

'Have a nice day,' Felix said to her.

'Don't tell me what to do.'

Felix puffed his cheeks out as she passed. 'Is it me or is Selena making people meaner?'

'Do you ever think there's nothing left to say,' Sail said. 'Out of all the words in the world, every single one of them has been spoken so many times they've lost their meaning, their importance.'

'Some still pack a punch,' Felix said.

'Like what?'

Mae dropped a C-bomb.

Felix nodded to that.

At school she passed a dozen kids she didn't know and saw the ink peeking from out of their sleeves, behind their watches. Most of them smiled at her, one boy nodded.

A supply teacher covered for Mr Starling.

They sat in silence, their heads in books, their minds somewhere far.

Halfway through, Mae walked to the front, picked up a pen and slowly got to work filling in the whiteboards, still smeared by Liam.

She used her textbook, went over what she could.

She looked to the right when Lexi joined her. Lexi wore a hat, didn't smile, just picked up another pen and worked another section. And then Hunter and Candice followed.

They worked in silence till they were done. Then they stood back and admired their work, and Mr Starling's.

At lunch Mae sat at a table of fifteen. Fanned out around her was their small army, but it was growing. Girls as young as thirteen didn't even hide their wrists, wore the word like a badge, like proof of a better world.

The stars shone brighter that night on the beach as Mae helped Candice and Lexi take back their forevers.

'You want to go next?' she said to Hunter, who held a bottle of wine and watched them.

'I'd rather cut off my arm.'

The fire burned.

They helped circle it with heavy stones.

'I think you should do it,' Hunter said, as Lexi stood in the centre and held the clippers in her hand.

'It might be my last chance,' Lexi said, a little slurry. 'I don't want to die with shit hair.'

'What about Callum?' Candice said.

'It's the ultimate test of his love,' Lexi said.

Callum stood with Hugo and Liam, looking nervous.

'*V for Vendetta*,' Lexi said. 'She's, like, the ultimate feminist. It's a power move.' She pressed the button and they heard the tinny buzz of the razor.

Lexi ran them through her hair, then held a lock aloft to wild cheers.

Hugo stepped forward, took the clippers and stripped Lexi of every hair on her head.

When he was done they sat and watched moonlight bounce

from Lexi's skull as she gently sobbed into Callum's arms.

'It's so short I can read her mind,' Sail said.

Mae laughed into the bottle.

He took her hand and led her from the group.

Behind them the music started.

Candice and Hunter danced around with locks of Lexi's hair.

Sail took her in his arms and they moved together. 'You want to be in my love story?'

'Pretty sure our love story is doomed, Jack Sail.'

'Sorry,' he said. 'About yesterday.'

She said nothing.

'I hate this life,' he said. 'I love it and I hate it. I hate that people still smile, that I still smile and laugh. I hate that it all just goes on. It should've paused, even for a second, everyone in the world should've stopped dead and . . . I don't know, crossed themselves or fucking sworn or something. Just taken a moment to acknowledge the fact that my perfect little sister had stopped breathing.'

She watched him speak.

'And I know you know this kind of . . . not pain, that doesn't sound . . . that's not enough. It's something else. It's a living, constant, concentrated kind of agony that stamps on everything good until the end of time.'

Mae swallowed dry.

'Maybe you make my world a little less shit, Mae. It's more than I thought I'd ever get.'

The rain came without warning.

It thundered down.

At midnight they stood in a circle.

Laura Matthews and Daniel Holland held hands in the centre, while Hunter waved around a piece of paper. It had taken her a day to get ordained online and print the certificate.

'I am the Reverend Silver,' she said, to laughter. 'Laura, do you really want to get married with braces on your teeth? Shit, do you really want to die with a mouth full of metal?'

Hunter clicked her fingers and Liam produced pliers, then got to work stripping the train-tracks from Laura's mouth.

When he was she done, she smiled widely. She wore shorts, a white bikini top and a veil, which might've been a piece of net curtain cut down to size.

For his part Daniel stood there bare-chested with a black bow tie.

They'd written their own vows.

Laura wanted to be obeyed.

Daniel wanted her to love him in sickness and in asteroid collision.

When Hunter declared them man and wife there was applause. Mae smiled as the two kissed, then they all stripped down to their underwear and sprinted at the water.

In a line they held hands.

The water was cold.

They swam for a while then lay on the beach.

There was talk of final plans, a couple of kids would leave West in the days before and head to family across the country.

The roads would be blocked, five hundred miles could take days.

Mae felt detached, like someone had cut the strings that kept them tethered to reality.

'We need music tonight. I want to dance.'

Lexi held up her phone and turned the music up.

'"If You Leave Me Now . . ."' Hunter screamed, jumped on Hugo and wrapped her legs around him as she kissed him.

When the noise died, they fell back to the sand and settled into silence.

A dozen of them lay back in a neat line.

Together the Forevers of West watched the night sky and thought of the impossible.

'I don't want to die.'

Whoever said it spoke for them all.

34

She broke into Sergeant Walters's house two hours before dawn.

Jack Sail stood in the shadows and kept watch.

In the driveway was a rusting Vauxhall and she carefully climbed on top, felt it flex a little as she clambered from there onto the roof of the carport.

She glanced up and down the street, saw a cat watching her intently from the neighbouring drive but other than that not a soul.

Across the roof and along to the open window, one of the perks of the sweltering summer.

Inside she stood on green carpet, then nearly retched when the smell hit her. Sickly sweet, so bad she leaned her head back out the window and gasped for breath.

The bedroom was empty.

Floral print on the walls, dark wood furniture. She hooked her T-shirt over her nose and crept out of the room and along the hallway.

And then she heard it.

A rumble so deep it was like the floor beneath her was shaking.

She passed black-and-white photographs in gaudy gold frames, a young Chief Walters in uniform. A photo of Beau on the beach, hand in hand with his mother. The smell got stronger, the rumble louder.

Mae fought back her fear, breathed shallow and tried each door.

Two other bedrooms were perfectly neat, unslept in. A vase of fake flowers on each windowsill. The house looked like a shrine to before.

She moved down the stairs slowly, the rumble so loud she almost placed her fingers in her ears.

A stack of letters by the front door, all addressed to Mrs Walters, his mother.

Another rumble.

It sounded like a monster, hungry and waiting.

And then she found it.

The source.

Sergeant Walters snoring.

He lay back in a leather recliner, eyes closed, the deep power of each rasping breath shook his whole body.

She saw his wallet beside him, her heart sinking when she saw his keys clipped to his belt.

Mae held her breath as she leaned over him and gently unclipped them.

It was as she stepped back that she stumbled and fell. She stared up, breathing hard, calmed a little as the rumble continued. And then she noticed the shoes by her head.

Black leather, buffed to a shine.

She followed them with her eyes.

Legs.

A belt.

The horror unfolded slowly.

And then Mae saw it. And she clamped a hand over her mouth to stop the scream.

Sitting in the matching recliner.

A glass of whisky on the table beside the chair.

And the grey face of Beau's father.

The Chief.

Dead.

She walked from the house, pale enough that Sail took her hand.

'What is it?'

She didn't tell him till they reached the station.

'Shit,' was all he could manage.

She thought of Sergeant Walters in there, sleeping beside his dead father, eating beside him. Mae didn't know about dead bodies, but she guessed from the smell and from the look of him it wasn't a recent thing.

All that wonder, all the times he had covered for the Chief. 'If people find out, it's over,' she said. 'Sergeant Walters, he's nothing without the threat of his father coming back.'

Mae unlocked the door to the police station.

She flipped a switch and light flooded in. She didn't care who saw her, she was tired of it all, tired of waiting for Sergeant Walters to find answers he wasn't even looking for, tired of waiting for the giant rock in the sky to flatten her dead.

'Look for Abi's file,' she said, as she opened the door at the back of the office and took the stairs down slowly. The walls were stone, painted white. She saw two doors, an old desk and a fan in the corner. There were hatches in each door, she pulled down the first and saw the empty cell inside, a single basin, a toilet and bed.

Sullivan Reed was in the second. Mae felt a stab of sorrow as she saw him lying there, his eyes on the ceiling as moonlight filtered in through the high window.

'Hey, are you okay?'

He sat up quickly, came to the door and peered out. He looked drained, his eyes red and his skin pale. 'Mae?'

'Can he keep you down here, is it even legal?'

'I'm eighteen. They'll take me away after. If there's an after.'

Mae pressed a hand to the cool of the door, then fished through the keys. She tried a couple before she found it.

They stood facing each other.

'Theodore told me.'

He looked down. 'What did he say?'

'You were with him, the night . . . Abi. Also said he loved you.'

He looked up. 'He said that? We haven't . . . I mean, not yet. We haven't said that yet. I haven't said that to anyone.'

'You should go and tell him, before it's too late.'

'Why are you doing this?'

She glanced at her wrist, he followed her eye.

'Tell me about Hunter Silver.'

He kept his eyes on the tattoo. 'I just . . . I just wanted to scare her. To let her know how it feels, you know, each day you wonder what it'll be this time. And if you make it through, if no one speaks to you the whole day, then that's a win.'

Mae looked at his face, properly, the tightness around his mouth, his eyes, the pain of it.

'It was you that night, you attacked me outside Abi's house.'

He swallowed. 'I take photos, Mae. I'm one of the night people. My mother, you've seen my house. I stay out as much as possible. I know . . . what you do, Mae. I saw you break into Hugo's place. I didn't tell Sergeant Walters because fuck Hugo Prince. But Abi . . . you can't take anything from that family, Mae. They've lost enough.'

She stepped aside. 'Go.'

'I can't leave Theo.'

'Take him with you. There's not time, Sullivan.'

He shook his head.

There was a lot Mae could have said then, about Theodore choosing God over him, but when she looked at him she could see that he knew all of it already, and it was enough, the stolen part of Theodore was more than enough, maybe more than he ever expected to find.

'He'll confess,' Sullivan said. 'After the concert, he'll come down here and tell Sergeant Walters everything. I can give him that. He'll stand in that hall and sing and his parents can have their son. Because after, the way they are, they'll have nothing.'

He took a step back inside the cell.

She took a deep breath and heard the door close on him. 'What if there's a fire?'

He laughed, it came out almost like a cry. 'Haven't you heard?' He pointed to the scar tissue on his cheek. 'In this town, I'll burn anyway.'

Upstairs she found Sail sitting at Sergeant Walters's desk, files spread out in front. They used the old copier to take what she needed.

And then she found the tapes. Mae knew Sergeant Walters had pulled them. The security cameras only covered the high street and marina, one at each end.

On his desk she saw a photo of his father, the two of them together.

She thought of that greyed face again, the smell still in her nose, in her mouth, in her hair.

Sergeant Walters would join him soon enough.

'You seen this?' Sail said, handing Mae another file. 'Hugo's mother – a neighbour reported her missing.'

'Small town. And maybe too hard to believe a mother could walk out on her son.' She thought of the bruises, of Hugo's belief she was somewhere better. Mae hoped it was true.

It was as she put the file back that another caught her eye. Mae opened it.

As she read, she felt the blood drain from her. 'Oh, Jesus. Oh no . . .' She whispered the words to herself.

Mae thought of Sally.

Of Abi.

Of everything she thought she knew about the world.

Sail read it over her shoulder, placed a hand on hers and squeezed.

She put the file back. But the name was burned into her brain.

OLIVER SWEENY

35

Mae used her last morning shift to watch the tapes.

Three weeks back, she propped her tired eyes open and saw the town of West, the people ambling by.

The old skywatchers, the young summer couples. Children ate ice creams, their parents walked behind, hand in hand. Something about the perfect normality of it helped Mae to breathe.

There was a timestamp in the corner. On the Sunday she watched hundreds march up towards the church, old men in suit and tie, young boys in smart trousers. She tried to pick out Abi but the cluster was too tight. She did see Jon Prince, and in a perfect pause she captured the way he looked over at Luke Manton. Mae wondered if business had come between them, money or something equally worthless. People still cared about their standing when they fell.

A few came into the store, dropped off their movies. She stamped cards, took payment, let people borrow whatever they wanted. The due date a day past Selena.

An old lady cried, took Mae's hand and told her sorry.

Across the street, Felix pressed a sign to the glass.

THE REVEREND IS HOME.

She wondered if the heart attack had brought Felix closer to God, or closer to the doctors that pumped his father's chest.

Mae stood in the open doorway.

She saw a couple of men on ladders, stringing bunting and fairy lights. From the top of the high street all the way down to the marina.

Mr Cleeves swept the pavements.

West was readying for the last days. The Final. The school concert. Stella's play. She'd seen adverts in the local newspaper, the excitement was muted among the adults, palpable in schools. West Fashion had posters in the windows.

END OF THE WORLD SALE.

The owner was Trixie, and she'd placed her own advert, telling anyone that was struggling they could come in and hire anything free of charge. Mae watched a couple of boys walk out carrying suit bags.

She turned back to the tape, saw Felix struggling with a box of papers, then trip and send them flying across the high street. Mae laughed to herself.

Another hour, Mae finally saw the girl on her screen.

'Abi,' she whispered, as she slowed it.

The clarity was good, she could see Abi's solemn face as she walked up, her head low as she disappeared into a shop.

Mae couldn't see from the angle exactly which shop.

She watched in real time.

Fifteen minutes passed before Abi walked out. She clutched a piece of paper in her hands. The paper was dark with bright lettering, too small to read but striking.

Tears streaked down Abi's cheeks.

And then she was gone.

Mae held her breath as she rewound and froze the tape on Abi's face.

Crying.

She knew she was close, she felt it then. All the wrong turns, the misdirection, she was closer than she'd been before.

Mae strained to see the shop, but still could not. So she counted, down from the salon.

Seven down.

Mae ran out into the street and up to the salon.

The shops were busy, the cafes hadn't yet run out of coffee.

She pushed by a couple of summer people, the last in town.

Mae counted carefully, one by one as she passed them.

Seven.

West Pharmacy.

She found Lexi eating lunch beside the tennis court.

'You mind if I sit?'

Lexi sighed, like she wanted to be alone.

Mae sat anyway.

Two boys played on the court, grunting and sweating as they powered the ball back and forth. Mae recognised one of them as Callum.

Lexi wore a stylish sunhat.

'How's the head?'

'Itchy.'

'I can imagine.'

'You ever got drunk and done something you regret?'

255

'Pretty sure that'll be my degree.'

Lexi took a drink from a sports bottle. 'I keep seeing girls with tattoos and they smile at me, and then I remember I have one too. I mean, I've always been in a gang. It used to be the hair, with Hunter.'

'We're not a gang. We're just . . . human.'

Lexi glanced over at the court. 'He likes me to watch him play. You know his parents came here because the tennis coach is some former player.'

'Part of the Sacred Heart gifted.'

'It's so boring. Back and forth.'

Lexi took the hat off, scratched her head and caught a look from Callum so put it back on quickly.

'He doesn't like it?' Mae said.

'He makes me keep it on when we . . . you know.'

Mae bit her lip, then saw Lexi begin to laugh so she laughed with her.

'You want to tell me why you came to sit here, Mae?'

'Your mother –'

'I can't get you drugs. Believe me, everyone thinks I can, but I can't.'

The sun crept from behind the old school building.

A group of younger girls sat in a circle and played some kind of game Mae couldn't work out the rules to.

'Abi went to the pharmacy. The day before she . . . the day before it happened.'

'Yeah.'

'You knew?'

Lexi sipped her water. 'I was helping out that day.'

256

'She was crying.'

'A lot of people come in crying. Or angry. Or just so sad. They want something to help them sleep, or something to help them smile. Or just something to take away all the feeling they've got.'

'That's what Abi wanted?'

Lexi shrugged. 'There's a room at the back, you can go there and talk to my mother. If you don't want the whole town knowing your business.'

'Abi went in there?'

'Yeah.'

'You think your mother would tell you what she wanted?'

'No.'

'Not even now she's dead?'

'Principles, Mae. My mother has them. I think maybe they skip a generation.'

They looked up when Callum started to walk over, a towel draped over his shoulders.

Callum saw them together and frowned.

'I thought her mother could get me drugs,' Mae said.

Callum shook his head, then slipped an arm round Lexi and they walked away.

The pharmacy was empty.

Mae walked down each aisle and looked at the myriad of placebos. Anything of use was locked away now.

Lexi's mother was tall and striking, and she had that look on her face like she was more than used to teens coming in with fake illnesses and trying it on without a prescription.

She had a white coat, smooth skin, almond eyes.

In the gene lottery, Lexi had won the jackpot.

Mae was so distracted she bumped right into Jeet Patel.

His bag fell to the floor, the contents spilling.

Mae bent to pick up a bottle, saw a dozen warnings printed all over it. Hydrochloric acid.

'Damn, Jeet. Are you building a bomb?'

He laughed as she passed him the bottle. 'I'm making the costumes for the concert. Distressed is in right now. Wait till you see us, Mae. Just . . .'

'Fabulous?'

He smiled widely.

'I've got to go,' he said. 'I have to pick up sequins from Trixie.'

Mae held the door for him. She wondered what it was like, that eternal optimism.

'Mae,' Lexi's mother said. 'How's your grandmother?'

'Still with us.'

No smile. 'What can I do for you?'

Mae cleared her throat, her shoulders dropped a little. 'Abi Manton came to see you.'

The woman's face softened then, her eyes filled with tears so quickly Mae was taken aback.

She sniffed, her composure returned quickly. 'You know I can't tell you anything.'

'I do. I just . . . I need to know she was okay. She tried to call me, I wasn't there for her.' Mae swallowed. 'I think maybe she needed me, and I let her down.'

'You can't blame yourself for this.'

'Do you think she killed herself?'

The question hung long in the air. Outside, the street lost its colours. Mae held her breath.

'I can't answer that.'

Mae breathed out slowly.

'But I do know that whatever Abi was going through wasn't your fault, Mae. Do you have someone you can talk to? Lexi tells me there's a school counsellor.'

'I just . . . I can't sleep any more. And I know that's a thing, right? I see it in the newspapers. No one can sleep. I don't know what I'm saying.'

Lexi's mother reached out and took her hand, gave it a squeeze and smiled gently. 'It can't be easy, your situation.' A smile. Pity.

Mae steeled herself, turned and walked towards the door.

And then she stopped deathly still.

The display, the bank of leaflets.

One stood out far.

The same leaflet Abi had left with.

Mae picked it up slowly, her throat dry as she took in the bright lettering.

ABORTION.

36

She was supposed to make pizzas with Stella, meet Felix at the church, hang out with Sail and the Forevers at the beach.

Instead Mae found herself sitting opposite Luke Manton as he tried damn hard to drink himself into the afterlife.

The bottles towered.

She saw through to the immaculate kitchen, to Lydia Manton's part of the home.

She wouldn't tell Luke that his daughter had been pregnant.

There was a chance he knew, but loyalty ran deep, it was all Mae could offer to her friend now.

'I've almost made it, Mae.'

His beard was long, his hair greasy and wild. In his eyes she saw nothing but a vodka fog.

She had more pieces of Abi's story, but they were scattered so far she couldn't bring the picture into any kind of focus.

'It's been a long month.' He slumped back, drank some more, slurred his words. He was done crying, there were no tears left, no life left to hold onto.

Morales was muted on the large flat screen.

'I need him to fail. But if he doesn't, then on July the

twenty-first I'll follow my little girl over the cliff. You think there's something noble about suicide?'

There was no answer she could give that would lessen his pain, or make more of Abi's death, so she went with the truth. 'Yes.'

He raised the bottle to the screen. 'Ten years I've listened to this guy. Ten years he's tried and failed. We hear the names, see the lab coats, the giant metal rockets and the probes and bombs and goddam paint. I try to be a man, but my fate's decided by people more powerful than me.'

He sat among hundreds of photos of his daughter, then looked up at the arched ceiling, through the panes of glass that opened to the dark sea. 'Ocean Drive,' he said. 'I used to ride down this road on my bike when I was a kid. We aspire. We push and drive and hope to make it, then when we do we take a look around and wonder exactly what it is.' He sniffed, then reached for another bottle, broke the cap and peered into the clear liquid. 'I thought the people here were better, because they had more. Their lives were . . . more.'

Mae watched as he sloshed the bottle and vodka spilled over his jeans.

'But you know what, Mae? Mortals and gods. The Greeks told it, *The Iliad*. Trojan War. The gods have no morals. They see something they want and they take it. And it ruins lives, but they don't care.'

He drank. 'Walk down this road, look in every house and what you see is nothing more than an act. To seduce you into believing you're worth less. They maintain power by diminishing your worth. True equality, that would be the real anarchy.'

Mae thought of his neighbours, of Abi and the lure of fitting in. The man she was seeing. It hit her suddenly, hard, so cold she shivered.

'Jon Prince,' she said, out loud. It clicked then, Luke attacking him in the street. Hugo talking about his father taking what he wanted.

Luke Manton closed his eyes, like the name alone was painful to hear.

'You knew,' Mae said.

He nodded, eyes still closed. 'She said she loved him.'

37

They ate breakfast in their spot, side by side, in silence only heightened by birdsong.

'Tomorrow they launch Saviour 10. They're calling her Faith. She'll blast off from Florida.'

'Have you practised your dance?' Mae said.

'I know every step. Every spin. Every thrust.'

'Thrust?'

'I'm gonna slay,' Stella said, then took a big bite of toast. Mae reached across and dabbed butter from her sister's cheek. It was the only time she was reminded of her tender years. They could talk relative velocity and kinetic energy, but still Stella could not eat without making some kind of mess.

'Did you ever think maybe I wanted to butter my cheek?'

Mae walked to the edge of the cracked patio, stepped onto the grass and breathed the summer air.

'There's no planes,' Stella said as they walked to school.

Mae looked up at the quiet sky.

Lady kept pace with them, occasionally sneezing.

'I think she's allergic to you,' Stella said.

'That's not a thing.'

They passed an old couple, eyes on the sky as usual, a dog walker. Stella stopped to pet the collie, knelt in front of it and looked as happy as Mae had ever seen her.

Lady growled.

Stella told her not to be jealous.

'It'll be okay, you know,' the dog walker said.

Stella looked like she might cry, so Mae placed an arm around her. 'What shall we do this summer?'

'We'll go to Hawaii and wear grass skirts.'

'And I'll play the ukulele while you sing about rainbows.'

At the gate Stella hugged her for longer than usual.

'Dress rehearsal today.'

'Yes.'

'Be brilliant, Stella.'

At Sacred Heart Mae arrived to a cluster of kids. She found Felix at the back.

'What's going on?'

'The caretaker didn't show. The gates are locked.'

'So what do we do now?' Candice said.

Hunter shrugged. 'We wait for my dad.'

'Or we go to the beach,' Hugo said.

Mae wondered if he knew about his father and Abi, guessed he didn't, not the detail, just that his father was the kind of man who did what he pleased. Mae had spent the night lying on the roof watching the stars. She reasoned it was likely Abi had jumped. Maybe she hadn't told Jon Prince she was pregnant, maybe she'd stolen Hunter's necklace and pawned it for the cash to take care of the problem herself. There were many variables, but the only constant was that Abi had found herself in an impossible situation.

They turned as a collective and began to walk away from the school.

Felix headed home to check on his father.

'You mind if we stop at my place first?' Sail said, appearing beside her.

'Forgot your trunks? No, you just swim in the suit, right.'

It wasn't till they walked through the towering gates that she realised it was a trap.

Flowers lined the driveway.

Rose petals were laid out in a trail.

Mae glanced at Sail, he walked on oblivious, like it was nothing to do with him. 'You know I don't like this.'

'I know.'

They followed the trail past the weeping willows, the heavenly scents, the garden awash with colour. Down past the infinity pool, the pathway carved into the rock.

She saw a small white motorboat at the end of the jetty.

'No grand gestures,' she said.

'It was this or I burned down your house.' He took hold of her hand and led her.

She stepped down into the boat. He pulled the cord and the engine gently hummed.

Sun caught the water. She kept her mind on the sky, on the hurtling end to keep the perfect day far from reach.

They moved off slowly, following the curve of the shore, passing the towering mansions, Hugo's house came into view, Hunter's in the distance.

Sail sat at the front, the wind in his hair. She noticed the hamper beside her.

Mae trailed a hand in the wake, the water cool against the soaring heat.

They passed the cliffs, white rock so sheer. The steeple of St Cecelia, the way it stood proud above the vista, the town looked spectacular enough that she could not tear her eyes from it, not even when the engine cut and Sail turned to face her.

They lay back, heads at either end of the boat as they pitched over gentle waves. Sail had had the good sense to pack wine but no glasses, so they passed the bottle back and forth.

They ate sandwiches and fancy crisps and chocolate cake so good she kept most of her piece for Stella.

'You know I'm going to ask you,' he said.

'I know.'

'You want me to get it over with now or wait?'

'Let's wait.'

She splashed her hand in the sea, brought it to her lips and tasted the salt on her fingers. The waves calmed till they stopped drifting, far enough from shore that they could have been the last people in the ocean.

'Three days,' she said, like she needed to break the perfect apart.

They saw another boat, this one older but the paint looked fresh.

It came slowly, so close Mae stood when she saw Mr Starling at the wheel.

She raised a hand, he saw her and slowed right beside them.

Sail stood and guided the motorboat closer, took a line and tied it off.

He helped Mae climb over, then sat back and bobbed with the waves.

'Of all the places in all the seas,' Mr Starling said.

She looked at the small deck, then down to the cabin below. She saw canned food, a sleeping bag and a case of wine. Beside that was a container of diesel.

'Are you taking a trip?'

'I mean, my boat can't compete with yours.'

She looked over at Sail, who was lying back in the sun, his eyes closed to the sky.

'How's school?' he said.

'I'm in a boat on a Tuesday morning.'

He laughed.

She sat on the edge, ran a hand over the polished wood. 'I found out some things about Abi.'

'Oh.'

'I'm not sure what to do about it.'

He sat beside her. He looked older then, like he'd lived too many lives. 'I read Abi's paper. In the service book. The Forevers.'

'Yeah,' she said.

'Even in death she'd get top marks. She was a brilliant student, Mae. With everything going on, she didn't miss a paper, didn't ever drop a grade.'

'So what are you saying?'

He smiled. 'Sometimes the fallout, it's too great. If we can't rewind time, do we sully the future?'

'I'm not sure I understand.' She watched a razorbill swoop, clutch at the water but come up empty handed. 'So I do nothing. I can't bring Abi back –'

'You're tough, Mae. Stronger than anyone I've ever met.'

'You're not making any sense.' She looked around again, his life all packed up. 'When will you be back, Mr Starling?'

He smiled but said nothing, and then she got it.

'You're not coming back?'

'None of us are, Mae. Despite what they say.' He reached into the cabin and took a framed photo from the side. 'My wife. She's all I ever had, and all I ever needed. So I'll aim my boat at the endless, and maybe I'll take my Forever back.'

'Saviour 10. Will it work?'

She could see him weighing options, but knew he would not lie to her.

'No, Mae. It won't. Not for us.'

She nodded, and then she stepped forward and hugged him briskly.

Sail helped her back.

She watched the small fishing boat till the horizon took it.

As the cliffs parted he eased the boat towards the rocks. She was about to ask when they rounded the furthest, and then she saw it. The cave mouth was low and he guided the boat with skill that told her how different their lives had been.

They went from sun to shade, the light cut to almost pitch black before she lay back and gasped.

'I didn't even know this was here, right beneath us,' she said.

Minerals caught what little light made it through and sparkled like lost treasure.

He sat beside her as they floated in the hidden world.

* * *

They lost an hour watching the colours before they headed back.

As they approached the jetty she turned to him. 'Thank you.'

'For what?'

'Not asking me to the Final today.'

'You said no, and I respect that. But could you do me a favour and not turn around.'

Mae turned, and on the jetty she saw it. The banner was large and crudely painted.

MAE AND SAIL.

THE FINAL?

'Stella helped me. And Felix tied it there.'

'Judas bastard.'

She looked up at the looming house, the tended grounds, and then down at her worn sandals, chipped polish on her nails.

'You know no good can come of this,' she said.

'I do.'

Mae suffered the inconvenience of falling in love three days before the world would end.

They lay on the deck and kissed.

She placed a hand on his chest, he placed a hand on her back.

She liked the way he said her name, the only way it could be said but from his lips it sounded better. His lips, full and pink.

They drank cold beer.

'I like the stars,' Sail said.

'I used to want their lives, girls like Sally and Abi. I used to want their . . . symmetry. Their parents, their parents' jobs. Their cars and their holidays. Their hopes didn't seem like dreams.'

'And now?'

'Now I just want to fix them.'

He kissed her and she thought of ice cream and vodka and lemon sherbet. Of perfectly cooked steak and pizza and tacos.

'What shall I eat for my last supper?' she said.

He went quiet in that way he sometimes did. He took her hand in his and she slipped it from him and he looked at her.

They talked politics and he spewed his father's opinions like they were his own. He adopted a posher accent and wagged a finger and talked about Iran and the crisis, Syria and plights. But she could hear the passion beneath, he cared, his cheeks flushed.

She climbed on top of him and kissed him and they discarded their clothes.

Mae ran her fingers up his arm, over the track of small scars, the times he had tried to say goodbye to their world.

I love you too much, she wanted to say.

Why did you make me do that?

38

She watched him sleep.

Matched her breathing to his.

She tried to calm, but the dream had been too vivid. Her and Abi on the beach, the first Forevers, so clear she woke with a start and for a few cruel seconds forgot Abi was gone.

She felt the heat in her chest, her hate for Jon Prince so hot she couldn't breathe.

Mae left him and walked along the cliff path that ran behind the sprawling gardens till she came to the Prince house.

She climbed over the back wall and stopped by the cavernous hole.

She saw the lift, the lights, but the garden was quiet. She guessed the men were done, that the bunker was complete.

The screen doors were open.

Net curtains caught the wind and billowed out towards her. As she slipped into the house she pressed close to the white wall and listened.

The decor was dark wood and leather, flat screens and a pool table.

She needed him to pay, for what he'd done to Abi, and to

Hugo. She'd find something in his office, a message, a note, something that linked him to a teenage girl. Maybe she'd paste it around town, let people see the real him, make him live his last hours under a cloud of shame.

She passed a painting of a sailing boat, thought of Mr Starling out there, setting a course for the end of the world and intending to sail right off it.

Upstairs she moved through the bedrooms, heard a shower running and found her way to the study.

She searched through draws, files, notes. She saw a leather diary and checked that too. She tried to imagine Abi with Jon Prince, shook the image from her mind and moved on into the spare bedroom. There was nothing in there but a bench, a barbell and a running machine.

Mae was about to turn and leave when she felt the rumble.

The whole house shook.

Mae ran into Hugo's room and shut herself in the wardrobe, breathing hard as she peered out through the slats.

Hugo came in, wet from the shower.

He dropped his towel and stood naked, staring at himself in the mirror.

Six two, his body pared back to nothing but muscle. He wasn't big like Liam, whose veins popped from injecting himself with steroids. He was the perfect size to cut through the water when he swam.

He flexed his arms and watched the biceps swell. Front on, the way he stood, you couldn't see them.

And then he turned slightly, his leg pivoting, and she saw the angry scars on his inner thighs.

He took a deep breath and tried to pinch the fat around his lower stomach. She saw him visibly relax when he couldn't.

Hugo moved to the wardrobe opposite and took the heavy box down.

Mae watched him carry the make-up case to the mirror by his door.

And then he got to work.

He concealed the dark bruise beneath his eye. And then he painted his lips, and contoured his cheekbones.

Mae smiled as she watched him.

When he was done, she saw someone else.

And maybe he did too.

Hugo Prince looked at himself in the mirror, smiled once and wiped the mask away.

And then he sat on the bed, found a small scalpel hidden in the bedside cabinet and tried not to cry out as he dragged it across his skin.

The scars opened.

He never let them heal.

Mae held her breath when she heard a knock at the door.

'Just a second.' Hugo moved instantly, put the box away and pulled on a pair of shorts. 'Yeah.'

Jon Prince crossed the threshold, arms folded tight across his chest as he stared at his son, the stare so cold Mae shivered.

'It was bigger this time. The house shook.'

Hugo nodded.

'Today,' Jon Prince said.

Hugo stood, hands by his side, his back military straight.

He watched his father as he spoke, the long hair tied back.

'You missed swim practice.'

Mae saw Hugo fight the tremble in his knees. 'I just . . . three days . . . Everyone went to the beach.'

'You haven't been the same since Abi. First it was the car, then that stupid tattoo, now this. You're losing focus.'

Jon reached out and squeezed his son's shoulder, hard enough that when he took his hand away a red print remained. 'Abi took her own life, correct?'

Hugo went to shrug.

'Correct?'

'That's what Sergeant Walters said.'

'So whatever happened, whatever was done to her, she couldn't cope with it. It's a test, Hugo. We can roll over and give up, or we can . . .' Jon stared at his son, willing him.

Hugo cleared his throat. 'Or we can pick up our shovel and dig.'

Jon nodded, no smile.

Mae thought of Abi's face, the way her body lay broken on the rocks.

'I'm sorry. It won't happen again.'

'This isn't the end, Hugo. No matter how it plays out, this won't be the end for us. And we can come out stronger on the other side, or we can join the rest of the town watching the sky and reddening our knees in church. Now get some sleep, you have training in the morning.'

At that Jon turned.

'I miss her,' Hugo said.

The words landed hard. Jon turned back and stared at his son like he couldn't work out who he was, where he'd come from.

'We don't talk about –'

'I miss her,' he said again.

Jon clenched his fists and Mae closed her eyes. She could not watch it again without doing something.

'You said it would get easier.'

Jon stared at him, eyes blazing so hot Mae felt the burn. 'I've given you everything. You can still be everything. You're a Prince.'

'I don't want to be you.'

Jon took a step nearer. 'Say that again?'

Mae willed Hugo to stay silent, to resist that urge that she could not.

She breathed again as Jon turned and left.

When Hugo's light cut, and his breathing changed, Mae crept quietly into the hallway. And then she heard it.

It was soft at first, then louder.

The regular thump of a headboard against a wall.

As she cracked open the door to Jon Prince's bedroom the world tilted on her again.

Mae thought of Luke Manton as she watched his wife lie back on Jon Prince's bed, eyes closed as Jon grunted away on top of her.

39

She took what she knew to the beach.

And she joined them in her daze, and was soon flanked by Matilda and Betty, who stood either side and took her hands in theirs.

She watched them wade into the dark water and float on their backs.

And then she noticed the small clusters of girls who stood waist deep, passing bottles of hair-dye as the sea took the silver away. Maybe they were showing affiliation, or maybe they'd just tired of looking up to Hunter.

'Hey.'

Mae was surprised to see him, sat down on the sand and leaned heavily, her head on his shoulder.

'Are you okay, Mae?'

She did not know where to begin, so much death already, so much more would come. 'I'm tired, Felix.'

Around were a hundred Forevers, they lay in groups, the fire crackled and music played softly.

'Did you do this?' he said.

'They did.'

He passed her the bottle of communion wine and she drank and passed it back.

'Anything with Abi?' he said.

'I thought maybe yes, but then everything . . . it just changed. And now I don't know anything, Felix. I don't who I am, and I don't know who these people are. I want it to go back, you know, just to before, not even before we knew, because I don't even remember that time.'

'Hey,' he said, and wiped her tears with his thumbs. 'You don't cry. You're Mae Cassidy and you're the toughest person I know. And you've been through more than any one of us here.' She cursed and he told her it was okay but she didn't feel okay then.

'Stella,' she said.

He nodded, and she saw tears of his own forming.

'It wouldn't be so bad if it wasn't for her. I never had siblings, never needed them because I had you and I had Stella. And I know I joke with her and I've messed up her dance but I . . .'

'I know.'

He took a moment to calm and she let him.

'Wait. What was that about her dance?' she said.

He climbed to his feet quickly but the rumble almost knocked him down again. This time it was savage, so deep, like West was about to split in two.

The hundred climbed to their feet and stood together.

And they gasped as the town behind was plunged into darkness.

So total it was like it no longer existed.

There were murmurs, calls to go get help.

But they stayed there and looked back, and then out to sea.

277

And then, finally, someone looked up.

'Up there.'

Mae wasn't sure who the voice belonged to, but she looked up too, and she felt Felix press close to her as they saw it too.

'Shit,' he said, quiet. 'Oh shit, Mae.'

It was the brightest light in their sky.

It was bigger than they could have imagined.

Maybe it had been the light pollution, or maybe it was that exact moment when it became visible to them, truly visible.

Selena set alight the sky over the town of West.

Mae ran from the beach and down the darkened streets, saw people at their doors carrying candles, all struck dumb by the wonder above their town.

She saw Sergeant Walters by the station, talking into his radio, calling for calm from the growing numbers gathered at the foot of the high street.

It's just a power cut.

She found Stella asleep in her bed.

Instead of waking her and sending her back to her own room, Mae grabbed Abi Manton's file and climbed out of the window, lay back on the flat roof and began to read through each page.

So tired her eyes burned.

The light from the bedroom was just enough to read the words and see the photographs. Sergeant Walters had done his best, photographed the scene from every angle, but Mae only had to close her eyes to see it again.

There was a close-up of Abi's face, and she forced herself to look at it.

'Mae.'

She turned to see Stella at the window behind her.

'Are you ready?'

Mae nodded.

Stella changed into her white pyjamas while Mae moved through the kitchen and found the popcorn she'd been saving.

As the microwave whirred she looked out the front window and saw lights blink on in every house on the street. Behind she saw the slow wake of West, hours before dawn.

Stella put on her space helmet and stood close to the TV.

Morales was sanguine.

This is it.

I know you've all read about it. I know you've seen dozens of TV programmes.

You can pray.

You can believe.

Stella cried when the rocket launched.

Mae held onto her tightly.

The popcorn sat on the table, untouched.

'Will it work, Mae?'

'Yes.'

'How do you know?'

'I just know.'

'What colour is the rocket. Paint it for me.'

Mae stared at the screen. 'It's every colour in our world. The darkest blue to the brightest yellow. It's beautiful, Stell.'

They sat on the sofa as the experts talked, charts were wheeled out, computer graphics loaded up.

Mae looked over at Stella fast asleep. She took a blanket

and covered her sister, then watched the break of dawn in the garden, the dog beside her.

Mae sat in the crisp air and turned the last pages of Abi's file. And then she came to an interview with Mr Silver. She skimmed it, knew she'd find nothing, chalk up another failure, another dead end.

Sergeant Walters: Mr Silver, thanks for coming in.
Edward Silver: Of course. And please, call me Edward.
Walters: Seems kind of wrong. In my day the headmaster was all formality. But I guess I've seen you so much over the past months I can call you a friend.
Silver: Well, in that case, my friends call me Teddy.

Mae skipped ahead, past the small talk, the school talk.

Walters: Tell me about Abi Manton.
Silver: She was friends with my daughter. Most of the girls are, actually.
Walters: And your daughter, I hear she's popular. Head girl. Someone the younger children look up to.
Silver: Going back to the Manton girl . . .

Mae skipped past Mr Silver detailing Abi's achievements, her talent for music and art.

Walters: Abi's suicide, it doesn't make sense to me.
Silver: And James and Melissa, that did?
Walters: That's why you have a school counsellor.

Silver: Jane. We brought her in months before we had to. We try to pre-empt these . . . situations.

Walters: You have Abi Manton, popular, lots of friends. No problems at home. She's doing well at school, likely to head to Cambridge.

Silver: Actually she . . . she had problems in that department.

Walters: Oh? Her parents didn't say.

Silver: We try to give students a chance before we involve the parents. Abi was struggling. Her grades had fallen sharply. I spoke to her about it, informally, just to see if she was okay.

Walters: And was she okay?

Silver: She was having trouble concentrating. She said her mind was all over the place. It was the noise, she said she couldn't shut out the noise from the outside world. It was deafening.

Walters: What did you tell her?

Silver: I arranged another session with Jane.

Walters: And how did that go?

Silver: She didn't turn up. I was due to follow up with her but then this . . .

Walters: I'll have to tell her parents about this. It won't bring them comfort, that Abi didn't go to them to say she was struggling.

Silver: They rarely do. The parents are always the last to know.

Walters: Of course you have experience in this. Gemma Dune. At Goldings. To us though, in West, three students.

Silver: It's devasting. Devasting.

Mae watched light shatter the night sky, breaking through in thin strips of gold. She thought of Abi, her world falling apart. No doubt finding out she was pregnant had taken a toll on her grades.

But as Mae glanced at the moon, holding in place, stubborn, she thought about what Mr Starling had said. How Abi maintained her grades. How strong she was.

Her mind swam before she reached the only conclusions.

One of them had it wrong . . .

Or one of them was lying.

40

They left West early.

Kitten screamed her way along the empty high street as dozens of people walked down to the beach.

Felix kept one hand on the wheel, the other on the gearstick. As he turned onto the B road the dice swung his way. He ripped them down and threw them out the window.

'You know there were near two hundred Forevers on the beach during the launch. Sergeant Walters stood there watching them, waiting for them to do something wrong so he could find a reason to break them up,' Felix said.

'You were with them?'

'Nah. I'm an F, remember.'

They stuck to the back roads, traced the coast because the motorways were jammed. They passed the Waterside Holiday Park, a line of caravans, the boats beyond them.

'I feel like we should be saying more . . . something profound,' Felix said.

'Live like there's no tomorrow.'

'What is coming is better than what has gone.'

Felix took his foot off the pedal as they passed the mouth

of Hamilton Bay, rocks towered on either side, the water was too clear, like an aquarium.

'I never said thank you,' she said.

He glanced over, then back at the road. 'For what?'

'You've always been there for me.'

'Shit, we really are getting profound.'

Mae smiled. 'When my parents . . . and Stella came home. I didn't leave the house that whole summer, remember?'

'Yeah.'

'You sat in the garden each night. And you read your book. Sometimes you sat there hours.'

He shrugged like it was nothing. 'In case you needed me.'

'I did need you. And you were there.'

She placed her hand over his, gripped it tight.

'Our friendship,' he said.

'The Reverend's son and the town slut.'

They watched a boy and girl, maybe ten years old, walk down to the water, hand in hand.

'This can't be the end,' Felix said.

'Then how come it is?'

They drove the last half-hour in perfect silence.

Goldings Secondary was half the size of Sacred Heart, and a quarter as grand. Mr Silver had been head there for three years before coming to Sacred Heart.

Mae and Felix slipped in among the others and filed through the gate.

They found themselves in the main corridor, beside a line of lockers. A couple of kids glanced their way but most ignored them.

The head's office was empty, they took a seat and waited. Mae had found out what she could online. Gemma Dune had been sixteen when she died. She'd looped a belt around her neck, then attached it to the automatic garage door at her house.

Mrs Charles entered and frowned. She was small but her face was all steel.

The second Mae mentioned Gemma Dune, Mrs Charles asked them to leave. Mae tried to argue till the headmistress threatened to call the police.

'That went well,' Mae said, as they walked back through the halls.

Just as they were about to head out the main door Felix stopped dead.

'What?' Mae said.

'Look.' He pointed.

The girl was maybe a year younger, she stood beside two others.

'And them,' Felix said.

Mae saw another group. 'Jesus.'

Felix grinned.

Mae walked over to them, didn't think of what to say because she was blinded by the tattoos on their wrists.

'You're Forevers,' Mae said.

They turned together. One was about to speak when Felix called out, 'Mae, we need to go.'

Mae looked past him and saw Mrs Charles coming, with another teacher beside her.

Mae smiled at the girls, who stared at her like they'd seen a ghost, then she jogged from the building with Felix beside her.

They'd almost made it to Kitten when Mae heard her name called.

'You're from West,' the girl said.

Mae nodded.

'Holy shit, it's you. It's really you.' She reached out and grasped Mae's hand, looked at the letters like she'd never seen them before, like they weren't printed on her own wrist.

'How –'

'My cousin goes to Sacred Heart. Freya Cannon.'

Mae drew a blank.

'She's in Year Nine. She emailed a photo . . . and then I printed it out and before long . . . I mean, there's twenty-six of us here now.'

Mae smiled.

'I can't believe it's you. The ultimate creep.'

'That's what they call her,' Felix said.

'We get together in the field behind my house and play music . . . and we've taken back Forever, just like you. I mean, two days, but we've got each other. I feel like we owe you.'

'You don't.'

'What are you doing here?'

'We were trying to find out about Gemma Dune,' Felix said.

'Oh.' The excitement died in a breath.

'Did you know her?'

'Not really, I mean, everyone knows about her. She had problems, she couldn't cope with it all. And she was majorly into drugs. She's like a cautionary tale in this town. Just say no.' Mae wasn't sure what she wanted to hear, maybe that Gemma had been just like Abi, and then she'd met Mr Silver and fallen apart. It would've been neat, but then she reasoned nothing about life was neat.

Another town.

Another dead girl.

'You're like a god to them,' Felix said, as they drove back towards West.

'Please.'

'Seriously. All hail Queen Margaret.'

She punched his arm.

They stopped at Adlers Bay, swam out into the clear water and floated on their backs.

'I'm going to miss this,' Felix said. 'I'm going to miss you.'

'Yeah.'

'Do you think we lived, Mae?'

Gentle waves, the sun so bright above. 'I think we survived.'

'I wanted more.'

'Everyone does.'

'I keep feeling . . . angry. I want to scream.'

'You should, Felix.'

'I think you're either a screamer or you're not.'

Mae screamed then. So loud Felix righted himself and began to tread water.

The beach was empty.

And so he screamed.

And she screamed again.

And together they screamed.

The road jammed five miles from West.

'Remember the time I broke my arm cliff-diving?' Felix said.

'Sprained your wrist jumping from the low board at the pool,' she corrected.

'How about the time I made out with Avni Laghari?'

'She was so drunk she puked into your mouth.'

'First kiss *and* a free meal.'

They crawled along for a couple of miles. Stopped and started.

She tapped the analogue clock in the centre of the dashboard.

'It's stuck at eleven. Maybe time has stopped for a while.'

'What's the real time?'

'Six.'

'Shit, my mother's going to kill me. I was supposed to be back by five at the latest. Said I'd help with the set for the concert. It's supposed to look like heaven, all white curtains and candles.'

'Sounds like you're coming around to the whole church thing.'

He leaned out the window and craned to see how far the traffic backed up.

'I'm just helping her because no one else will.'

Mae stretched her legs out. 'I thought Jeet Patel was doing all that.'

'Please, that kid's the water boy. He spends all his time hoping something will happen to Theodore so he can step up. Eternal understudy, it's gotta sting.'

Mae turned to Felix. 'What do you mean?'

'He pours the water, Mae. He makes sure everyone has a glass in case they choke up there.'

She thought back to seeing Jeet Patel in the chemist's.

Mae opened the door and sprinted towards town.

41

The queue stretched from the bay up the high street to the church.

She pushed past, ignored the complaints.

Inside the church was transformed.

White netting draped from each wall, white flowers rose from tall vases at the end of each pew. Mae looked to the ceiling and saw lanterns had been hung from the wooden arches.

The concert had already started.

She realised then that the people outside wouldn't get in, they'd just come to show their support, maybe to get close enough to hear Theodore sing.

She stood at the back and looked out over five hundred.

Sally sat behind the piano and played those same notes Mae had heard outside her house, those notes that broke her heart all over again.

Theodore sat there with others.

They'd left a chair for Abi, her violin on the seat.

Mae crept her way along the stone. Between the nets she caught sight of townspeople. Mrs Abbott and her husband. Theodore's parents. She saw Jon Prince sitting beside Hugo, who wore a tie and kept his eyes down, like he was carrying the weight of his father's sins.

Mae caught sight of Jeet, who sat in the wings on a plastic chair, his hands pressed neatly between his knees. There was something pure about the way he watched them, the way his breath caught when Theodore stood.

Mae moved closer, so close she could almost reach the stage.

She saw the small tables to the side of them.

The glass of water on Theodore's.

Mae thought of Jeet Patel waiting for his chance, his time to stand in the light.

She edged closer.

Mae crept low, avoiding everyone's eye, trying to look official as she grabbed the glass from in front of Theodore. She took it back to the corner, out of sight, her heart still racing, her hair matted down with sweat.

She breathed.

And then she froze as Theodore sang.

Sally matched him on the piano.

Mae recognised the song. The words.

His voice cannoned from the old roof, rattling it till the wood splintered and light fell on them.

Mae let her eyes drift to the stained glass. And she remembered sitting there between her parents, back when the world made some kind of sense. Back when Selena was a faraway thing in a faraway sky.

She thought of Abi, of everything they knew and everything they dreamed of. She needed her then, despite Felix, despite the Forevers all around her, she needed her friend, to hold her hand when she jumped, to tell her everything didn't need to be okay, so long as they had each other.

Mae saw Lydia Manton sitting alone in a corner.

Theodore's parents were uniform in their smiles.

Sergeant Walters cried silently. Mae thought of his father, still in that room, in that chair.

As Theodore sang about the creeps and the weirdos, Candice was the first to turn, and she nudged Lexi. Others turned as Sullivan Reed appeared at the back of the church.

The notes died and people stood, their applause so thunderous Mae felt it in her bones.

Theodore took a brief bow and walked down the aisle.

And Sullivan walked towards him.

They met in the centre, and melted into one perfect kiss.

The applause didn't stop.

They held each other, lost, the words on their wrists so bold.

Mae looked over at Jeet Patel, who smiled at her with such sadness in his eyes.

She wanted to be wrong, more than anything, right then she needed to be wrong.

Mae brought the glass to her nose, inhaled and breathed out slow.

She crossed the stone floor and hugged Jeet tightly. 'Thank you.'

He smiled. 'For what?'

'For being everything good.'

42

Mae stood in the graveyard as the crowds broke and drifted away.

She walked over to Theodore.

'You told Sergeant Walters,' she said.

'It took me too long.'

Mae smiled. 'But you did the right thing in the end.'

'I think you helped me realise. You and the rest of them . . . on the beach, at school. Everywhere I looked.'

'Realise what?'

'That my Forever is Sullivan.'

She watched him walk over to his group. Mae guessed Theodore didn't know his parents quite as well as he'd thought, because they wrapped their arms around him. And then his father shook hands with Sullivan.

The four walked together down towards the bay front.

Mae nodded at Sergeant Walters, who tipped his hat in reply.

'Sally . . .' Mae called, and caught up with her.

Sally turned.

'That was . . .'

'Did you see them?'

'Yeah. And I saw you. Everyone was crying in there.'

'Two days left, it was like shooting fish in a barrel.'

Someone had strung fairy lights around Abi's gravestone. They stopped in front of it.

'You want to come down to the beach?' Mae said.

Sally smiled, then shook her head.

'Are you okay, Sally?'

'I'm always okay. It's just . . . I used to dream of more than that. I'll see you around, Mae.'

Mae sat by Abi's grave until the last of the church people left, until they were alone. She told Abi how close she came to being there for her, all the roads she had run down. She told her about the Forevers, how they'd given hope to so many. She talked about Sail, how she was going to a school dance. At that point she imagined Abi turning in her grave.

She stood by the far wall and saw the beach a long way below. The light of a fire.

She knew Sail would be down there waiting for her, and maybe Betty and Matilda and dozens of others. Time had never been more precious, but right then Mae knew where she was needed most.

She knocked on the cottage door, waited a long time before it was opened.

'Some people think the world is cruel,' Mae said.

Sally blocked the doorway, her face pale and drawn. 'And you?'

'I really wanted to believe in karma. I mean, I needed it to be true. I needed there to be balance.'

293

'Matching tattoos don't fix everything, Mae.'

Mae glanced around at the picture-perfect scene, the wildflower lawn, the wishing well in the centre.

'I know,' Mae said.

At that Sally closed her eyes.

'You've got me, and I've got you. Whatever you need to say.'

Sally, her tears fell then. 'You don't want this, Mae.'

Mae took her hand.

'I thought I could disappear. If I ate enough.' She looked at the stars. 'I thought I'd be someone new. People still look, but they see something else.'

'Your stepfather –'

Sally smiled. 'He still saw me, Mae. How could anyone want this?' She held up an arm and grabbed a fistful of the flesh that hung from it. 'How could he still want this?'

Mae stepped forward.

Sally cried harder. 'Please, Mae. Just turn around and go to the beach. Be with Jack Sail.'

Mae took Sally's hand. 'That's not how this works, Sally.'

They walked through the house in half-darkness, up stairs that groaned under Sally's weight.

There was a nameplate on her door.

SALLY, spelled in pink letters.

Mae thought she was ready.

And then Sally opened her bedroom door.

And Mae closed her eyes to the scene.

Oliver Sweeny lay on his stepdaughter's bed, face down, his trousers around his ankles.

A large kitchen knife buried in his back.

So deep only the handle showed.

Mae stood there for a long time, just looking, taking in the pink wallpaper, the thick white rug, the blood soaking into the mattress.

'Sally. Where's your mother?'

Sally's eyes never left him. 'She said I was making it up. All those years ago. Even afterwards. She said he only confessed so I wouldn't have to go to court. She said he was selfless, that he was protecting me. Barbara. Barbie. She wanted to play happy families. *There's only a few days left, Sally. You can be good for a few days. Isn't it nice to have your father back?*'

'Where is she?'

'Where she always is when things happen. Lying in bed, pretending to sleep.'

Mae left Sally in her room, then crossed the hallway. She took a deep breath before she opened the door.

She saw the shape in the bed.

Mae felt her heart thundering.

Barbie lay unmoving, her eyes open, her mouth fixed in a scream.

Mae pressed a hand to her and felt the cold skin. Then she turned and saw Sally at the door. 'What did you –'

'I sat on her. Right on her chest. I just sat there and asked her why. She didn't answer, Mae. For the first time in Barbie's life she couldn't say a single thing to me. Couldn't tell me I was disgusting. Greedy. Vile. That I was ruining everything.'

Mae steeled herself as she thought back to Oliver Sweeny's file. The things he'd done to Sally. The things he'd made her do.

'Have you called anyone?'

Sally seemed to shake herself out of it. 'Sergeant Walters will come. I have to tell him what I've done.'

'He'll lock you up. You'll die in a cell, Sally. Your . . . Oliver. You can say it was self-defence, but Barbie. I mean, temporary insanity or something. Sergeant Walters, he'll follow the letter of the law. Selena will come and you'll die alone.'

'I've lived alone.'

'Not any more.' Mae looked at her, her mind beginning to turn. 'When's he coming?'

'Tomorrow morning at eight. Oliver's out early on parole. He comes into the house and has a coffee.'

'You'll say they left town. They're leavers.'

'He'll come in. He'll check the house.'

'Then we have to get them out of here.'

'Us?'

'Not just the two of us. We'll need help.'

'You're not thinking clearly, Mae. This . . . If Saviour 10 works then you have to live with this.'

Mae took her hand. 'We do what's right. We made a promise to do what's right.'

Sally cried again.

Mae hugged her tightly.

'But who'll help us? Who'll help me?'

'You're not alone any more.'

She found Sail on the beach.

He stood with Matilda and Betty and read the look on her face.

'Sally's in trouble. She needs help.'

'Okay,' Sail said.

'Okay,' Matilda and Betty said.

'It's serious. Like, the most serious. And even asking you to do this is –'

'We said okay,' Matilda said, and took Mae's hand. 'It's not like any of us were heading up anyway, doll.'

In the old cottage Matilda clapped her hands briskly. 'Sometimes it comes in handy having a mother who runs a cleaning business.'

Sail had taken charge quickly, poured Sally a large drink and sent her into the garden where she sat on her swing and watched the stars.

If they had been horrified, which they were, when they saw the position Oliver Sweeny was in, they quickly, and grimly, put the pieces together. Matilda's eyes burned for a moment, and then she went to her mother's small van and returned with a host of cleaning products.

Sail took off his jacket and worked quietly, wrapped the bodies in bedding and did not look at their faces.

Oliver was heavy.

Mae felt her heart pumping as they struggled down the stairs and out to Sail's idling Mercedes.

Betty found the CD player and cranked the volume.

'Blondie?' Mae said, as Barbie's shoe fell off.

'Our love . . . it's divine,' Betty said, and winked at Matilda, who pulled on a pair of latex gloves and shook her arse in time to the music.

They dropped low when car lights swung in front of the house.

Breathed again when they faded into the distance.

They left Matilda and Betty dancing and climbed into Sail's car.

'You think there's something wrong with Matilda and Betty?' Sail said, looking back at the house.

Neither mentioned the back seat, or what would happen if Sergeant Walters was out and pulled them over.

'I had no right to ask for your help with this,' Mae said, still coasting on the shock.

Sail drove slow. 'They deserved it.'

'That's it?'

He nodded.

They limped the car through the gates of Sail's house and down a service road that curved through the rocks and came out by the jetty.

'I wanted to get them on the boat, but it'll be light soon.'

'What then?' Mae said.

'The caves.' Sail pointed up the beach a little.

It took them an hour to manoeuvre Sally's parents across the beach.

Above them the sheer cliff rose to St Cecelia. 'And if someone finds them?'

'The tide . . . We'll be dead by then,' Sail said.

'And if we're not? DNA?'

'We are an army of each other.'

'But this . . . what Sally did, what we've done. I dragged you into this,' Mae said. 'I'll find a way out.'

Sail took her hand. 'Whatever happens, people like this don't deserve our Forever.'

'And if we get caught.' Mae looked up at the church.

'Then we'll pray for a miracle. I think it's time for God to prove his worth.'

They lay together on the jetty.

'I thought you were soft, when I met you,' she said.

'I am.'

'You're not, Jack Sail.' When he slept she leaned over and touched the water. And for the last time she crossed the town and broke silently into the Silvers' pool house.

Hunter's bed was made, Mae guessed she'd spend her last nights with Hugo.

The jewellery box was hidden at the back of an antique wardrobe.

Mae took the moon necklace from her pocket and placed it back carefully.

And then she noticed the false bottom.

She lifted the panel out carefully, and gasped when she saw it.

43

When she got home she washed her face and stared into the mirror and did not know the girl who stared back.

She changed her clothes and opened the fridge and found her hands shook so much she almost could not mix the batter.

'Pancakes,' Stella said, from the door. 'Is it my birthday?'

Mae attempted a flip. 'It's stuck to the ceiling.'

Stella applauded as the pancake gently unpeeled and landed on the green tiles with a splat. Lady appeared and gulped it down in one bite.

That morning there was a picture so big Mae switched off the television and the radio. She did her best to shrink their world by so much it was just the two of them, sitting in the garden and eating their pancakes on a perfect summer morning.

She tried not to think of the night before. It seemed like a different world, Sally's parents and where they were. Maybe they'd crossed over, maybe they were burning. Or maybe they just existed in the kind of nowhere Sally had spent much of her life. Unable to feel, unable to see or hear or enjoy anything at all.

'It's the concert tonight.'

'It is.'

'And the Final.'

'And the Final.'

Stella took a large bite of her fifth pancake. 'You know I finish at lunch today? Don't forget to collect me.'

'I won't.'

'And you have to dress up for my show.'

'I know.'

'Are you going to wear black? You always wear black, but Miss Hart wants the room to be filled with colour and happiness and –'

'I know.'

Mae felt hollow on the walk. She was aware of her bones, how they fit together, the way her heart pumped her blood.

She tried to smile at the old ladies who came out of their front doors and waved to the children of West Primary as they passed, like some kind of dying parade.

'What's going on?' Stella said.

'I don't know.'

Lady stayed beside them instead of running ahead.

Mae kept her eyes down as they neared the school, willed all the mothers and fathers to keep their shit together as they packed off their children for a last morning of normal.

'I'm worried about my dance,' Stella said.

'You'll be brilliant.'

'Felix said he's the lord of the dance, but I asked Miss Hart and she'd never heard of him.'

Mae hugged her a little tighter that morning.

And then she held her hand.

And ran her finger over the Forever on her sister's tiny wrist.

'Permanent marker,' Stella said. 'All the girls did it. Miss Hart is going to go crazy.'

'Ask her to join.'

'I think my glasses are too big to dance in. But if I take them off people will see my eyes.'

'You have beautiful eyes.'

She watched her sister walk into school.

They cut that day.

Every single kid at Sacred Heart.

Five hundred of them went down to the beach, stripped their uniforms off and lay on the sand. Dozens had left town.

'If God created the universe, then who created God?' Lexi said.

'Sometimes I think we should leave,' Hunter said.

'And go where?'

'Somewhere. I want to be doing something.'

'If they stop Selena, do you think we'll be different? Maybe we'll appreciate –'

'Don't say life,' Mae said.

'Each other.'

'No. We'll make exactly the same mistakes over again. We're flawed by design to ensure we live our lives racking up the kind of debt that can never be settled.'

She cupped the breeze with her hand as Sail lay beside.

'Matilda and Betty stayed with her.'

Sail nodded.

'We have one day left,' Mae said. 'We can dwell on the past –'

'We have no past.'

At lunch they collected Stella.

Mae had brought her swimming costume and watched Felix, Stella and Lady splash in the shallows.

'I let her down,' Mae said.

Sail turned to her.

'Abi. I let her down.' She looked across at the sea of bodies. Hugo tossed a frisbee with Liam, while Hunter and Candice sunned themselves. 'I needed it to be more than just suicide. I needed someone to have done it to her.'

Sail milled the sand with his fingers. 'We can't all be well, Mae.'

'I know. I didn't –'

'Equal and opposite.'

'For every happy person, someone has to be sad?'

'It's not about happy and sad, bad and good. There's a bigger picture today, right? The news this morning, across the world, people are queuing at the Louvre, the Guggenheim. Thousands are surrounding the pyramids. They cut to garden parties, families coming together.'

'The closer you look, the less you see.'

'The less you need to see.'

That afternoon they sat with their grandmother.

Mae brought out Stella's favourite books and read to her of Lucy and the wardrobe and Max's search for his family. Stella did not say much.

They stood together when they heard the heavy thump of the helicopter above.

Stella waved frantically.

Mae watched it pass.

'Where's it going?'

'Somewhere.'

At three o'clock they turned on the television and watched as Morales took to the stand for the final time. He had cropped his hair close, shaved and put on a smart shirt and tie. Gone was the lab coat, the sense of despair and urgency. He wished them good luck, told them to remember who they were, and he told them to pray if they had faith. It would work or it would not, there was no second chance, the time had come to focus on what was important, family, friends, loved ones. He spoke of his team, some of the greatest minds this world had known had gathered and worked alongside him for the past decade, and they would be there till whatever end came to be.

Morales signed off with a smile, with a final goodbye and another weighted line.

Tomorrow will happen.

'What the hell are you wearing?' Felix said.

The dress was pink and poofy. She'd found it in Stella's dressing-up box. On her head was a pink tiara, also borrowed from Stella. She carried a wand, at the end was a silver star which she aimed at Felix, attempting to turn him to stone.

'I need to get my camera,' he said.

'Do that and I'll cut off your hands.'

They walked across the street. Felix kept having to stop, he was laughing so hard.

They fell in with a crowd of princes and princesses.

'Stella's nervous about the dance. You did teach her the waltz, right?'

Felix nodded. 'I'm doing the music, and the lights. Perks of being president of the AV Club.'

'President and only member.'

She took a seat in the front row. Mae saw familiar faces, kids from school, Hugo sat a few rows behind with his grandparents.

'Are you going to wear that tonight?' Sail said, as he sat beside her.

'I don't have anything to wear tonight. And I have no idea how to do make-up. Or style my hair. You got a problem with that?'

He shook his head quickly.

Mae felt her stomach tighten when the curtain opened and Stella appeared, wearing old rags and pushing a broom around the stage.

Mae mouthed every word her sister spoke, clapped her hands and laughed and lived Stella's perfect performance.

And as Stella slipped the glass shoe onto her foot, and Prince Charming asked her to dance, Stella turned to Felix and told him to hit it.

Prince Charming held out a hand, only for Stella to slap it away. 'Boys make everything worse.'

Mae sank low in her seat.

'I can dance on my own.'

There was nervous laughter.

'Felix was supposed to teach her to waltz,' Mae said, watching from between her fingers as her sister spun a dozen times, then offered a hand to the ugly sisters and told them not to be defined by their looks.

Mae closed her eyes when the speakers crackled and Barry White rang out loud.

There were gasps when Stella gyrated, winces when she slut-dropped.

'Felix is a dead man.'

The other kids stopped waltzing and stared.

The Fairy Godmother pressed a hand to her mouth.

Sail got to his feet. 'Stella's a Forever, right. I'm going up there to join her.'

He crossed the floor and climbed up onto the stage.

Mae looked into the audience with something like pleading in her eyes as it slowly dawned on Stella that her perfect moment was being met with a stony silence.

And then Theodore stood, and people turned as he began to sing.

Sail took Stella's hands and she stepped onto his feet as they danced together.

'You know how badass you are,' Sail said.

'Totally badass,' Stella said.

Mrs Abbott stood and began to clap her hands.

The other kids moved around them, spinning and laughing.

Even Miss Hart got to her feet.

Mae frowned at Sail, who held out his hand.

Mae took it. 'I'm dancing on stage wearing a pink tutu. I think I'm ready for Selena now.'

When the music finally died, Stella and the class took a bow as the parents stood and cheered through their tears.

Felix joined them on stage. 'Awesome, right? Barry, sending us all off.'

Mae kept her smile in place. 'When this is over, you better start running.'

44

'You could wear the dress Sail sent over,' Stella said, holding up the navy dress and declaring it the most beautiful thing she'd ever seen in her life.

Mae sighed heavily.

'But it *feels* so beautiful.'

'There's something *Pretty Woman* about Sail sending me a dress. Do I look like a whore to you, Stella?'

'What's a whore?'

'The kind of girl Sail apparently wants me to be.'

'Then, yes. I think you should put it on and look like a whore.'

Mae turned a little and looked at the old dress of her own she'd put on. Worn to a shine. She went to straighten it again, found it tight around the waist so gave it a tug and heard the brutal sound of fabric tearing.

Stella grimaced. 'Mummy must have been so skinny.'

'Anorexia was all the rage back then.'

Mae bent, watched the dress split apart and then swore so furiously Stella placed her fingers in her ears.

And then their grandmother wandered in.

She clutched an armful of emerald silk and held it out.

Mae remembered the dress well.

'It's too big. I told you, it won't fit.'

The old lady said nothing, just shook the dress a couple of times till Mae took it.

Stella was grinning.

'What?'

'Just try the damn dress,' Stella said.

Mae slipped it on, then she stood back and glanced at her grandmother. 'You fixed it.'

'And I helped,' Stella said.

Mae did not speak for a long time. 'I suppose it'll have to do then.'

'I bet you look just like Mummy.' Stella jumped down from the bed and hugged her sister tightly.

'You just need someone to do your make-up now,' Stella said.

'Let's get this over with then.'

Mae looked up when she heard his voice.

Hugo stood by the bedroom door with a large make-up box in his arms. 'Time to make this goose into a swan.'

Mae frowned.

'I overheard you at the play,' he said, then turned to Stella. 'You were awesome by the way.'

'I know,' Stella said. 'Now turn my sister into a whore.'

Sail wore a dark tux, his hair combed neatly back.

He leaned on a classic red Porsche, the roof down, the engine idling.

'Wait there,' Mae said.

He fired off a salute.

Mae walked back to the doorway and knelt beside Stella. 'You'll watch the sunset tonight? Grandma said she'd paint it.'

Stella nodded.

'It's important.'

'I know.'

'I don't want to go,' Mae said. 'I could stay here. We could watch a film, anything you like. We've still got some of that popcorn. I saved it.'

Stella hugged her tightly. 'I danced with my Prince Charming earlier, now you have to dance with yours.'

Mae smiled. 'When did you get so grown-up?'

'When you were drunk at the beach.'

'Well played.'

'You have to go say goodnight to Grandma now,' Stella said.

Mae glanced back at Sail.

'Please, Mae.'

She found her grandmother in the kitchen. She looked older then, so old and frail. Mae thought of the changes, so severe, so hard. The times she'd lashed out, the times she'd taken Mae's hand and told her everything would be okay. Mae had stopped looking for perfect a long time ago, stopped looking for normal.

She fixed her watery blue eyes on Mae. 'So . . .'

'Yeah.'

She patted the seat beside her. 'I'll be asleep when you get in. And I don't want you to wake me in the morning.'

'But –'

'Some nights I dream of your grandfather. Maybe tonight will be one of those nights. I know I haven't –'

Mae swallowed. 'No.'

'But you know that I . . .'

'Yes.'

Her grandmother stood, and Mae hugged her quickly. 'Goodnight, Grandma.'

'Goodnight, Mae.'

He drove slow, behind a procession of limos.

There were people on the street, watching the cars pass, a horse and carriage. She saw girls in long dresses posing while proud parents fired off photographs.

Mrs Abbott had opened her salon for the last time, brought in a team of friends to help style hair free of charge.

They left the car at Felix's house, stood on the pavement and watched him kiss his parents goodbye.

Felix wore all white, the buttons gold, his shoes polished to a deep shine, a captain's hat pulled low. 'This is it. The last roll. The last movie she rented. *An Officer and an effing Gentleman.*'

Mrs Baxter glared at him. 'Can we have one night where you don't swear? Just one.'

He bent down and kissed her cheek. 'Don't wait up. I'll be slamming Candice all night long.'

Mrs Baxter sighed. 'Making love, son. Making love.'

Felix flexed his bicep. 'Not the way I do it.'

'Into a tissue in the bathroom?' Mae said.

Felix walked them over to Kitten, to which his mother had tied a ribbon. 'Like a goddam wedding car.'

'We can't all fit in the Porsche,' Mae said.

'I prefer Kitten,' Sail said.

'You won't when you hear the engine.'

They piled in and Felix gunned the accelerator. Mae opened her window to the howl of neighbourhood dogs while Sail winced. 'It actually hurts.'

They stopped outside the Sweeny house and Felix pressed the horn.

Mae glanced at Sail, the memory would not have time to soften.

'She's wearing a dress,' Mae said.

Sally climbed in, her face drawn, her eyes red. 'You look like a magician, Matchstick.'

'You look lovely, Sweeny,' Felix said, smiling into the rear-view mirror.

'Lesbian crew did my make-up,' Sally said.

Mae reached a hand back and Sally squeezed it limply.

As they reached Sacred Heart Mae saw a dense crowd, expensive dresses and heels, black bow ties and wide smiles.

Cameras flashed, the air smelled of perfume, she managed to smile as Sail gripped her hand tightly.

Felix pulled into the car park and they all got out.

'Have you seen Hunter and Hugo?' Mae said.

'Hugo's probably picking up our Viagra so we can bang all night,' Liam said, getting out of a limo.

Mae raised an eyebrow.

'I mean bang our girls, not each other,' Liam clarified.

Candice soon arrived, then Lexi and a group of others.

'Jeez, that car,' Liam said, kicking the side of Kitten. 'You couldn't afford something better for your date?' He looked at Felix, then saw Sally climb out of the back and laughed. 'Actually maybe it's you that'll need Viagra tonight.'

'Shut the fuck up,' Felix said.

Liam cocked his head a little, like he couldn't believe what he'd heard, then he took a step forward.

'Just leave it, Liam,' Candice said.

Sail moved in front, squared up to Liam, a slight smile on his face. But Felix pulled him back. 'I've got this.'

'You sure?' Sail said.

'Yeah.'

Liam slipped off his jacket. 'This night just keeps getting better.'

He was big, his arms bulged beneath his shirt as he clicked his neck from side to side.

'Why does his neck make that noise?' Felix whispered to Mae.

'Could be arthritic,' Mae said.

'Can I use that against him?'

'Possibly in the future.'

'We have no future.'

'Good point.'

'Am I about to have a fight?'

Mae nodded. 'Looks that way. You want me to kick him in the nuts?'

Felix shook his head. 'It's time for me to step up.' He took his glasses off and handed them to Mae.

'Can you still see?'

'No, but that wouldn't stop Stella.'

'Kill him, Felix. Dead dead.' Mae turned to see Matilda and Betty, both watching Liam like prey.

312

Matilda smiled. 'We're creating a new world. If you want to make an omelette . . .'

'You have to spill some blood,' Betty finished.

'I think they're insane,' Felix whispered to Mae.

A crowd was quick to form. They made a circle. The noise grew loud, kids hollering for blood, baying and jostling for a spot at the front.

Felix stepped forward.

Liam stepped forward.

'Please leave it, Liam,' Candice said.

'Shut up, bitch.'

Mae looked at Felix. Maybe it was the fact that Candice didn't see him, that no one really saw him, or maybe it was the way Liam talked to the love of his life, but right then he began to move like he knew what he was doing, like months of midnight karate sessions with a possible sex predator would finally pay off.

Liam lunged.

Felix twirled out the way like a bullfighter, a blur of white polyester.

And then he moved in and swung hard.

The crowd watched in stunned silence as Felix finally stepped out of the shadows.

He connected flush, and might have done some damage had he clenched his fist.

'Did you just chop me?' Liam said, rubbing his forehead.

'Karate,' Felix said, quietly, then glanced at Mae.

'Chop him again?' she said.

And then Liam stepped forward, and there was collective flinching as Felix closed his eyes tightly.

The sound of flesh on flesh echoed around the car park, silencing everyone there.

When Felix opened his eyes he saw Liam laid out on the ground.

He glanced to his right and saw Sally Sweeny holding her hand. She winked at Felix. 'I kind of owed you that one, Toothpick.'

As Liam's friends tried to help him sit up, Felix walked over to Candice.

She stood tall in heels, her make-up flawless.

Felix produced a single rose, the same white as his suit.

'"Up where we belong",' Felix said.

'It was you,' Candice said.

He nodded.

'You're the arsonist zombie raper?'

'That's what they call him,' Mae said.

'Maybe I should punch you myself,' Candice said.

Felix dropped to his knees.

Candice clenched a fist. 'Any last words?'

For the second time that night Felix closed his eyes tightly. 'I love you.' He continued, his eyes still closed, 'I've loved you since the first day of primary school. When you carried an Aristocats backpack. I'm the O'Malley to your Duchess.'

Sail frowned.

'Whenever it rained we used to stay in at breaktime and watch a movie. There were loads of choices but my uncle was the caretaker and I used to make him grab *The Aristocats* every time. And then you'd get up and dance during that song . . . remember? O'Malley's friend, Scat Cat.'

Sally wrinkled her nose. 'Is that porn or something?'

'"Everybody Wants to Be a Cat",' Candice said, slowly, quietly.

'And then in Year Five, you once forgot your PE kit and you cried because you didn't want to be the only one doing PE in your underwear. So I said I'd forgotten my PE kit too. And I was wearing Toy Story underpants so no one took any notice of you and just ripped me to pieces instead.'

'I remember – Buzz Lightqueer,' Candice said.

Felix nodded. 'They called me that for two years straight. But it was worth it. You wear Chanel No. 5, because it reminds you of your grandmother, whose bush I did not mean to desecrate. You hate llamas.'

Sail mouthed, 'Llamas?' to Mae, who shrugged.

'Your bedroom is blue because you love the water. I know that because some nights, when everyone is watching the sky, I aim my telescope at your window, because you're more beautiful than all of the stars.'

'I think he's gone too far,' Mae whispered.

Sail nodded.

'See, even now,' Felix said, 'while everyone watches the last colours of the very last sunset on Earth, I watch you. I can die tomorrow, and that'll be okay, because I had the balls to say it to your face. I love you, Candice Harper.'

Felix was still braced for impact when Candice dropped to her knees.

He wasn't prepared for the kiss so forgot to move his lips.

'This is horrific,' Mae said.

'And yet I can't look away,' Sail said.

315

Mae watched them and smiled, because, finally, Candice saw Felix Baxter.

Sail led her inside, where the school hall had been transformed into an homage to the world they lived in. Planets spun above designated areas, an Arctic bar, a beach where another photographer stood, and a rainforest dance floor where leaves hung from branches draped from the ceiling.

Locals had volunteered to help out. A man from the local pub had stocked the bar, the lady from the beachfront cafe was in charge of catering. The food was courtesy of Reverend Baxter.

The music was loud, kids ran to the dance floor. Across were teachers, Miss Holmes dabbed her eyes, until the tears became a deluge and she shook her head as kids and other teachers crowded around and hugged her tight.

Sail brought them fruit punch. Mae pulled vodka from her small bag and poured liberally. 'I need this to get me through.'

'Of course.'

When he asked her to dance she did not fight him, just let herself be led, held and swayed. She pressed close to him, her head on his chest as she looked out at the others.

Matilda held Betty tightly, by the wall Sally stood with a group of Forevers, she didn't once glance at the food.

They wandered outside and gathered for a group shot as the photographer knelt, his back to the view, a better one on show.

As the camera flashed they called out, 'Forever.'

Mae was about to head back inside when she saw Hunter.

She took a breath and walked towards her.

45

'Looking good, slut.'

Hunter wore a gold dress, gold shoes, gold tiara. Her confidence bordered on ferocious.

'You seen my date?'

'He's not here yet,' Mae said.

'Fashionably late and he still upstages me.' Hunter began to walk past as Mae steeled herself. 'I know,' she said.

Hunter stopped and watched the sky, her back to Mae. That night the stars shone almost as bright as Selena, like a reminder of everything beautiful as they faced the coldest truth.

Hunter grasped the necklace as she turned, the blue stone caught the light. 'You put it back.'

'And found the tape.'

Hunter nodded, her face straight, no tears, she was too strong for that.

'It's your job to take the mail. Counsellor Jane . . . the Abi tape was supposed to go . . . Did you listen to this one?'

Hunter reached into her bag and took out a silver flask, drank deeply from it. 'I didn't need to. I already knew what was on it.'

'Because your father has done this before.'

'Gemma Dune was a druggie slut,' Hunter said. 'No one believed her. I mean, my father and her . . .' She shook her head.

'But she was telling the truth.'

'There's more than one truth, Mae.'

Mae shook her head. 'There isn't.'

Hunter drank again.

'So you moved to West to start again.'

'At first I thought Abi was sweet. A little sad, what with her mother and all. It was like she'd been wandering around in the dark her whole life, and I showed her the light. She dressed like me. Talked like me. I caught her once copying the way I flick my hair back. She did it over and over – Tom Ripley, you know? Minus the talent.'

Mae said nothing, just listened.

'I tired of her quick. Stopped taking her calls, left her to Lexi and Candice. She could hang out with us, but I didn't want her on my back.' Another long drink. 'She was so . . . young. The kind of girl who dotted the *i* in her name with a heart, who talked true love like it's actually real. I thought she was lying when she told me she was late.' She laughed then. 'Prissy Abi Manton wasn't dumb enough to get knocked up, not by accident.'

'But she was.'

Hunter nodded. 'Took the test at my house. Cried her eyes out. I sat there and watched. You ever feel detached, Mae?' Hunter glanced at her then laughed. 'Look who I'm asking. Of course you do. So I sat there, detached.'

Behind they heard distant laughter.

'I told her to tell Theodore to sort it. Or not, whatever. It's not like she'd ever meet the thing, right?'

318

'And that was that?' Mae said, knowing it wasn't.

Another drink. 'She wanted me to go with her. Actually, she wanted you to go with her, but you weren't there, Mae.' Hunter laughed. 'Coming to me with her shit. Like I cared.'

'You were in the woods when she came to you?'

Hunter shrugged. 'Everyone's got their part of West. I like the cliff. I like to know I could just . . . it's my choice, right? I like knowing that. So goddam perfect. I'd die that way too. A little perfect mystery.'

'Tell me what happened.'

Hunter waved the bottle. 'I told her again, "Get Theodore to go with you."'

'But it wasn't his.'

Hunter smiled. 'She didn't want to tell me, and I didn't really give a damn. But we were drunk. I mean, Abi couldn't drink for shit, but that night I had a bottle and she did half. I was impressed.'

Mae held her breath.

'I thought I was so blessed. I didn't even see the fatal flaw, or maybe I did but I looked past it. Is that what we do, is that how we absolve ourselves? We look but we don't see. I see girls around my father, even Lexi, they get all . . . tits up, arse out. I fucking coined that move.'

'The necklace, I didn't steal it. Your father gave it to Abi. She sold it to get the money for the abortion.'

The slightest flinch. 'She calmed the second his name left her lips, like she'd been holding it too tight. She wanted to tell someone, her parents. Me. Theodore, someone. But you see, Mae, that day she'd already told Counsellor Jane.'

'What did you do, Hunter?'

'I did nothing. I stood beside her. And we held out our arms like we could fly. I don't even know if she jumped, or if she slipped.'

Mae closed her eyes, and when she opened them she saw a flash of sadness, a single crack in Hunter Silver's immaculate face. Hunter caught it quick, smoothed it away like it'd never been.

'You need to make it right,' Mae said.

'There is no right. No wrong.'

'There has to be.'

'I used to think you were bad, Mae, now I just think you're just naive.'

Mae stepped closer to her. 'You can still take your Forever back.'

'I never had it to begin with.'

She danced with Sail for a long time.

'Are you brilliant?' he said.

Mae thought of Abi Manton, of everything they had been through. 'I am.'

She thought they were done with the drama, and then she heard the noise.

A space cleared as the crowd parted.

He wore a fitted tux. His lips were painted dusky pink, his eyes smoky, his lashes long.

There were murmurs. Liam looked at Hugo like it was some kind of prank he wasn't in on. Hugo stood tall as he stepped beneath the spotlight.

320

And then people laughed.

They laughed and pointed and Hugo flashed a practised smile at all of them.

'You look ridiculous,' Liam said.

'He looks hot.'

They turned towards the voice. Hunter stood there, sparkling in gold, and she extended a hand.

Hugo walked through them. 'Dance?' he said.

'First I have to do something.'

They watched her climb onto the stage. The music died as she took hold of the microphone.

She thanked them for coming. 'You look fierce, Hugo. And I love you.'

He mouthed it back.

And then she pointed to her father. 'I just want to say a thank you to my dad, who's always been there for me.'

Mr Silver smiled.

'I mean, always.' Hunter stopped smiling. Mae could see the microphone shaking in her hands. 'Except for those nights when he said he was working late.'

Heavy silence fell.

'I thought I was lucky, you know? I have a father that works hard so we can have all this . . .' She took off her diamond earrings and tossed them to the floor. 'But I know. Gemma. And now Abi.'

Mae glanced at Mr Silver, who stood there frozen, his eyes locked on his daughter as she bared her soul.

'I know everyone looks at me . . . girls dress like me, cut their hair like mine. They copy the things I say and do because they think it'll make them better. It won't. Abi did all that. And my father got her pregnant.'

There were gasps.

'And Abi jumped from that cliff because she felt like she had no one. I know that feeling. I know what it's like to have everyone look at you and nobody see you. Tonight someone told me I could take back my Forever. I don't think that's true. But fuck it, I'm going to try.'

46

'Shit, it effing stings,' Hunter said, as Mae worked on her wrist.

They were sat on a bench at the bottom of the driveway.

They'd all marched through West like an army in black tie and ballgowns.

The party was at the Prince house.

Spotlights shone into the sky as a heavy bassline thumped.

'Are you okay?' Mae said.

'Now, yeah. I'm drunk. But when I get home, and I see my mother . . .'

Mae and Hunter watched Hugo as he tussled with Liam, just playing, Liam joked Hugo was too worried about losing a nail to get into it properly.

'Your boyfriend likes to wear make-up.'

'I've always known, Mae. Always. I caught him with my lipstick when he thought I was asleep.'

'It doesn't bother you?'

'Hugo's a good guy, he just hides it well.'

'Under a thick layer of foundation.'

'He learned from the master.'

They stood.

'Something I forgot to ask – what did you do with the other tapes?' Mae said.

'Please, that wasn't me. You really think I wanted Abi Manton coming back from the dead?'

The house had been transformed. Lights were strung from every tree, a butler stood by the door and handed out champagne while Final banners were draped from the windows.

Dry ice smoked from machines by the garage block and drifted like fog across the driveway And behind that was the hole, the reminder that nothing about their night was normal, no matter how they pretended otherwise.

Hugo stood in the shadows. Mae could see his hands shaking.

'You don't have to do this,' Hunter said.

'You stand up to your father, I'll stand up to mine. That was what we agreed.'

Maybe Hunter would've done it anyway. Mae looked at her, in that perfect gold dress, and she wondered just how little she knew about her.

Hunter kissed him, then fixed both of their lipstick. Hugo took a deep breath, grabbed Hunter's hand and they began to walk up the driveway.

Inside the music was deafening.

People spilled from every room.

In the kitchen kids played beer pong. Mae watched a boy run past clutching his mouth, looking for somewhere to puke.

'We need a room,' Candice said to Hugo.

She grasped Felix's hand. He made eyes at Mae, who leaned close so she could hear him.

'I'm scared,' he said.

Hunter pointed to the stairs. 'Take your pick.'

Felix leaned closer to Mae. 'Those pills I've been taking to keep me up, they don't keep all of me up. In fact they kind of do the opposite.'

'Jesus.'

'Yeah, he still hasn't helped either.'

Candice dragged him towards the stairs.

Felix looked close to tears as he followed her up, his fingers crossed behind him, like he was hoping for a miracle.

And then the music died.

Sergeant Walters walked into the room, clutching his hat, his mouth tight. Mae thought of his life, working on the last night, his commitment to keeping order.

He walked up to Sally Sweeny and asked her to step outside.

Mae moved in front of her.

'I need to talk to Sally alone.'

'No,' Mae said. 'It's the last night, she's at a party. She needs this.'

Sergeant Walters seemed to weigh things, then looked directly at Sally. 'Is there anything you need to talk to me about, Sally?'

Sally looked at Mae.

Sergeant Walters continued to watch her. 'Mitch Travers was out fishing today. On his way back in he saw something by the cove. White as a ghost when he told me.'

'What did he see?' Sally said, so quiet Mae could hear her own breathing.

'Two of them. Only people I've got missing from this town since I closed the road in.'

Sally closed her eyes.

'Thought he saw,' Mae cut in. She felt every eye on her, on Sally and Sail and Sergeant Walters.

'The tide, it goes out at sunrise. I'll be able to get to them. But I think I have a good idea what I'll find. It'll be easier if you just tell me. You need to come now, Sally.'

'And then what happens?' Sally said.

Sergeant Walters smiled at her, the kind of sorry smile that almost broke Mae. 'I do my job. I keep you all safe and I uphold the law. And it doesn't matter if Selena comes, or if she doesn't. I'll die protecting this town and the values that built it. I have to take you in, Sally.'

Sally went to step forward but Mae stayed in place.

'Don't make this harder,' he said.

'Sally was at the concert last night,' Mae said.

'And after that?'

'She was at the beach with me,' Matilda said.

'I saw her at eleven,' Betty said.

'I saw her at midnight,' Sail said.

'I was there till dawn. Right beside her,' Hunter said.

Sergeant Walters looked at each of them in turn. 'And before the concert?'

There was silence for a while.

'She was with me. We rehearsed all day.' They all turned to see Theodore, beyond reproach.

Sergeant Walters looked down at Theodore's wrist, then shook his head sadly, like he was disappointed in every one of them. 'Your house, Sally. That feeling I got. All that bleach I could smell. I understand, believe me I do. You should have come to me. You have a duty to report it.'

'To report it?' Mae said.

He faced her.

'How's your father, Sergeant Walters?'

Time froze between them.

And then he looked around, at all the faces watching him, and he made his decision, because he knew Mae, he knew she wouldn't back down.

'At dawn I'll find out. And this just got a whole lot worse for all of you.'

They watched him leave.

For a while nobody spoke, and then Mae followed Sally out to the pool as the music started up again.

They watched the blue of the water.

'I'll tell him what I did. I'll say I did it alone and –'

There was a moment when Jon Prince saw his son. The make-up on his face.

And that moment seemed to stretch for so long that Mae stood close to Sail and felt his body tense.

The hatred he felt for his all-star son was plain to see.

Mae spotted a couple of Forevers, and they didn't turn away, just silently moved towards Hugo, till they stood beside him.

And then others from the house came out, maybe twenty of them, and they joined the line.

Jon Prince started to laugh. 'Out here in the open now? I didn't beat it out of you?'

Hugo watched his father.

Jon Prince kept the sneer in place, though the laughter died.

Hunter kept hold of Hugo's hand.

Jon Prince took a step towards his son.

But so did Liam.

And Sail.

And a dozen other Forevers.

'You've got your gang together now,' Jon Prince said, sneering. 'I tried with you, Hugo. I always did my best, but you were too much like your mother. Shit, you're even starting to look like her.'

And then the tirade began. Maybe he was drunk, or frighteningly sober, but he swore at Hugo. He told him he was a freak, that he was weak, that he wasn't a Prince.

Mae watched Hugo. He said nothing back but she could see the hurt and the strength there.

'Maybe I didn't hit you hard enough,' Jon Prince said.

'Like you hit Mum hard enough?'

'You watch your mouth.'

'Why? I thought we were telling each other how we really feel. We confess all our sins before the morning comes.'

'You shut your mouth, Hugo.'

'The night you started digging was the night Mum left us. Only she didn't really leave, did she?'

'I'm warning you.'

Hugo took a step forward, alone. 'You didn't mean it, that's what you told me. She hit her head when she fell. The Wright girl next door, she was looking out, always watching the sky. And she saw you digging. So you told everyone you were digging a bunker.'

Jon Prince watched his son with hatred burning in his eyes.

'That's why you don't let building control in here. Why

you've done all the work yourself. Why the town keeps shaking the way it does. Because you're wrecking it. Because you know what they'll find.'

Jon Prince took a deep breath, and then he smiled. 'You could've had it all, Hugo. But now you'll rot, just like your mother. And your freak friends.'

'We're not freaks,' Hugo said.

'We're creeps,' Hunter said.

'And weirdos,' Mae said.

Jon Prince looked at them like they were crazy. And then he took a step back, and they watched him as the lift began to descend.

'There's no room for you in here,' he said to Hugo, as he took a last look at his son, and then he disappeared below.

They heard the heavy, steel door begin to close for the first time. It groaned and moved and dislodged itself from its place.

No one spoke for a long time.

Hunter cuddled close to Hugo.

He didn't look sad, that was what Mae thought, there was something different about him, like he'd finally found his Forever.

47

The party raged till the sky lightened.

And then the Forevers gathered on Ocean Drive. Together they walked down to the beach, Sally at the heart of them. Maybe the shock was beginning to wear off, because when Mae looked at her she saw tears falling from Sally's eyes.

At the bay they saw Sergeant Walters, his head down as he trudged along the sand like a man condemned to his calling.

They walked a little way behind him.

'We could skip town,' Mae said.

Sally shook her head. 'I think I'm done being afraid.'

'I won't let him take you.'

'None of us will,' Matilda said.

Sally stopped then, right in front of them, and she hugged them each in turn. 'You've had my back. Now it's time for me to have yours. I've got this.'

They watched her walk across the sand, trailing Sergeant Walters as the water began to creep from the rocks. They knew what he'd find, they knew Sally would confess. She would die alone.

'Are we going to let her do this?' Mae said.

'Hell no,' Betty said.

They caught up with Sally and walked beside her. Five Forevers in perfect step with each other.

The moon pulled the tide.

'All right,' Sergeant Walters said, as his pathway cleared.

They were about to move with him when they heard it.

That familiar rumble.

This time it came from above them.

And it was louder, so loud they each took a step back into the water.

Sail was the first to notice the crack.

'Jesus . . .' Mae said.

The crack in the cliff edge was joined by another.

Betty pointed high ahead of them.

'It's the Prince house,' Sergeant Walters said.

The lines snaked from the steel bunker buried deep in the earth. The bunker Jon Prince hadn't got permission to build. The bunker that rumbled the town of West.

They watched the cliff begin to crumble. And then large chunks of rock rained down. They stood frozen as the steel of the Prince bunker was bared.

And West was silent again.

Mae was the only one to look ahead to the cove, her breath held as she saw two shapes almost uncovered.

Sergeant Walters was about to turn when the second rumble hit.

This time it was savage, so deep and loud Mae saw dozens running towards them, motioning them back.

A scream as another crack opened.

It raced along the white face of the cliff and twisted its way up till it met the graveyard high above them.

Time slowed.

The church that had stood there two hundred years began to lean towards them.

'Run,' Sergeant Walters shouted.

They turned and ran along the water edge. Sail helped Sally.

Only when they heard the final rumble did they stop, breathless as they turned and watched the church tear from its foundations and crash to the rocks below.

The dust cloud rose high.

In the distance Mae saw dozens run from it, then take their place at the edge of the road to watch the spectacle.

She heard screams, saw people gather and cry.

They stood there stunned, the cove gone, replaced with rubble that continued to rain down. Sergeant Walters left them and ran towards the bay, to try to seal off the area above to keep people away.

'Jesus,' Felix greeted them, as they arrived back at the crowd.

'We've already covered that,' Mae said.

'The church,' Hunter said. She stood barefoot on the sand, carrying her heels.

They were joined by others, still wearing their suits, their dresses.

'As last nights go,' Hugo said.

'Yeah,' Sail said.

They all looked up to the top of the cliff, to the gap where their faith used to be, where they spent a million Sundays asking why and pleading for more.

'It fell on the cove?' Sail said. 'I'll be damned.'

'No, you won't. None of us will.'

The waves lapped.

The sun rose higher.

'We lived,' Hugo said.

Mae didn't notice the boy behind them.

For the second time that morning time slowed, sounds muffled, birds circled above them.

The surprised look on Hunter's face.

The way Candice's scream floated high above them all.

At first Hugo didn't move, just looked at Mae and Hunter, confusion in his eyes. He smiled again as the colour drained from his face, and he dropped to his knees.

Sail tried to catch him.

And then they saw it.

The blood.

'I'm sorry,' Jeet Patel said, as he let the knife fall to the sand.

48

Whatever was left of them died that morning on the beach. Died as they watched Hunter Silver, the newest Forever, cradle the love of her life.

Sail tried to stop the blood but there was just too much.

Sergeant Walters knelt beside them.

'Hell,' he said. 'Hell.'

He took Hugo himself. Carried him with the help of Liam up towards the old police car and sped from their lives. Mae held Hunter tightly.

She did not cry.

When the crowds began to drift away Hunter sat with Candice and Lexi, Hugo's blood sticky on her palms as she closed her eyes and the sun warmed her face.

Mae sat on the flat rock and finished his tattoo.

This time he didn't cry.

'I know it was you,' Mae said.

Felix kept his eyes on his wrist.

'I saw you on the security tape. It's your job, right. You collect the service sheets from the printers. You added your own. You know how the school audio system works. AV Club.

I think I know why you did it. I just want . . . I mean, I wanted to say –'

He pressed his head to hers. 'I wanted to give you your Forever back. But I knew only Abi could do that.'

She hugged him tightly.

They saw the Reverend standing at the water's edge, Felix's mother beside.

'The last service. He won't do it,' Felix said. 'The church falling, he took that as a sign. That and the fact that his son will burn. He thinks he failed.'

'You know what you have to do,' she said.

'I do.'

'You want a pep talk?'

'I do.'

'You helped give me my Forever. So maybe it's time you gave them theirs.'

Felix stood. 'Is that it?'

'It's been a long night.'

'I'm no longer a virgin.'

'How was it?'

'Turns out Liam wasn't joking when he said they were getting some Viagra.'

They looked over to Liam, who sat alone, as broken as Hunter.

The large cross had been rescued from outside the ruins of the church and carried by a dozen to the edge of the bay, almost touching the water.

Almost the whole town turned up for that last service on the break of the last day.

They expected the Reverend Baxter, instead they got his son.

In his white dinner suit, Felix stood on a piece of driftwood and took the microphone.

Mae sat, Stella on her lap, her hand in Sail's.

She looked around and saw crowds gathered on the promenade, some stood ankle deep in the water.

She heard the fear in his voice as he began. 'I used to wonder about faith. I tried to weigh up the pros and cons. Religion, and what it means. I saw people hiding behind it, using it as an excuse to commit cruelties in someone else's name. To compare. To judge.

'I never thought I'd be standing here like this. My father, he always wanted me to. I always said no. I didn't want to be part of something I don't believe in. But then I realised it wasn't about God, your god or mine. It was about more than that. This past month I've seen the best of humankind, and the worst.'

Mae looked from Sail to Sally Sweeny, to Matilda and Betty.

'Someone once told me that the closer you look, the less you see. So last Sunday I stood outside church and watched. I watched my father tell stories, I watched people draw comfort from his words. That's all. Comfort. Hope. Faith, in people.

'I don't know what will happen this morning. I don't know what happens after. To be honest, I don't think anyone does. No matter what they promise, no matter which book they read from or which heaven they look up at. So instead of praying with you for what might be, I want you to look around now and realise what is. What you can hear and see and touch. Don't say your last goodbye, say your first hello.

'I've spent the past years trying to work out which version of myself people will see, people will like. It's taken until now, the last hour of the last day, to work out that I am imperfectly, uniquely and gloriously me. And that my faith is in my friends. And that's all I'll ever need.

'And for the briefest time, I, Felix Baxter, was lucky enough to live.'

Sail squeezed her hand as she kissed her sister's head and breathed in the smell of her hair.

'At least he didn't swear,' Stella whispered.

Felix cleared his throat and opened his arms. 'We're fucking amazing. Each and every one of us.'

They stayed in their place.

Together.

'You have to finish,' Stella said. 'You have to tell me about Saviour 1. You promised.'

'You know I once said that exact same thing to Dad.'

'You never talk about Daddy.'

Mae held her sister close, Sail leaned in. Felix sat beside them, smiled across at his parents and closed his eyes.

'Tell me about the Saviours,' Mae said.

Her father held her hand as they walked barefoot along the sand. She was nine and the world was hers.

Summer was infinite and though people talked about the rock in space it was nothing more than something to be gossiped about over TV dinners.

A dozen movies were spawned. Mae and her father would stay up late on a Saturday night and watch them. She would fall asleep long before the end.

'There's plans to save us. The people . . . from all over the world. They formed a task force. Do you know what that means?'

'They come together to complete a task.'

He smiled like she was clever.

He was average height,

average build,

average at everything except for loving her.

He was brilliant at that.

'The Saviour rocket will launch in a few days.' They stopped and faced the water.

'Will the baby come soon?'

He nodded. He wore an old watch and sometimes when he came in from work he'd slip it over her wrist and she'd take his briefcase and his overcoat and pretend she worked in an office.

'And we'll be living somewhere else?'

He dropped to kneel in the sand. He wore shorts and the water came in and reached his knees. 'We'll be living somewhere else. Does that scare you?'

'Yes.'

'We'll be together. Me and you and your mum . . . and your sister.'

Mae looked over at him.

He was smiling.

'It's a girl?'

'Your mum said I could be the one to tell you. You'll have to look after her. She'll look up to you.'

'I'll teach her the bad words.'

'Of course. And maybe you could teach her to be kind, like you.'

'I'll protect her. That's what I'll do.'

'Promise?'

'I promise.'

Mae hugged him, so hard he lost his balance and they fell back. She screamed as the water soaked them.

Mae looked across the beach to that same spot, and she wondered if in three billion years another little girl would make that same promise and keep it.

And then she looked to her friend, Felix Baxter, who had finally fallen into a deep sleep.

'It's time,' Sail said.

'Will we stay together?' Stella said.

'Yes.'

She pressed her hands to Stella's ears.

The calm lasted till the first scream.

People turned and began to run.

Mae held her sister tightly.

Someone once asked her how you make your death count.

'I love you,' Sail spoke the words close to her ear.

'I love you.'

The light was blinding.

It made their world brighter.

Acknowledgements

The brilliant Gordon L. Dillow, whose book *Fire in the Sky* helped shape this story.

Victoria, Charlie, George and Isabella. There's no one I'd rather lock down with.

Cath Summerhayes. When life gets tough I turn to you, and you make things better. I love you.

Fliss Alexander, who started on this journey with me.

Maurice Lyon, for taking the reins, always being so kind and patient, and helping me to tell this story.

Emma Quick, Molly Holt and the amazing team at Hot Key. You are so incredibly talented and I'm very lucky to be working with you.

Isobel Taylor, for creating the most beautiful proof I have ever seen.

Ruth Logan, it's hard to put into words just how much I love you. I tend to say that a lot, but when it comes to you I really mean it.

Talya Baker. Thank you for making this book better in every single way, for catching my endless mistakes and for being so funny and lovely when I (relentlessly) mess things up.

Sasha Baker, for casting your expert eye over this story, and for teaching me how to pick a lock.

Rebecca Elphick and everyone at Easypress.

Sophie McDonnell and Muhammad Nafay. The cover you have

created is so staggeringly special. The words inside do not do it justice.

Fran Burgoyne. It takes such skill to narrate an audiobook and I am in in awe of your talent. And Marina Stavropoulou, for championing the audiobook and finding Fran.

Katie McGowan and Cal Mollison, for inspiring so many exotic meals. Your passion and support is something I will always be grateful for. I love you both.

Luke Speed, for making it rain, and for inspiring my indoor-Aviator-look. I'm so Hollywood now.

The Lovely Jess Molloy, for ridiculous levels of loveliness.

Everyone at Curtis Brown, the finest agency in all the land.

Frankie Pellatt, my cat friend, moral compass and wizard of all things tech. Packets. Analytics. Interweb. Spet.

Isabelle, Lisa and Tom. At the time of writing this we haven't drunk from the salmon jug in over a year. My heart aches for you (though my liver is healing).

Nick Matthew, for the love and laughter. And for never giving up. We've come a long way since breakfast.

Everyone at Bishop's Stortford Library. My second, much nicer, family.

My family. This is awkward.

The wonderful booksellers who have championed me/my stories. Thank you for making me feel so at home when I visit.

The book blogging community. You are the best.

Liz Barnsley, the tonic to my gin.

Siobhan O'Neill. Always.

My amazing author friends, who are, as always, unremittingly kind and beautiful.

Thank you for choosing a Hot Key book.

If you want to know more about our authors
and what we publish, you can find us online.

You can start at our website

www.hotkeybooks.com

And you can also find us on:

We hope to see you soon!